CW00431036

Emily Kerr has been scribbling st [...]
since she learnt how to write. She [...]
is based in Yorkshire.

She can generally be found with her nose in a book, or
hunched up over her laptop typing away, though she has
been known to venture outside every so often to take part in
various running-based activities.

www.emilykerrwrites.com

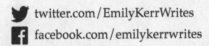
twitter.com/EmilyKerrWrites
facebook.com/emilykerrwrites

DUVET DAY

EMILY KERR

One More Chapter
a division of HarperCollins*Publishers* Ltd
1 London Bridge Street
London SE1 9GF
www.harpercollins.co.uk

HarperCollins*Publishers*
1st Floor, Watermarque Building, Ringsend Road
Dublin 4, Ireland

This paperback edition 2021
First published in Great Britain in ebook format
by HarperCollins*Publishers* 2021

A catalogue record of this book is available from the British Library

ISBN: 978-0-00-843357-4

Printed and bound in the UK using 100% Renewable
Electricity at CPI Group (UK) Ltd

To M and D, with love

Chapter One

Tuesday 23rd April

4.57 a.m.

There's nothing quite like snuggling in the warm embrace of my one true love. It's where I feel utterly content. Here I am safe, happy, and briefly able to remove the mask of sensible, Grown-Up Lawyer that I have to show to the rest of the world. Here, for a few blissful moments, I can finally feel like Alexa Humphries, actual human being, rather than Alexa Humphries, corporate drone. But the trouble is, that's all it ever is. A few blissful moments. For my darling, king-size, 13.5 tog duvet and I spend most of our time apart, cruelly separated by the ever-growing demands of my job, which has become more of a lifestyle choice than just a career. This is so not how I imagined my dream life in London would turn out.

Take today, for example. It's still dark outside. The foxes are scavenging by the bins on the street corner, and the noise of traffic has quietened to an occasional grumble from its usual constant roar. Anyone with any sense is deep in the land of nod, and according to my employment contract, I'm not expected at work for at least another four hours. But whereas lawyers are steely-eyed and detail-oriented in pretty much every other aspect of our business, when it comes to following the letter of our own working hours, we're expected to become forgetful and instead do what is necessary. And it turns out that my employers consider it necessary for me to be on call. Permanently. Which is why I didn't get to my beloved bed until nearly 1.30 a.m. and why I've been awake for the last half hour stressing about the day ahead and panic-reading obscure bits of contract law for a particularly complicated merger that's looming on the horizon.

It's not like I'm extremely senior and important either. When it comes to the food chain of office politics, I know I'm the pond life. But if I want to make it from plant to herbivore and beyond, I need to play the game. I'm just not sure I like this particular game that much any more.

Despite that old cliché of lawyers being bloodsuckers out to make as much money as possible, whatever the cost to others, I've always had a rosy-eyed view of the profession. It started when I was six and the local solicitor helped my grandma prevent developers from forcibly buying the family farm, and then was solidified by my addiction to the movie *Legally Blonde* during my formative years. Sure, the main

2

character, Elle, went through tough times, being patronised by a pervy professor and being constantly underestimated because of her hair colour. But she triumphed as the underdog and rose to great heights, all while wearing killer heels and carrying her faithful pooch in her designer handbag. I would sit in my teenage bedroom, teeth aching from my latest trip to the orthodontist, face covered in bits of toothpaste in a vain attempt to dry out my spots, and promise myself that, one day, I would be like Elle: a confident, successful woman full of integrity, standing up for justice, and fighting for those without the power to fight for themselves.

The spots vanished (mostly), and the teeth were straightened, but somewhere between law school and venturing into the big, wide world, I got lost. It's been two years since I became the envy of my university buddies by joining Richmond Woods. But I didn't realise when I signed on the dotted line that I might as well have signed in blood. It's one of London's leading law firms, notable for having one of the biggest budgets for pro bono work in the city, which is why I was so desperate to get the job in the first place. Alas, while the people on the fifth floor get to make use of that philanthropic power and do some good in the world, I'm trapped on a treadmill on the second floor, charged with applying my skills to help a lot of rich, bossy men become even richer and bossier. The richer bit is from using my legal know-how to help them negotiate company mergers and takeovers, the bossier bit is from being a real-life Alexa who they can enjoy ordering around with the same lack of respect they use to operate their voice-activated devices. The only way it could be worse was if I was called Siri instead.

I stretch out my toes to take full advantage of the still-toasty hot-water bottle at my feet. My room in the house-share has beautiful big windows, making it a light and airy space, or so the girl moving out promised me when she showed me round. I unfortunately failed to consider the fact that the stately Victorian sash windows with their glorious view of the squat opposite were single-glazed. Add into the mix ill-fitting wooden frames which are suspiciously squishy, and it's a recipe for a permanent draught akin to a gale. Even during last summer's heatwave, there was only about one week where I didn't need some extra form of warmth to get me through the night. I suppose what I could really do with is a hot bedmate – in both senses of the word – but as I appear to have formed an unhealthy, all-encompassing relationship with my job, I can't see that happening any time soon.

Instead, I'm trying to keep warm with my current bed attire, an anything-but-sexy unicorn onesie. It's all the colours of the rainbow, fleece-lined, with a furry exterior, complete with tail and silver horn. Don't get me wrong, I love a cosy pair of PJs as much as the next girl, but a unicorn onesie is definitely at the extreme end of things, and when my twin brother Charlie handed it over to me for Christmas with a wicked grin on his face, I swore I'd never lower myself to actually wearing it. But what can I say? Needs must. My laundry pile has been growing its own ecosystem because I've been getting back from work late, and I'm too scared of incurring the wrath of my Queen Bee

4

housemate Zara to turn on the washing machine after dark. In desperation last night, I'd dug out this little number from the back of my wardrobe, where it had been languishing in a cocoon of torn wrapping paper. I'm trying not to imagine the look of triumph on Charlie's face if he knew I was wearing it. He's always on at me to "Chill out and go with the flow", which is all well and good if you're content coasting your way through life by occasionally busking in the local market town back home, like he does, but it doesn't really cut it in the corporate world I've ended up stuck in.

The windows rattle as a lorry rumbles down the road, sending another chilly blast of morning air over my face, and making the curtains flutter. Shards of orange light from the streetlamps dance their way around the walls, sharpening the fuzzy details of my room. I gaze around, nostalgic thoughts of my childhood home making me see my current surroundings as if for the first time. I'm barely ever in here when I'm not sleeping, and I can't remember when I last actually paused and considered my surroundings. It's a depressing sight; wardrobe doors hanging open to reveal a row of identikit suits, the pile of dirty washing overflowing out of a bag in the corner, and stacks of musty legal tomes leaning precariously by the bed. It's more of a habitat than a bedroom, certainly not what someone would associate with a so-called professional woman in her mid-twenties. The only uplifting feature is the collection of pictures on my walls. They're bright abstract prints of some of the most famous London landmarks, images which adorned my student bedroom to

5

inspire me during the long days of learning case law and wading through incomprehensible legal jargon.

When I first moved here, I had visions of changing the world during the week, and then ticking off each famous landmark during the weekends, but I'm always too knackered to be bothered. Most of my weekends are spent comatose, wrapped up in my duvet and trying to catch up on all the sleep I've missed out on during the weekdays of corporate kowtowing. The realisation saddens me. It's like I've blinked and suddenly two years have passed without me getting any closer to the dreams of making a difference that I'd once held so dear. How have I let things get to this position?

I turn onto my side, blocking out the too-cheery images, and try to ignore the crushing sense of failure which threatens to overwhelm me. I need to get a grip. Nobody likes a misery-guts and this one-person pity party needs to stop. Time to focus on the day ahead. Right on cue, my phone buzzes, warning me that yet another email has landed in my inbox. When I first started at Richmond Woods, being gifted a work phone and being told that I could also use it for my personal calls felt like a demonstration of trust and respect. However, after the thrill of being able to ring utility companies' premium-rate phone lines without having to worry about the cost had worn off, I realised the hard reality of the apparently generous gesture. I started to resent the fact that I was expected to carry a device akin to my own personal slave master in my pocket all the time. Even in my supposed downtime I find myself obsessively checking messages and feeling stressed if I don't reply to my seniors within half an hour. Sometimes it feels like my head might explode with the pressure of keeping on top of everything.

Despite my best efforts last night, my inbox is still at the higher end of double figures, and suddenly it seems impossible that I'll ever get through it all. Several of the emails have been sent with bright red exclamation marks in the subject line to denote them as extremely urgent, and just in case I haven't got the message, "SORT THIS NOW" has been added in shouty capital letters. I cringe as if I was actually being yelled at. Of course, no one at Richmond Woods would be so coarse as to raise their voice in person, but they've developed all kinds of passive-aggressive methods of creating the same horrible effect on us lowly minions.

I know I should start chipping away at my replies, but I'm desperate for just a few more minutes of peace. I find myself grabbing my own battered mobile and falling into my usual procrastination habit of scrolling through Instagram, trying to escape reality into a world of hashtags promising glossy positivity.

Pictures of cute animals and gorgeous holiday destinations normally do the trick in cheering me up, but today all I can notice are my friends' posts about their perfect lives. Instead of putting a smile on my face, they increase my sense of melancholy. I gaze at the shiny picture of my best friend from school, carefree and laughing with her fiancé on Sydney Harbour Bridge, and try to remember the last time I saw any of these people in real life.

When I make my weekly call to my parents, they always

ask after my old school and uni mates, and the answers trip off my tongue. Laura's engaged, Michael's got another promotion and oh, did I tell you that Sara thought she bumped into Prince William at Waitrose the other day? But now I'm stopping and actually thinking about it, I realise my friends haven't told me these charming anecdotes personally. They've made general announcements to me and several hundred others of their closest online followers. I've double-tapped my appreciation and sometimes there's even been the briefest exchange in the comments along the lines of, "Congratulations lovely, we must meet for a proper catch up soon", but I can't remember the last time it actually translated into a real-life interaction. Have I allowed social media to paper over the cracks of where an actual social life should be? I always assumed everyone was too busy, but a growing fear is telling me that maybe I'm the only one struggling, while everyone else really has got it sorted so that they're #livingthedream.

Suddenly my body jerks and the sick sensation of being about to fall off a cliff jolts me back to full consciousness. That was close. Much as I need the sleep, I can't afford to drift off again. Regretfully, I push the hot-water bottle out of reach so I don't get too comfortable. I know I should be getting on with work. The senior partner I report to has flown out to Japan to help a client finalise a deal, and her flight is due to land in Tokyo at any moment. I'd be prepared to bet next month's rent money that she'll ping a dozen missives my way as soon as she does. Genevieve's notorious for expecting an instant acknowledgement and I daren't let her down. Besides, she's on the appointments board for the pro bono department and maybe, just maybe, one day she'll recognise my hard work and reward me for it with a position there, and then all this will have been worth it. Or that's what I keep telling myself, anyway.

My work phone buzzes once again as the expected emails arrive. My fingers hover over the screen, but just the thought of sending even one more reply makes me feel like a steel band is tightening around my head, and I find myself pushing the phone away. Despite my good intentions, I shuffle back down my mattress, burrowing myself into my duvet like a hibernating animal. If I can't see the emails, maybe I can pretend they don't exist, I tell myself, much like a small child playing hide and seek by merely covering their eyes.

The phone's buzzing continues, and through the thin party wall, I hear the distinctive thumps of Zara jumping out of bed and switching her light on. It's a badge of pride among us junior lawyers if we can count the number of hours of sleep we've had on one hand. Zara claims to thrive on this, but anything less than six hours and I find my brain becoming sluggish and my reactions slowing until I feel like I have jet lag. Sometimes, I'll have a whole conversation with someone and feel like they're talking to me on a time delay, so it takes me several seconds to be able to process what they're saying and be able to respond appropriately.

Now she's in circulation, I know I should look at my emails. Zara and I work for the same firm and in the same department – another reason why I feel I can't even switch off when I get home. When I first moved to London, it seemed like the easiest solution to share a house with a colleague. Yes, I know, what was I thinking? But by the time I'd realised quite how ruthlessly competitive Zara is, I'd already signed a six-month lease. Somehow, it's gone on a lot longer than that initial agreement, but I'll just add that to my long list of things that I've let slip. I barely have time to buy a pint of milk, let alone look into moving house. And on the plus side, our other housemate Sam is no bother. In fact, she's no bother to the point that we've only ever communicated through the house WhatsApp group. She moved in at Christmas when I was home visiting my family for a brief forty-eight hours, and she appears to work weird shifts too. Or maybe the reason we've never met is that she's got a much better social life than me. Most people have, after all.

Now the clattering sound of Zara typing on her laptop punches its way into my room. She's attacking the keys as if they are promotion rivals. Even when I pull a pillow over my head, I can still hear her tapping away, each jab nagging at my growing sense of anxiety. It's like she's doing it deliberately, making sure I know she's already hard at work while I'm being a lazy layabout. I know I should pick up the work phone again, send out my own replies and signal that my working day has begun. But somehow today it seems impossible. The very thought of rolling out of bed, getting dressed and dragging myself into the office for yet another day of thrashing myself to the limit is enough to make me groan out loud. I wish I could carry on pretending to myself that everything is OK, but this morning, I just don't have the energy to even try.

I poke my nose out of my duvet and stare wistfully at

the family picture teetering precariously on what was meant to be my dressing table, but which I use instead as a makeshift desk. It's a classic Humphries image, illustrating the family pecking order perfectly, with me the default target for teasing. My older brothers are cracking up, my mum and dad are hiding their amusement with mock outrage, while I'm rolling my eyes at Charlie who was taking the picture. I can remember the suggestion he made to elicit such a response. I'd been in a hurry to make my train back to London, and being delayed for a family snap was not helping my stress levels. After dragging me back to the doorstep and plonking me in position, Charlie had peeked above the lens of the ancient camera and fixed me with a stern stare as I protested my urgent need to get going, right now.

"Lighten up, sis. Just throw a sickie. What's the worst that can happen?"

His words echo around my mind.

Throw a sickie…

I can't.

Charlie wouldn't think twice about it. But I'm the sensible twin. It would be completely out of character for me to do something so spontaneous and rebellious. I'm expected at work. I've got deadlines to meet, clients to appease, bosses to impress. I can't let my colleagues down. But Charlie's voice in my head is insistent.

What's the worst that can happen?

I know the answer to this. A day out of the loop could leave me on the back foot for weeks. I could lose the respect and trust of my colleagues, my job even, were I to get found out. I can't do it. It would be foolhardy.

But even as I try to bully myself into getting up and getting on with what needs to be done, my gaze travels back to those pictures of London, images which used to stand for hope and now represent nothing but personal failure. How long can I keep lying to myself that things are going to get better? I realise I've had enough. I am done with feeling like this. I need to do something about it.

Before I lose courage, I reach out, pick up my phone and find myself typing an email I never imagined I would dare to write. It's time I took my destiny into my own hands.

Chapter Two

5.43 a.m.

My fingers are trembling and my heart pounds with adrenalin as I sit bolt upright in bed, startled at my own daring. What have I done? Am I mad? Did I really just write that message and hit send? I check my outbox to make sure I haven't dreamt the whole thing. It wouldn't be the first time I've indulged in a fantasy like this. But there, in black and white, is the email I've sent off into the ether declaring that I'm ill and won't be coming into work today.

It's something thousands of employees do without even thinking about it, but for me, this feels like a huge deal. I remember on my induction day at Richmond Woods being told in no uncertain terms that to call in sick, we had to be on our actual deathbeds, or at least missing a limb. There have been occasions when I've dragged myself in with a throat so sore I couldn't even speak, and a chest so congested I could barely breathe, because I was that terrified of breaking the rules, but today I haven't even got the slightest trace of a sniffle.

I lie still, hardly daring to move as I think about my deceitful email, a contradictory mix of guilt and something like excitement churning around my stomach. I've never been so impulsive and daring. In the Humphries family, I'm the sensible, logical twin, while Charlie corners the market in being carefree and impetuous. But there's nothing sensible about the way I'm feeling right now. From the moment I woke up, everything just felt off. I tried to ignore it and carry on as normal, but today, that insidious drip-drip-drip of inadequacy and disappointment in myself got the better of me. I just couldn't face another day of the same old treadmill. If I were a stronger, better person, I'd recall the email, explain it away as a mistake and get on with my working day. But I'm not, and in the spirit of full disclosure, I'll admit that I don't want to do that. Because doing battle with my guilt is a growing sense of relief at the thought that stretching ahead of me is a blissful day I can truly call my own. Wonderful hours of time in which there will be no unreasonable deadlines, no entitled clients, no ambitious colleagues trying to get ahead by showing me up. For twenty-four hours, I am free. I know what I've done is wrong, but I desperately need this duvet day. Maybe after a day of sheer relaxation and what is fashionably called 'self-care', I'll find the energy to approach things afresh.

For the first time in months, I turn my work phone off and then hide it away in my bedside table. I'm determined I'm not going to change my mind about staying at home, but I'd rather limit the ways in which my firm can pressure me into doing so. It's about time I claimed back some autonomy. Today I am my own boss, free to do absolutely nothing at all.

I settle back into bed and contemplate the day stretching ahead of me. I'm going to do nothing but sleep, eat chocolate and watch crappy telly. I can feel the tension easing out of my muscles just at the thought of such decadent relaxation. For once, my mind is buzzing about which boxsets I should be bingeing on, rather than wondering how I'll meet Genevieve's latest demands. But with so much TV to catch up on, I reckon I'll need to be strategic about how I do it. I grab my notebook and on a fresh page I start mapping out a schedule which will help me maximise my impromptu day of rest. Sleep until ten, a leisurely breakfast until ten thirty, and then maybe start on my first boxset. Or I could even maximise the TV viewing time by eating and watching simultaneously. And then I catch myself. What is the point of having a duvet day if I spend it organising myself into another strict regime? I really need to learn how to switch off.

I toss the notebook to one side, manoeuvre the hot-water bottle to warm up my cold toes again and allow my eyes to droop shut. Today I need to go with the flow *à la* Charlie, and let myself properly chill out. I am answerable to nobody but me today, and I am not going to chivvy myself to do anything I don't want to. The tightness around my forehead is already easing. My limbs grow heavy and I start to gradually drift away. Clearly my body is telling me it needs sleep, so that's exactly what I intend to do.

"Do I need to call an ambulance or something?"

Zara barges her way into my room without so much as pausing to knock on the door. Her sudden appearance ramps my anxiety levels back up into overdrive. I clutch the duvet tightly to me, half-expecting her to rip it off and order me out of bed. A wave of guilt washes over me, and I'm convinced that she'll be able to read the deception in my features. Why did I think sending the email would be the end of it? I suppose I should have realised the firm would send Zara in to check up on me. Either that, or she's doing it off her own bat to see if I'm close enough to my deathbed to allow her to move into my office with its slightly superior proximity to the coffee machine. I need to think quickly. Too much time has passed for me to claim the email was sent in error. And having had the prospect of a day of relaxation dangled in front of me, I'm loathe to sacrifice it. I'm committed to my duvet day now.

It's all well and good typing something about being poorly, but having to feign it in the flesh is quite a different matter. Zara's incredibly sharp and if I'm not careful, she'll see straight through my little charade and then I'll be in a whole heap of trouble. But I didn't take GCSE Drama for nothing. Time to throw everything at this.

I blink a few times, as if it's taking me a while to process who is standing in front of me.

"Zara?" I say in affected confusion, deliberately keeping my tongue near the roof of my mouth so my speech is groggy and slurred.

She purses her lips and I catch her checking my pupils suspiciously, looking for signs of drunkenness or drugs. I'd better be careful not to ham it up too much or she'll take great delight in starting damaging rumours at the office and I'm not sure I like the idea of having to deal with the longer-term consequences of that.

"You do sound rough," she says, folding her arms and watching me closely. But just as I start to feel touched by her sympathy and a little ashamed for deceiving her, she whips out a thermometer and lunges in my direction. "Best to be on the safe side."

For a moment, I think she's going to stab it into my mouth and cause me some serious injury. But at the last minute she hesitates, perhaps fearing the danger of catching my non-existent germs, and instead throws the thermometer in my direction. It lands millimetres from my right eye and I have to fight the urge to flinch. Making my movements as slow and wobbly as possible, I pick it up, my brain going at a million miles an hour while I try to plot my way out of this predicament. Why didn't I pretend to have lost my voice? That would have been so much easier than faking a fever. She's definitely going to catch me out. And then just when I think I'm going to have to confess to my deception, I have an idea.

I make a retching sound. "Oh God, eurgh. Zara, I think I'm going to throw up."

I turn my head towards her, clutching my stomach and opening my mouth wide, to make sure my pantomime works. Sure enough, she leaps back in horror.

"Watch out," she says irritably, no doubt fearing for the safety of her designer trouser suit. She sighs, as if she's being massively put out. "I suppose I'd better go and find a bucket."

As soon as the door slams behind her, I whip the thermometer out of my mouth and slip it against my hot-water bottle, praying there's enough time to allow it to heat up to disease level. I briefly contemplate dabbing water on my forehead to create the impression of beads of sweat, but quickly dismiss the idea as ridiculous. I'll only end up spending the rest of the day in a damp bed, and that's not going to be pleasant.

The creaking floorboards down the hallway indicate that Zara is on her way back, and for the first time, I'm grateful that our house is as old and battered as it is. I quickly replace the thermometer in my mouth and sink back against the pillows, channelling my best suffering hospital patient vibes.

Zara dumps the overflowing kitchen bin by my head and snatches the thermometer from my mouth. I shrink away from the odour of old banana skins and tea bags, and meekly allow her to check the reading. She raises an eyebrow in surprise.

"Christ, maybe I should call that ambulance." There's an actual edge of concern in her voice now and my guilt complex kicks in again.

"No, don't worry. I'll be OK. I just need to sleep," I protest in a quavering voice. As I close my eyes again, I catch her smiling to herself and suddenly I don't feel quite so bad about my actions.

"Fine, I'll leave you to it." She's obviously had enough of playing Florence Nightingale, thank goodness. "Genevieve's landed in Japan, by the way. There's a lot she needs doing, but she knows that *I'm* on top of it, so you needn't concern yourself with that."

If it was anyone else, I'd be touched and grateful for the apparent gesture of support in picking up my workload, but I've worked alongside Zara for long enough to know that she never does anything for free. I'll have to pay the price eventually, but I tell myself that that's a worry for another day.

Despite saying she'd be on her way, she's still hanging around. Through half-open eyelids, I see her inspecting my bedside table. I mentally heave a sigh of relief that I managed to close my notebook with its potentially incriminating list of Netflix series. Zara's a naturally suspicious person and although I've given my all to this charade, I wouldn't put it past her to rumble me and drop me in it. I've learnt from bitter experience that she's not to be trusted.

Eventually she meanders towards the door, loudly knocking over my pile of books and switching on the main light as she goes. I muster my best am-dram skills and flinch at the noise and cover my eyes from the light. If I were genuinely poorly, she'd definitely have finished me off by now. I'm beginning to wonder if that's her intention.

"I suppose I'd better call you later to check you're still breathing," she says with a sigh.

"Please don't worry, I'll be fine," I protest wheezily. I'm rapidly coming to the end of my illness repertoire, and the last thing I want interrupting my day of indulgence is a phone call from the ice queen.

She tuts, then bangs the door for good measure on the

way out. I listen carefully, knowing that she's still lurking out there. I fake-gag loudly and groan a little, then berate myself for overdoing it. However, it seems to do the trick because the hallway creaks as she heads back to her own room.

I lie in bed with my eyes closed and try to relax back into that lovely sleepy state, but I'm too het up after my dramatic efforts and my brain is going into overdrive again. It's an effort to tune out the sounds of Zara squirting hairspray and humming to herself as she puts on her power lipstick. Anyone would think she was pleased her housemate and colleague was ill.

My personal mobile chirrups, normally the warning that this is the last possible moment I can leave the house and not get completely crushed in the rush hour on the Tube. I silence the alarm quickly before Zara registers it. I definitely won't be missing that bunfight this morning. I'd like to say I've gradually grown accustomed to the sensation of being forced to stand with my face in a complete stranger's armpit, but the feeling of horror is just as strong as that very first commute.

Anyway, the furthest I intend to travel today is to the kitchen and back again. Why venture out into the big wide world when I have everything I need right here? Besides, it would be just my luck to bump into one of the partners and get rumbled if I did leave the house.

Finally, I hear Zara banging her way out of the front door. Just Sam to go and then I'll have the house to myself for a blissful ten hours at least. I snuggle down into my cosy nest and quickly go back to sleep.

Chapter Three

9.06 a.m.

I'm dragged back to wakefulness from my Caribbean beach, where I'm about to dance with a chiselled god of a man in a Hawaiian shirt, by the clatter of the front door slamming once again. Was that Sam leaving for work? My windows rattle in response, sending another gust of chilled air in my direction. I blink sleepily, thinking longingly about the warm, golden sands and sparkling turquoise sea I've just been dreaming about. The reality of a Bethnal Green house-share couldn't be further from the delights of Barbados. My hot-water bottle isn't doing the business any more, and my stomach is grumbling at having missed the Pret porridge I normally grab en route to the Tube.

I'd quite like to stay in bed for a bit longer, sink back into the dream which was just getting interesting, and achieve a proper lie-in, but in addition to my feeling of hunger and coldness, my bladder is protesting. I stay still, trying to ignore it in the hope it will go away, but I'm bordering on the desperate stage. I suppose if I get up, at least I can combine the bathroom trip with grabbing some food from the kitchen and topping up the hot-water bottle. I fully intend to move as little as possible today, so I might as well be efficient when I am up and about.

It's so much easier leaving my bed at this hour than my normal alarm time. In fact, there's a spring in my step as I slip on my fluffy slippers and the tail of my oh-so-stylish unicorn onesie swishes enthusiastically as I meander around the house. It's good to have the place to myself. If I'm feeling really energetic this afternoon, I might even go and hunker down on the sofa in the living room for a bit, if I can remember how to work the telly in there. I tend to avoid the communal areas of the house if I can possibly help it. When I first moved in, I hadn't got around to contributing to the television licence yet, and whenever Zara heard me approaching the living room, she'd mute the TV so I didn't get the benefit of hearing programme sound when I hadn't paid for it. That pettiness should have made me wary of her from the start, but it took me a little longer to learn that lesson properly.

Peering in the bathroom mirror as I wash my hands, I realise with delight that the bags under my eyes have reduced from weekly-shop size to grabbing-a-few-bits-on-the-way-home levels. Admittedly, my hair looks like I've done battle with a Van der Graaff generator, the way it's sticking up on end, but sod it, no one's seeing me today, so I'm not going to waste my energy doing battle with a brush. Later I might treat myself to a bath with some of the aromatherapy salts I got for Christmas from my grandma, but I'm happy to fester in my sleepiness for now, and turn my attention to the next priority: food.

Venturing into the kitchen at a normal pace rather than my usual smash and grab, I realise with a shock how much mess three supposed professionals can generate between them. Even my student digs didn't have this much filth accumulating on the work surfaces. It's quite possible I'll pick up a genuine germ from this muck heap to support today's little white lie. I would put the blame on my housemates, but if I'm being completely honest with myself, I'm probably equally responsible. We do notionally have a timetable for taking it in turns to do the cleaning, but life happens, and it would appear we've all been too busy to be bothered to follow it. Oh well. Today is not going to be the day that I change that situation. Maybe at the weekend.

I open my cupboard and check the contents. A spider scurries out of a corner, emphasising the disappointingly empty level of my supplies. I tend to eat on the go – when I remember I'm hungry, that is – and I don't think I've done a big shop since I arrived back from my Christmas mini-break, which is shameful to admit. I'm left with a choice of a tin of baked beans, which I think I possessed when I first moved in, and a sticky jar of Nutella, which is a month past its sell-by date. Telling myself that a sell-by date is very different from a use-by date, I grab the cleanest-looking spoon I can find in the drawer, and retreat back to the bedroom with my jar of chocolatey goodness. No judging, please.

And then I curl up in bed, reach for the remote and settle

down with the only thing I want to interact with today: Netflix. Today I intend to get my money's worth from the subscription that I pay for, and the rest of my beloved family leeches off. The minutes melt past as I scroll my way through the myriad of choices I'm presented with. I'm pretty sure Charlie's been messing around with my account again, because I'm bombarded with loads of recommendations for horror movies and weird cult action films. It's almost too much effort for a duvet day, but eventually I find the stuff I actually like watching, and settle on an old favourite, *Queer Eye*. Nothing can boost a girl's mood like those lovely guys with their endless optimism and enthusiasm for life. I probably shouldn't admit this, but sometimes when I'm at work slaving away over a stack of documents, I imagine what it would be like to have them as my friends. They'd descend on my office, wrap me up in a bundle of positivity and transform my lifestyle with one elegant snap of their fingers. I scoop another big spoonful of Nutella into my mouth and idly wonder what the boys would think of my current bohemian nightwear look. They'd love the rainbow onesie, right?

I'm enjoying a chunk of crystallised sugar and getting a bit emotional as the boys match a lonely guy with an abandoned dog from a rescue shelter, when there's a bang at the door. My heart skips a beat. I hit the mute button and freeze in position, as if whoever is outside has the ability to sense my presence upstairs if I make even the tiniest movement. All I want is a quiet day being left alone by the rest of the world. Whoever it is can jog off.

There's another efficient knock at the door, and then,

inevitably, the niggling overthinking begins. Who's out there? Why are they visiting? What if I've been rumbled? Surely the bosses wouldn't send in the heavies to check up on me? I tell myself firmly that I'm overreacting and being ridiculous. I'm entitled to take sick leave. Then I remember that occasion where they caught an intern posting on Facebook when he was supposedly on an errand for Genevieve. The bosses sent security to escort him off the premises and people didn't stop talking about it for weeks. But confronting someone at home when they're poorly would be a bit much, even by their standards, wouldn't it?

The handle is being rattled now, and I catch myself holding my breath with the tension of not knowing who's at the door. Whoever is there is pretty determined to attract my attention. I'm starting to feel hunted. I nearly hide under the duvet again.

"Parcel delivery," bellows a man through the letterbox.

I sigh with relief. Trust me to be at home when the most diligent deliverer in London calls round. It's really unusual to get someone who actually bothers to ring the doorbell. The last time I ordered something to be delivered to this address, they shoved a card through the door claiming they'd called when I wasn't in and had left the parcel in a 'safe place'. I found said item three hours later balancing on top of the dog-poo bin in the patch of green around the corner which claims to be a community garden. I'd like to say I left it there and complained vociferously to the company, but it was an extremely expensive dress I'd ordered for the year-end social and I had literally no time to find something else suitable to wear. I told myself the packaging had protected the fabric from its disgusting surroundings, but I spent the whole evening being paranoid that I smelt like dog mess, which didn't make for a great night. Anyway, since then, I've always got my parcels sent to work, and I know Zara does the same because Bill in the post room ends up giving half of them to me to look after, so by process of elimination, it must be something for Sam. Would she bother to get out of bed to collect a parcel for me?

I'm all ready to hit play and see the *Queer Eye* makeover through to the end, but the letterbox clatters again and I finally relent. Reluctantly putting my jar of Nutella to one side, I heave myself out of bed and shuffle my way slowly downstairs, half-hoping the guy will give up before I get there. Without wishing to sound completely antisocial, I'm really not in the mood for talking to people today.

It takes several minutes for me to undo the myriad of locks which shut out the dodgier elements of this particular part of the world, but eventually I manage to haul the door open. To my disappointment, the delivery man is still there waiting for me, although he is looking anxiously at his watch.

"Alright darlin', parcel for Sam Harris. Can you sign on the dotted line?"

I blink a few times as my eyes adjust to the light outside. It's turned into a bright spring day and beneath the typical London aroma of exhaust and litter, I can almost convince myself that there is a smell of fresh foliage in the air.

"I'm not Sam, but can I sign on her behalf?" My voice is

claggy from not being used much today and my words come out in an adolescent-sounding waver.

The delivery guy gazes at me critically, unimpressed by my lack of authority.

"Not sure unicorns count as a responsible recipient," he says, looking pointedly at my furry hood, resplendent with its gleaming silver horn sticking up above my forehead. I hastily pull it down, revealing the full extent of my bed-head. He takes a step back in surprise, or perhaps fear, and silently hands over his tablet device.

I attempt to trace out my autograph with my index finger. My signature is a scrawl at the best of times, but trying to do it without a pen renders it completely illegible. I guess at least this way it means it can't be used as incriminating evidence against me. After all, I am meant to be too sick to even leave my bedroom.

He raises an eyebrow at the collection of weird loops and then looks at me expectantly.

"Parcel's in the van."

He gestures for me to follow him to the dirty Transit behind him and that's when my suspicions start to grow. When was the last time someone was this dedicated to delivering a parcel? And shouldn't he have brought it to the front door in the first place? Perhaps this is some kind of scam to lure me out of the house. I mean, on TV shows, this is always how the lead character gets abducted. I know that's just my imagination getting carried away, but this could be a classic distraction technique to get me out of the way while his mate zips in and robs the place, and how could I explain that?

I decide it's best not to take any chances. I close the door carefully behind me, making sure the delivery man has heard the decisive click of the locks sliding shut. We walk to the van, me keeping a few paces behind him and constantly looking back to check on the house, just in case. He bangs the back door, and it opens with a rusty clatter. After rummaging around for a few seconds, he hands over a long, thin box, nearly as tall as me. I wonder what on earth Sam has been ordering for herself.

"Have a good day," he says, jumping into the cab and speeding off in a swirl of exhaust.

I tramp back to the front door, balancing my unwieldy parcel and berating myself for my stupid paranoia. And that's when I realise.

I've locked myself out.

Chapter Four

9.45 a.m.

A whole heap of words come to mind, none of which should be said by a respectable lawyer. I take a deep breath and try to think about my situation logically while the panic rages around my brain. My law tutor always told us there are no circumstances which cannot be improved by a calm, analytical response. It's all very well, Professor Eaton preaching about making a considered list of your assets in challenging circumstances, but I'd like to see how well she'd cope standing on an east London street, assets bouncing free *sans* bra, while dressed in a ludicrous unicorn onesie and fluffy teddy slippers. I make an effort to run through what's going in my favour, but I quickly draw a blank. There's Sam's parcel, of course, but unless it contains skeleton keys, it's a fat lot of good. I'm a walking invitation for ridicule and my considered assessment of this situation is that I am utterly screwed.

29

Muttering prayers under my breath, I lean heavily against the door, just in case the catch hasn't quite engaged, but it doesn't give even the slightest millimetre. Damn those efficient locks. I'd quite happily take dodgy security over being locked out in my PJs any day. My sense of impending doom is rising. I step back, take a deep breath, and then try again, battering my shoulder against the door like a police officer raiding a drugs den. Funnily enough, the only damage I manage to achieve is to my own person. It looks so much easier on the news. Despite the risk of breaking myself, I persist in sheer desperation. They say the definition of madness is trying the same thing over and over again and expecting the outcome to change. Well, that's my invitation to the asylum sorted.

I pause on the threshold and try to get my breath back while I contemplate my lot. It's weird how it's possible in a city of nine million people to feel so utterly alone. If I was locked out back home in Yorkshire, it would be a simple matter of digging out the spare key from under the mat, or summoning one of my many siblings to let me in, or worst-case scenario, walking into the village and asking the neighbourhood odd-job man, Mr Potts, to come up and help me get back into the house. But here in London, I'm struggling to think of anyone who could come to my aid. The realisation that there's no one in this vast city that I can turn to in an emergency is a sobering one.

I'm feeling more and more exposed standing out here. Although the street is currently deserted, I can sense the twitching of the net curtains and the sniggering behind closed doors. It's a horrible sensation. Not only am I alone in my misfortune, I'm surrounded by malevolent beings who are delighting in it. It's like being back at work. I may be standing like a muppet on my front doorstep, but I can't help thinking about this time two weeks ago, when I was feeling similarly humiliated and alone, but for a very different reason.

I'd wandered into the office kitchen to grab a drink of water to stave off the caffeine headache which was making its presence felt, when I was cornered by Genevieve. Being pounced on by the bosses is not an unusual occurrence at Richmond Woods, but at that particular moment I had not psychologically prepared myself for a confrontation about an issue of which I knew nothing. The fact that it was Genevieve doing the confronting made the situation a whole lot worse. It's never good to appear incompetent in front of someone who could hold your future in their hands, especially when it's someone like Genevieve who puts a high price on reliability. Although I'd looked desperately around the kitchen, hoping against hope that one of my colleagues would take pity and step in to help me out, they'd all vanished, apparently sensing trouble approaching. All, except Zara, who'd loitered by the coffee machine, the expression of glee growing on her face as Genevieve quizzed me about a pile of paperwork I'd never received. As Genevieve's words of disappointment rained down on me (why is disappointment so much harder to deal with than out-and-out anger?), a suspicion had started worrying away at me that Zara's smirk and the disappearance of the paperwork were in some way connected. I'd tried to ignore it, telling myself that despite our differences, she wouldn't have betrayed me in that way. But the other part of my mind, the dispassionate, logical lawyer part, reminded me that it wasn't the first time she'd acted like this. Zara would trip up her own grandfather to get ahead. Screwing over her housemate would be practically small fry to her. I hadn't dared to confront her about it, especially as I was too busy trying to make up lost ground with Genevieve, but I knew I was right. I bet Zara would love to see me in my current predicament and turn it to her own advantage. And that's another reason why I've absolutely got to get back in the house as soon as possible.

I finally accept that the door is not going to magically open itself, and start to examine my other options. The ground floor of our house is home only to a windowless downstairs toilet, and a bedroom, which was probably originally intended to be the living room, but which our landlord, being the entrepreneur that he is, has transformed into Sam's bedroom, complete with even steeper rent than mine because it has a precious extra two square feet of floor space. For security reasons, the lower windows of Sam's room are sealed shut (I dread to think what the health and safety regulators would have to say about that particular fire hazard) and only the top two open. They're currently cracked ajar. Leaving windows open is something Zara has nagged about on the house WhatsApp group, but for now I thank my lucky stars that Sam is less security conscious than Zara would like her to be. Maybe if I could open the upper window wider, I could somehow haul myself up the wall and pour myself through the gap?

As I contemplate this, I know it's a completely harebrained scheme. Even if I don't seriously damage myself by clambering up the wall, I can guarantee that this would be the one occasion our neighbours suddenly find a sense of community spirit and summon the police to catch me in the act. And after all that Nutella this morning, I'm not convinced I'll actually fit through the miniscule gap. But not many other options are presenting themselves to me right now, and desperate times call for desperate measures. And perhaps here's where Sam's parcel can come into its own.

Balancing on the low wall which separates the foot of scrubland we laughingly call the front garden from the pavement, I manoeuvre the parcel towards the open window, hoping to use it as a prop to open the casement further. I hold this object responsible for my current predicament, so I am happy to sacrifice its safety in the cause of getting back to my relaxing duvet day. Fortunately, it's light enough for me to be able to hold it above my head and cautiously direct it towards the window like it's a giant piece of thread trying to fit into a tiny needle eye. My tongue is sticking out of the corner of my mouth in concentration as I gingerly hook open the latch. Not even pausing to celebrate my small moment of triumph, I take a deep breath and summon up every bit of strength I possess to try to lever the frame upwards. It doesn't budge. Cursing my piddly arm muscles, I lean forward, balancing one foot on the lower frame and the other on the wall so I can get a better purchase on the parcel. Out of the corner of my eye, I see an elderly man crossing himself and turning around to avoid having to pass the weird unicorn who's apparently attempting the splits in her front garden. Here's hoping he's not on his way to call the authorities on me.

I seesaw the parcel up and down a few times, gradually increasing my tempo to build up momentum. To my complete astonishment, the window groans and then starts to open wider. Just one more push upwards and I reckon I can get it fully open.

I give one last shove and yelp as I lose my purchase on the parcel. I tumble to the ground and watch in slow motion as the parcel miraculously slides through the gap, and the window slams firmly shut behind it.

I am having the worst luck today.

"I suppose at least Sam's parcel is safe," I mutter to myself, trying to look on the bright side while wondering what on earth I'm going to do now.

Checking up and down the road to see if anyone witnessed that disastrous chain of events, I jump up quickly before the damp dirt can seep through the fabric of my onesie. If I'm going to look ridiculous standing on the street in a furry unicorn suit, I'm jolly well going to keep it as clean as I can.

Dignity not quite intact, I turn my attention back to the task in hand. From where I'm standing, the front of the house looks as impenetrable as a fortress. If I'm to have any chance of finishing off that jar of Nutella, I'm going to have to try approaching this challenge from a different angle.

One of the selling points of the house is that we have a back garden (again, for "garden", read five-feet-square patch of debris), but I've not ventured out into it since Sam moved in because the access door is in her bedroom. From what I remember from the one barbeque I attempted to host in there when I first moved in, I seem to recall there is a fairly high wall around the garden, but it's worth a try. Given the open windows at the front, there's a chance Sam might have left the back door on the latch, allowing me to get inside. It's a slim chance, I'll admit that, but I'm trying to cling onto some hope.

The first challenge, of course, is to find the entrance to the alleyway which the garden backs onto. Hopefully it'll be slightly more discreet than my current surroundings. Londoners are famous for ignoring other people's eccentricities, but I have a feeling they might make an exception for an outfit as bizarre as mine. I feel like there's a neon sign pointing at my head saying "Lazy skiver", and the longer I stay out here, the more exposed I feel.

I pad down the road, picking my way along the cracked pavement, bemoaning the damage I'm doing to my lovely slippers. The trouble is, a lot of the houses around here look very similar and I'm worried I'm not going to recognise ours from the rear. God forbid I end up climbing into the wrong person's back yard. That's a recipe for arrest or worse if ever I heard one.

Eventually I find the entrance to the alleyway. It's piled high with rotting bits of cardboard and the stench of urine is almost thick enough to taste. I hover on the main road, torn between my desire to return to the safe haven of my house, and my instinct for self-preservation. However, the lure of Netflix, combined with the fear of being spotted by someone who might report me to my bosses, is too strong, and I slowly, hesitantly, venture down the gloomy passage.

Chapter Five

10.02 a.m.

I emerge about ten seconds later at a run, and keep sprinting until the sound of barking dogs has faded into a sufficiently safe distance. Their owners would probably protest they were only being friendly, but I wasn't going to hang around and prove them wrong.

I lean against a bus stop as I try to get my breath back. This is the last time I ever pay attention to something my brother suggests. Bloody Charlie and his bloody stupid idea to throw a sickie. And idiot me for actually following his advice. What on earth am I meant to do now?

The stabbing sensation of a stitch makes me double up and clutch my side. As I do so, my hand connects with something rectangular and hard. Barely believing my luck, I reach into the capacious side pocket of my onesie and fish out my mobile phone, which I must have automatically slipped in there on my way downstairs to answer the front door. Thank goodness for pockets. Something is finally going my way today. There is no need for me to waste any more precious relaxation time when I can ring a locksmith and get back into the house easy as anything.

I'm halfway through googling numbers for local locksmiths when I realise that perhaps my brilliant plan isn't quite so brilliant after all. A locksmith should be able to help me get back into the building, but will they be able to do it without having to put a replacement lock in? And if they can't, how will I explain to Zara her sudden need for a new key? She'd be highly suspicious and I know she wouldn't rest until she uncovered the truth. The thought of being on the receiving end of one of her grillings is too much to contemplate when I'm already feeling pretty vulnerable. And if she gets the slightest whiff of suspicion that my sick day isn't quite as I've sold it, she'll inevitably report back to Genevieve and the other partners, and I'll be lucky to be allowed to use the photocopier, let alone be given the keys to the pro bono department.

But it wouldn't just be Zara who would need a new key, Sam would be affected too. Why didn't I think of her earlier? Why am I worrying about locksmiths, when I can ring Sam and ask her to come back and let me in? OK, we've never spoken in person, but I've taken in her parcel, and surely a sense of housemate solidarity will send her to my aid? I'd like to think I'd do the same for her.

I scroll through my contacts until I find Sam's number, under H for Housemate. Before I press dial, I rehearse my pitch, keeping it simple and to the point, glossing over why I was at home in the first place, and emphasising the fact that I got locked out in the act of doing her a favour by taking in her parcel. It's a big deal to be asking Sam for help, especially when I don't know whether I can trust her not to dob me in to Zara, but I have to do something. Who knows, maybe she'll find the whole thing hilarious and it could be the start of a wonderful new friendship? After all, if I had a better social life, maybe I wouldn't have driven myself to the point of having to skip work for a recovery day.

The phone rings for ages and then clicks onto a generic answer machine response, which doesn't give me much hope that Sam actually checks her messages. I don't waste time leaving one, but hit redial, hoping the sight of two missed calls will make her realise the urgency of the situation. And then I settle down on a wall on the street corner and wait, passing the time by counting the number of idiots in cars who decide to hoot their horns at me, thinking they're oh-so-hilarious.

The hope that Sam will call me back sustains me for around five minutes, then I finally acknowledge that she's not going to any time soon. She's either up to her neck in work, as I should be right now, or she thinks I'm going to nag her about the broadband bill or something. It's my own fault. I should have made more effort to be friendly when she first moved in.

But there's no time for regrets now. There's nothing for it. If Sam won't come to me, I'll have to go to her. I scroll back through the house WhatsApp group analysing the conversation and picking up clues until I piece together what she does for a living and where she is based, again feeling deeply ashamed that this is not information that I know off the top of my head.

I experience a moment of misgiving when I realise she's a photojournalist for one of the more notoriously gossipy tabloids. One of the junior partners at work was exposed by that very publication only a matter of weeks ago for snorting coke at a city party which had descended into debauchery. Suffice to say, they're no longer in employment at Richmond Woods, and the bosses sent around a diktat about 'appropriate behaviour' and the risks of consorting with members of the press. I quickly dismiss my silly fears. No one will be interested in reading about a lowly lawyer skipping work for one day, and Sam will have bigger fish to fry than little old me. The best thing to do is make my way to her office near London Bridge, borrow her key and I'll still be back home with plenty of time to spare for rest and relaxation before Zara returns from work.

I check the distance to London Bridge from here on my phone, and decide against walking it. I've already been wolf-whistled and yelled at several times for my strange get-up. The more I can minimise my time on the street, the better. The Tube will have quietened down by now, but this is still my day of indulgence, even if it hasn't turned out quite as planned, so I'm not going to hop on the Underground unless I absolutely have to. The taxi apps on my personal phone are still connected to work accounts, so there's no way I'm using those, which leaves me just one option. Cycling.

I signed up for a bike rental account during my early days in the city when I thought I'd still have time to care about things like my carbon footprint, but since then, as with many other things, I've had to compromise my principles for the greater good, in this particular instance, not arriving at work as a sweaty mess. Besides, the pace of traffic in my area is always terrifying and people seem to have little patience for cyclists. I've seen a fair few near misses and it seems like people take their lives into their hands when they get on a bike. However, the traffic couldn't fail to see me today, shining brightly in my rainbow colours. Surely the unicorn uniform will encourage cars and buses to give me a wide berth? I'd really rather not suffer the ignominy of being knocked down while wearing granny pants which would be the envy of Bridget Jones. Besides, pedalling will be better for my slippers than walking, I tell myself. I just hope security will let me through in this get-up to speak to Sam, but I'll worry about that when I get to her work.

I hurry to the bike rack, half-expecting to find they've all been checked out for people's morning commutes, but I'm in luck, as a Transport for London van has just arrived with a collection of cycles.

"Are these good to go?" I ask.

The van's occupants openly smirk at my strange get-up.

"Yeah, we're redistributing them from the racks where they're running out of space. Where you off to then?"

First it was the diligent delivery driver, and now I'm

encountering chatty transport managers. It feels like everyone in London is playing against type today.

"Fancy dress party," I say, figuring it's easier than explaining the real situation. I'm only grateful I don't sleep in a skimpy little negligee as I'd be attracting an even more dangerous kind of attention.

"Funny time of day for it. Student life, eh?" says one of them.

I smile for the first time since I got locked out. It's been a while since I've been mistaken for a student, probably due to stress adding about a decade to my facial features, so I'll definitely take that sideways compliment.

"It's the best," I say, thinking longingly of those halcyon days where everything seemed so simple. Feeling particularly generous, I help the guys unload the bikes from their van. However, my good turn backfires on me, because despite my pleas to leave one ready to go, they diligently lock them all up so I have to start from scratch. Even worse, they hang around to watch my attempts to fathom the incomprehensible information on the app so I can set one free again. Normally, I'm quite good at following instructions, but I'm particularly cack-handed today. Before long, a streak of oil is tarnishing the brightness of my onesie and I have a horrible feeling I might have a smudge of it on my face as well. Maybe I'd have been better off going to work after all. That thought gives me the impetus I need to tap in the final code, and at last I am in possession of my transport.

"Good luck, sweetheart," says the smaller of the two men, then he pulls my unicorn tail which I'm pretty sure constitutes sexual harassment, even in the world of mythical creatures.

I twitch it out of his reach, and then loop it up so it won't dangle in the spokes of the bicycle. Conscious of my audience, I set off with a nervous wobble but holding my head high. Nothing to see here.

Chapter Six

10.16 a.m.

I manage to get around the corner without mishap, and then quickly dismount to re-check the directions to Sam's workplace. My phone reassuringly tells me that it's under three miles away and that the route is "mostly flat". I mentally add a minimum of an extra ten minutes to the sixteen it promises me it will take to cycle it. When I did my cycling proficiency badge back in the Guides, our leader described all the routes as "mostly flat" too, something we disputed as we panted our way up the near-vertical slopes of the crags.

I set off again at a stately pace, trying to muster the dignity of a Victorian lady as the breeze whips my hair into an even greater tangle. To be honest, I'm grateful for the wind providing a bit of air conditioning to counteract the cosiness of my apparel. The fleece and fur combination is far too insulating for exercise, and I'm getting a sweat on.

But despite the less than optimum cycling clothes, I start to enjoy myself. I guess this is what they mean about exercise giving you endorphins. I must make more of an effort to use this as my mode of transport to work in the future. I mentally kick myself. Why do all thoughts lead back to that place? I need to stop obsessing about it and instead concentrate on the task in hand.

I'm starting to gain some confidence in my cycling-in-slippers technique when another cyclist suddenly overtakes me at speed, and yells, "Hurry up, you slag!" in my direction. I instantly feel like I'm on the set of *EastEnders* and my mood crashes accordingly. I send another curse in Charlie's direction. He would definitely be laughing his head off at me now, plus he'd probably be lapping me on that ridiculous unicycle he learnt how to ride at circus school. Thoughts of my brother bring out my competitive edge, and I put on another burst of speed.

Two more cyclists effortlessly whip past me, and I swear I can hear their laughter on the breeze long after they've gone out of sight. I grit my teeth together and push on regardless, the beads of sweat dripping down my forehead and making my eyes sting. I bet this is tougher than the bootcamp workout sessions Zara boasts about going to at ridiculous-o'clock on a Saturday morning. I'm seriously regretting my decision not to sign up for the electric bike subscription offer.

However, I am finally making progress. The rows of terrace houses have fallen behind me, and I'm now cycling between the glossier buildings of corporate London which only serve to increase my feeling of scruffiness. My firm isn't in this part of the city – I certainly wouldn't be cycling anywhere near it if they were – and I'm not familiar with the purposes of these buildings, but I can recognise their type, and the sort of people who will work in them. They won't suffer fools gladly and anyone who doesn't conform to what they regard as the norm will be an object of derision at best, and suspicion at worst. I'm going to stand out like a hippy at a death metal gig. As I cycle past the mirrored walls, I spot my own crazy reflection and imagine the security guards whispering warnings to each other on their radios. I half-expect to see a welcome party emerge to escort me out of the area.

I'm about to take to the back streets in the hope of finding a less conspicuous route when someone on the pavement opposite sends a cheery wave in my direction, with no apparent edge behind the interaction. What differentiates them from the countless other people who've felt the need to attract my attention in my current state is the fact that they are dressed as a tiger. I wave back in amusement, wondering what on earth someone is doing wandering around central London in a tiger outfit. Mind you, he's probably thinking the same thing about my current style.

As I cycle past the imposing Gherkin building, all steel and endless panels of shimmering glass, I'm suddenly joined by a whole group of furry creatures, including two polar bears, a koala and a penguin. They ring their bike bells at me cheerily, greeting me like a friend. I have literally no idea who they are or where they're going, but surrounded by a phalanx of onesie-wearers, I no longer feel like I stick out like a sore thumb and I happily ring my bell in response. There's a lot to be said for safety in numbers, so I allow myself to be swept up in their merry convoy.

"First time?" one of the polar bears asks conversationally as we wheel around a corner and start to slow down near the imposing entrance to the Bank of England.

I glance across and realise that my new companions all have placards balancing in their bike baskets. The polar bear lets go of her handlebars and leans across to shake my hand, introducing herself as a resting actor called Libby. I feel pretty proud to be able to return the gesture without face-planting on the pavement, although I do keep one hand firmly gripping my bike throughout. I try to read the slogan on the banner, but it's a step too far for my meagre city cycling skills, so I go ahead and ask the question instead.

She laughs. "We're here for the climate change demo. Hence the costumes of endangered species. All of these animals are losing their habitats because of the actions of mankind."

Her companions boo and a few cries of "shame on us" are uttered.

Libby continues her explanation. "When you get to the bottom of it, money is what drives it all. So, we're protesting at as many high-profile, wealthy institutions as we can, until someone listens to us. We've been doing it every week so far this year. The police are getting pretty pissed off. But once you start pissing off authority figures, then you know that you're getting somewhere."

I think about how Genevieve and the partners would react if I tried that tactic at work and quickly decide I'm not brave enough to even consider it.

"Are you going to join us? You look the part, although I'm not sure where unicorns fit on the endangered list," says the penguin, who turns out to be a former investment banker called Graham. He's a clone of the suits who haunt the corridors at Richmond Woods, and for a few moments I worry in case he's clocked who I am. I'm fairly sure my bosses would view getting involved in a political protest like this as a serious misdemeanour, one which would bring the firm into disrepute. Off the top of my head, I can count several clients we've dealt with whose attitude to climate change would be exactly what this group of protesters are campaigning against.

I'm about to toe the party line, make my excuses and leave on my key-fetching mission, when out of the corner of my eye, I spot someone dressed as a rhinoceros whizzing past on a unicycle and I experience a pang of nostalgia. Charlie wouldn't think twice about staying here and joining in with the protest. Mind you, back in my school days, neither would I. We both had a reputation for standing up for what we believed in, and were fervent card-carrying members of Greenpeace, spending our free time spamming our local MP with letters demanding she vote in favour of green bills. When I applied for law school, I had visions of turning up at police stations and defending protesters who'd chained themselves to railings outside nuclear power stations. But as I started applying for jobs, I allowed myself to be persuaded by a tutor to let my Greenpeace membership lapse in case it was misinterpreted by potential employers. It was my first step on the slippery slope of compromise, and there's always been a feeling of regret at the back of my mind that I let it happen. There have been too many occasions in the past few years where I've allowed myself to be railroaded into doing things that don't sit well with me in the pursuit of a greater good which I fear I will never achieve.

"Come on, join the movement," urges Graham. "You dressed for the occasion – don't let yourself back out of it now."

"Not exactly," I reply, and find myself confessing exactly why I'm cycling through central London in a unicorn onesie. I don't know why I'm trusting complete strangers with the story, but there's something about their friendly, easy-going attitude that makes me feel safe telling them the tale.

Graham and Libby hoot with laughter, especially when I describe trying to break back into the house. I remind myself that hopefully before long I too will be able to look upon this day as an amusing anecdote.

"As you're stuck and it sounds like you've nothing better to do today, you should join the fun," says Libby, leaping off her bike and gesturing for me to follow. "Come and make a stand with us. There's plenty of time to get the key off your housemate later."

I look around at the sea of people in their colourful costumes clutching banners with slogans ranging from the hilarious to the downright rude, and suddenly sitting at home and binge-watching *Queer Eye* seems rather dull in comparison. I do have most of the day ahead of me to rescue the key, and I'm being presented with the perfect opportunity to reboot my activism. When was the last time I got the opportunity to stand up for something I really believe in? Wouldn't it be good to feel like I was actually taking positive action, rather than just daydreaming about it in between meetings with selfish millionaires? This time it's my own voice I can hear in my head urging me to act the rebel and go with my instincts.

The brakes squeal as I come to an abrupt halt next to the bike hire rack. I may be about to become a protester on my illicit day off work, but there's no need for me to break the rules still further by illegally keeping hold of the bike for longer than the rental period. I hurry to catch up with my new furry companions.

Chapter Seven

10.56 a.m.

The sun is shining, the traffic has been stopped by the efforts of my campaigning compatriots so the area is strangely tranquil, and I'm lustily singing a rather rude, but funny, song I've just learnt about climate change featuring one Derek the Duck who doesn't care very much about his effect on the environment. Everyone has linked arms in front of the Bank of England, a sea of endangered animals in human form dancing and swaying to put our message across. The atmosphere is lit with excitement and enthusiasm, and I know that this is exactly where I'm meant to be.

It's so much better than being in the office and I'm feeling a surging sense of joy at being part of something so important. For once, I'm standing up for what I believe in. I have a voice, and it's so good to be able to use it, without feeling constrained by the conventions of my workplace. I can see people smiling as they walk past, putting their thumbs up in support and occasionally snapping photos on their phones to share with their friends. There are even a few press photographers with their long-lens cameras recording the demo for posterity. I'm glad they're spreading the word about such an important issue, but their presence sparks a niggling concern about who else might see those images. It certainly wouldn't do for a partner to spot me mid-protest song, when I'm meant to be vomiting my guts up at home. I pull my hood as low as I can over my face and hope the photographers focus their lenses on the much more photogenic polar bears instead of me.

We're now doing a hokey-cokey style dance to accompany the chanting. Nobody's going to be winning *Strictly Come Dancing* any time soon, but who cares about that? All that matters is that a group of strangers have come together to stand in solidarity for a cause everyone feels strongly about. Even the act of singing as a group is uplifting and I feel happier than I have done in weeks, no, make that months. I'd forgotten what it was like to share jokes and laugh with such ease, without wondering if there's a hidden agenda behind the interaction.

Just as we're getting to the lyrics about Derek driving a tanker, what a… well, you can fill in the gap, my phone buzzes and I quickly reach for it in case it's Sam finally responding to my missed calls. I'm not in a hurry to leave the demo, but I would like the reassurance of having the ability to return to the house under my own steam well before Zara is due back.

No such luck. My heart sinks as I fight to control the

feeling of anxiety which automatically rises. I've not got the number saved in my personal phone, but I know it off by heart. Genevieve. How did she get my private number? It's either another example of her being all-seeing and all-knowing, or Zara has maliciously passed it on to her. I'm halfway through the process of unlocking the phone to read the full message when I catch myself doing it and force myself to stop. As far as anyone else is concerned, I am off sick. If Genevieve has descended to the level of bombarding my personal mobile with messages when, as far as she knows, I could be on my deathbed, then she really is the lowest of the low. But even full of outrage, I find myself drawn back to the text. It's hard to change a reaction that's been programmed into me for the last two years. Besides, what if this is her response to seeing pictures of me at this protest? If I don't check, I'm going to worry about it until I do.

I detach myself from the frontline group and retreat a bit further back to where there's space for me to read the message and hopefully put my mind at rest. I really shouldn't have bothered. It's a missive from Genevieve asking me to put my sick leave to good use by reading up on a particular new directive from the tax office. If I wasn't feeling ill before, I certainly am now. That feeling of being trapped in a pressure cooker momentarily returns, closing in on me, leaving me fighting for control. I close my eyes, and try to concentrate on my breathing, steadily counting out the seconds for each inhale and exhale, until I've steadied myself. Gradually, I can focus once again on the cheery whistles and shouts of my fellow protesters.

Now the feeling of mounting stress is overtaken by righteous indignation that my boss dares harass me when I've signed off sick. Do other companies act like this towards their employees? Sometimes I really feel like I've sold my soul to the devil, and I so desperately want it back. I delete the text in a rage, thanking my lucky stars that I don't have the "read message" facility activated on this phone. I hurry back to the group and launch into the protest chants with even more vigour than before, putting my anger at work's appalling attitude to good use.

Graham high-fives me, clearly impressed at what he sees as the passion I am demonstrating for the cause.

"It's great to have fresh blood at these things," he says. "I hope you'll join us again at the next one."

I beam in delight, pleased that I've made the grade. It's so refreshing spending time with new people in a completely different context from my normal surroundings. Maybe this could be the beginning of me being able to build some meaningful friendships in London.

"I'll add you to the WhatsApp group so you can keep up to date with what we're doing." Graham whips out a very expensive new mobile, taking care to shield it from the rest of the crowd as if he's slightly ashamed of it. "Oh, I know, it's probably hypocritical of me to have this thing when so much pollution and stripping of natural resources is caused by making them, but it's either have one and keep informed, or be ignorant without one. Besides, my wife insisted so she can keep an eye on what I'm up to. She's convinced I'm going to get arrested one of these days, but I'm working to bring her round to my way of thinking."

"You don't have to justify yourself to me, Graham," I hurry to reassure him. It would be hypocritical of me to have a go when I have two mobiles and probably facilitate a lot of climate unfriendly businesses through my job. Yet another reason to make it to the pro bono department, or even reassess my career completely.

Just as we're exchanging numbers, the line of protesters staggers back. The police are surging forward, shoving against the ranks of fluffy campaigners in a bid to get the traffic flowing again. The protesters are having none of it, pushing back with everything they've got. Suddenly there are elbows jabbing into ribs and boots tramping on toes, as people try to stand their ground. Angry drivers hoot in support and the noise levels increase to near deafening. It feels like there's not enough room to draw breath, let alone shout as everyone jostles around, but somehow it doesn't stop the bellows of "Police brutality!" as the campaigners refuse to back down. In all the confusion, Graham stumbles backwards, and I only just manage to stop him falling. His shiny phone isn't quite so lucky. Despite the din of my surroundings, I swear I hear the distinctive crack of its screen shattering into a thousand pieces. Graham turns puce with rage and throws himself into the heart of the fracas.

"I say, watch out, you thugs!" he says, his voice becoming even more refined and plummy in his anger. It's like the Earl of Grantham from *Downton Abbey* has arrived on the scene with his sleeves rolled up, spoiling for a fight. Graham pushes back against a constable, dislodging his helmet so it's now at a rakish angle over one ear. It's so ridiculous that everyone starts laughing, which doesn't endear us to the police line. The PC tries to defend his dignity by shoving even harder against the crowd of protesters. Libby stumbles, and Graham kicks out to defend her, and then I lose track of who's doing what, because suddenly it's everyone for themselves and fur is flying as the endangered species lash out and the police respond with heavy tactics. The relaxed mood of the protest has vanished, to be replaced by bristling rage and aggression, chants turning into grunting shouts of fury. I've never been in the middle of a skirmish before and I'm both terrified and elated, probably something to do with the adrenalin which is now being pumped at double-speed around my body. I find myself shouting alongside everyone else, although I couldn't tell you what words are coming out of my mouth.

Then, suddenly, the breath is knocked out of me as a stray fist clips my stomach. Gasping in shock more than pain, I realise how vulnerable my position is and that's when the fear wins out. However much I value the cause, I do not believe in violence to get the message across. It's time I got out of here. I hold my arms up, as if in surrender, trying to make myself look as unassuming as possible. But I know that I'm fighting a losing battle. My outfit stands out from the crowd, the rainbow unicorn a splash of colour among the monochrome of the polar bears, penguins and police uniforms. In a weird way, I can almost visualise the scene as if I'm not part of it, and I can picture how distinctive I appear in comparison to everyone around me.

It would seem I'm not the only one to have come to that conclusion. Just beyond the police line, I can see a photographer taking shots, his finger held down to get a rapid-fire collection of images. I'm pretty sure he's framed up the picture with me at the centre of it. I turn cold with fear as I quickly assess the dire consequences of appearing in the press in my current predicament.

Chapter Eight

11.50 a.m.

Who would have thought a protest could go from peace to carnage in a just over an hour? Libby and Graham look like they're quite enjoying the growing scuffle, wielding their placards merrily with little care of the consequences. But within seconds, they've been swallowed up by the rest of the crowd and then I'm alone in a group of yelling and screaming strangers. Their polar bear costumes don't look quite so friendly any more, and they're revealing themselves to be quite the fighting force, wildly swinging banners around, the fabric delivering stinging blows to anyone in their way. The police, meanwhile, are shouting antagonistically, their words indistinguishable among the piercing whistles and roars of the crowd. As much as I care about the cause, I cannot risk being caught up in this carnage any longer. The mood of the protest has turned dark and I'm finding all the noise and chaos really intimidating. The air is thick with anger and aggression. The all-too-familiar feeling of panic is rising in my stomach and my breath is catching in my throat. It feels like if I don't get out of here soon, I'm going to suffocate.

I stumble forward, my fluffy slippers providing zero protection against the sturdy boots of the demonstrators. But I don't get very far before my path is blocked by a growing line of angry-looking police, who are impervious to my pleas to be allowed past. My only choice is to go backwards, straight into the heaving mass of campaigners, in the hope that I can somehow duck and dive my way through and find safety.

Shielding my head with my arms, I try to negotiate a path for myself, my breathing coming quick and shallow now, but with horror I realise I'm being prevented from moving by someone holding onto my tail and aggressively trying to yank me towards the police line. It's like being in one of those nightmares where you're trying to run from something terrible but your legs won't move fast enough to get away. I try to jerk myself away, but the fabric is stretching and straining, and it's only a matter of time before it rips altogether, leaving my naked form exposed to the world. My tormentor clutches at me again, and this time they succeed in grabbing my waist with a bruising grip, hauling me close enough to feel their hot breath on the back of my neck. The hold feels disturbingly intimate, especially when the hand slips a little further down, allowing their fingers to press into the top of my thigh. A shudder of horror goes down my spine, but I refuse to be paralysed by fear any longer. I jab up and backwards, and hear a faint "whoomph" as my right elbow connects with something hard. Then I spin around and slap the guilty hand away, preparing to deliver an angry lecture on sexual harassment. I became a lawyer to stand up for the powerless. Well, I'm feeling pretty powerless right now, so I'm jolly well going to stand up for myself for a change.

But the words of condemnation die on my lips as I realise that the person who'd been grabbing at me was a police officer. The plastic casing of his radio is broken, and I have a horrible feeling that's why my elbow is now stinging. He seizes his handcuffs from his belt and launches himself at me again, spittle flying through the air as he bellows threats of arrest and worse.

It takes me a split second to decide I'm not going to hang around and argue self-defence. In a crowd this big, it's going to be a case of "he said, she said". And examining the situation dispassionately, it's not looking too good for me. Respectable lawyer I may be on most days, but today in the eyes of the authorities, I'm a law-breaker in a furry onesie, a ridiculous tree-hugging troublemaker who's smashed up a policeman's radio. Criminal law isn't my speciality, but I know enough to realise that this incident could see me landed with a charge of assaulting an emergency services worker, despite the fact that he was the one attacking me. That's a prison-worthy crime, punishable by up to twelve months in jail. I don't think I could survive twelve seconds behind bars. What kind of a mess have I got myself into? I actually feel sick with fear. I have got to get away.

Throwing all caution to the wind, I lower my head and charge my way through the crowd. I daren't look back to see if I'm being chased, so I keep moving forward, heart pounding, breath catching in my chest. My fluffy slippers are grimy and matted, and I can feel every imperfection in the pavement through them, but I keep on going, determined to make my escape. All the way, I'm repeating the mantra, "Please don't arrest me, please don't arrest me", as I imagine the police officer in hot pursuit, ready to grab at my tail once more and clap the handcuffs onto me.

Eventually, the atmosphere lightens, the noise of the crowd fades into the distance and there is space around me where before there was a squirming mass of bodies. I'm probably safe to stop now, but the instinct for self-preservation keeps propelling me onwards, head still down, not looking back, until I end up charging stuffed horn first into something very solid. The shock of the impact makes me see stars briefly.

"Eurgh," I moan, winded and disorientated by the abrupt halt of my flight. I stagger back and clutch my head for a few seconds, feeling thoroughly discombobulated. Eventually, I muster the strength to rub my eyes and brush the hoody back from my face so I can see what I've collided with. And then I wonder if I've been knocked out by the collision, because the guy standing in front of me can only be a figment of my imagination. Admittedly, a rather grumpy figment of my imagination, but he's definitely an improvement on the insipid suits I normally spend my time surrounded by, with his broad shoulders, artfully dishevelled hair and sexy glasses. In slow motion, I watch as he leans towards me, reaches out with a surprisingly elegant hand and delicately tweaks the squishy silver horn on my hood back into shape.

"Watch what you're doing with that horn," he says. "You could have caused a lesser person some quite serious damage."

"I'm perfectly capable of controlling my own horn, thank you very much," I snap back, annoyingly befuddled by my response to his general hotness and instantly irritated by his superior attitude. A lesser person? Who says that? I quickly decide that he's one of those annoying blokes who know they're super attractive and use it to get away with throwing their weight around.

He sniggers like a schoolboy and I realise what I've just said, but I refuse to show any sign of embarrassment. Although try telling that to my face, which is currently glowing in a way which tells me it's turning a particularly vibrant shade of red.

There's a shout behind us, and I look back nervously, worried that the scrummage is heading my way again.

"Been caught up in that lot, have you?" he asks with apparent innocence.

I'm about to answer when I spot he's pulled a notebook out of his pocket. I follow the line of a strap that's hanging off his shoulders and realise it leads to a camera. I'm instantly on my guard. If I'm not mistaken, he's the guy who was taking pictures of me in the protest. I'd have put two and two together earlier if I hadn't been so thrown by the collision.

"Why do you want to know?" I ask defensively.

He quirks his mouth in a lopsided grin. "I always like to

make sure I spell people's names correctly when they go in the paper."

I fight to keep my face neutral. I'm pretty sure he's trying to rattle me, but if I remain calm, maybe I can get away with this.

"I don't understand."

His grin widens. "Don't you want the credit for that little escapade back there? From where I was watching, it looked like you were right in the centre of the trouble, showing that copper what for, poor bloke."

I'm about to retort that it was the police constable who was in the wrong and I was only defending myself from his over-familiar tactics, but I stop myself just in time. As every good lawyer knows, sometimes it's best to say nothing at all, that way there's no danger of getting yourself into more trouble. If Mr Paparazzo here thinks he's going to catch me out with these tactics and trick me into saying something compromising, then he's very much mistaken.

"I have no idea what you're talking about," I assert, with as much dignity as I can muster.

He sighs and picks up his camera, making a great show of checking through the shots on screen, raising his eyebrows occasionally, and whistling as if in shock at particularly incriminating pictures. I fight the urge to shuffle nervously on the spot and instead fold my arms, and stand in as brave a stance as I can muster while I rack my brains for an idea. He could be playing a game to manipulate me into giving a quote for his paper. I'm desperate to have a look at the images, and he knows it, but

I'm not going to give him the satisfaction of asking to see them.

Our stand-off lasts for a good few minutes, my tension levels increasing horribly with every second. Eventually, I can't stand it any longer.

"How about you just show me the pictures instead of pulling all those silly faces while you look at them?" I ask, hating myself for caving. But it's better to be armed with knowledge than to let my imagination fill in the gaps, I tell myself.

"In the good old days, I'd answer that you can buy a copy of the paper tomorrow to see the images, but of course nowadays everything is online within minutes," he replies. "I'm sure you can check them out there."

He starts spelling out the web address, complete with the laborious "www dot" at the beginning. I know he's trying to wind me up still further and he succeeds.

I snort derisively. "Come off it, grandpa. You're not old enough to have been working before the invention of newspaper websites."

He takes a sharp intake of breath. "Oh, it's like that, is it?" he says. He clicks through a few photos. "Fair enough. I've got all I need here. I'm sure once we put the pictures online with a number for people to call if they recognise the 'Unicorn Thug', we'll soon get a response. Thanks for giving the story an interesting top line, by the way. It was turning into another standard protest piece, but I reckon these snaps can get it off the sidebar and into the headlines. So nice to have met you." His voice is dripping in sarcasm.

He makes a great show of packing his notebook away

and putting the camera back in its case while I berate myself for being all kinds of a fool. I am in deep, deep poo now. If he does print that appeal, one of my colleagues is bound to recognise me, even though they all claim not to bother with the "fake news" media. Even worse, the police will probably come after me for that little misunderstanding back at the protest. It's no exaggeration to say that my entire future now rests in this man's hands, and I don't like it, not one little bit.

I take a deep breath, and try to turn on the charm, desperate to make amends and save myself.

"Look, I'm really sorry." I pause to give him a chance to say his name, but he doesn't respond. "I'm really sorry, but it was a complete accident, charging into you like that. I inadvertently got caught up in the protest and I was trying to get away to safety and I wasn't paying proper attention to where I was going. You've got the wrong end of the stick, I promise you."

He raises an eyebrow, then unpacks his notebook and pencil again, and starts scrawling notes. I try to read what he's writing but it's all in shorthand. Every time I utter a word, he traces out incomprehensible squiggles on the page.

"Would you mind not doing that?" I ask. "It's really off-putting when I'm trying to apologise and you're writing down everything I'm saying. Please, could you stop?"

"Please, could you stop," he spells out, and then looks up expectantly, as if waiting for further dictation, an infuriating expression on his face.

"What are you, a teenager trapped in the body of a

grown man? You're not exactly behaving in a very mature fashion, are you?"

Once again, I find myself lashing out verbally at him. There's something about him which is making me really riled. Aesthetically, he's hot, I'll admit it, but that can't make up for his terrible personality.

He does at least briefly put down his pencil. "The same could be said about you," he replies. "What kind of grown woman wanders around central London in a unicorn onesie? I can only presume you dressed like that because you fully intended to join the protest. Are you trying to tell me you voluntarily look that ridiculous? Were you doing it for a dare or something?"

"It was a complete coincidence, I swear. And I know perfectly well that I look like a complete prat, thank you very much. In fact, the constant harassment I've been facing since I had the great misfortune to lock myself out in my pyjamas has made me very aware of how much of a freak I appear to be. I've had enough, and I don't need you, Hack Man, adding to it."

Again, his lips twitch in that annoying way.

"Hack Man, that's a new one. Sounds like a superhero. I'll take that." He looks me up and down and pulls a face. "You sleep in that get-up? Lucky boyfriend."

I'm so frustrated at his infuriating superiority and lack of sympathy for my predicament, I actually jab my finger on his notebook. "I am a grown woman, and I have every right to wear what I damn well want to bed without needing to ask permission from a man, thank you very much."

He holds his arms up in surrender. "Fair enough, I take your point."

"Too right," I say, the wind slightly knocked out of my sails in surprise at his agreement. Then he undoes the tiny bit of ground he's won.

"So, is he more of a teddy bear man, or maybe his mystical onesie creature of choice is a dragon?"

"You seem to have extensive knowledge of male onesies," I respond, and he nods his head to acknowledge the blow.

"Locked out, you say. That sucks. But it doesn't really explain how you ended up in central London taking part in a climate change demonstration."

I throw my arms up in the air in exasperation. I need to stop allowing myself to be distracted by this man. He's definitely trying to wheedle details out of me for his article.

"If I tell you the story of how it happened, will you promise not to publish my picture?" I change tack and attempt to negotiate with him.

"An interesting proposition," he says. "Would I be allowed to publish this story?"

I could kick myself. I'm getting myself into even more trouble here.

"No way," I say quickly. "I'm trying to appeal to your good nature."

He laughs at this. "But you don't really think I have a good nature, do you?"

"What else would I think? You're threatening to publish incriminating photos of me and all those other people, when all we were doing was trying to show the world the threat posed to us all by climate change."

He shrugs. "But it wasn't exactly a peaceful protest, was it? Violence is never the answer. Do you guys really think it's the right way to get your message across, disrupting honest, hard-working people who are trying to go about their everyday lives and get to their jobs?"

He's hit a sore point there. I'd normally count myself among their number, but after making the decision to take a duvet day today, I now find myself outside of this respectable part of society.

He continues with his grumbling. "Call me a cynic, but we've had weeks of these protests now, and what have they achieved? Precisely nothing. At best, you're a bunch of naïve troublemakers. At worst, well, you're thugs using a random cause as an excuse to throw your weight around. I for one have had enough of it all."

"You really are a cynic," I say. "I feel sorry for you. How can it be wrong to want to make a positive difference in the world?"

He sighs. "As I suspected. A naïve troublemaker. Well, it was an interesting experience making your acquaintance. But I have a story to file, so if you're not going to tell me anything of use, I'd best be on my way. I'll find out the facts for myself, one way or another." He pulls his mobile out of his top pocket. "How is it that time already? See you later, Bambi. I've got a couple of calls to return."

"Bambi's a deer, not a unicorn, you muppet," I yell after him as he strides off down the street.

I am literally sweating with anxiety. Why am I letting

him get away from me when he still has those incriminating photos in his possession?

But before I can start chasing after him, my phone starts vibrating in my pocket. If this is Genevieve calling me again, I'm so het up I might very well confess all and throw myself on her mercy. Then I see the name on the screen and nearly do a dance of joy.

Housemate Sam.

Chapter Nine

12.12 p.m.

I nearly drop the phone in my haste to answer.

"Oh my goodness, Sam, thank you so much for calling me back. You are my absolute heroine."

"Gratifying to hear, but to what do I owe the honour?" replies a very male, and somewhat familiar voice.

"Um, who is this please?" I say in confusion, trying to place where I know that voice from and failing miserably. "I think there might be some mix-up with the number. I thought I'd rung my housemate Sam. Is she there, please?"

"This is Sam Harris, as requested. I'm your heroine, remember. Although I think 'hero' might be more factually accurate." There's a rumble of amusement in his gravelly voice.

"But you can't be Sam," I say, still failing to get the very obvious solution which should have presented itself to me.

"Why not?" asks the man at the other end of the phone. His voice is getting louder for some reason.

"Because Sam's a girl," I reply stupidly.

"What gave you that impression?" Sam replies. Only this time it's not over the phone because he's standing right in front of me. Again. And now I know why the voice at the other end sounded vaguely familiar. Because the person who's calling from my housemate Sam's number appears to be the irritating photojournalist I've just been locking horns with.

My mouth falls open and I stand there like a gormless fool as everything I thought I knew spins around in my head and falls back in a new order. Apparently, my housemate Sam is a man. But then again, why wouldn't he be? I don't know why, but I always assumed Sam was female, and yes, I know it's really shameful that I never took the time to find out if I was right. I guess I made the assumption because when I first moved into the property, it was advertised as an all-women household, and I assumed it continued to be that way through some stipulation of the landlord. Although now I think about it, there has been a male razor in the bathroom for a while, but everyone knows it's cheaper to buy men's products because of the woman tax which charges extra for pink stuff. If I'd even considered it for a second, I'd made the assumption Sam was one of those savvy buyers who refuses to bow to the patriarchy.

"Sorry," I say lamely, feeling extremely uncomfortable and embarrassed at the awkwardness of the situation.

"No offence taken," says Sam. "I suppose it's a pretty bad reflection on both of us that we'd not bothered to introduce ourselves properly, even though we've been living under the same roof for several months."

I nearly dive into my usual excuse of explaining how busy I am at work, but it's not good enough, and I know it. How many more ways can the job change me into a heartless drone?

I hold my hand out, although I'm still annoyed at him for the farce with the photos earlier.

"I guess it's time to remedy that. I'm Alexa Humphries, occupant of the smallest bedroom in the house. Over-worked lawyer, currently locked out and in a bit of a pickle. Nice to meet you, finally."

"And Humphries is spelt how?" says Sam, that irritating glint back in his eyes again. He doesn't bother to respond with pleasantries of his own.

"Why do you want to know?" I ask suspiciously. "Surely now you know I'm your housemate, you're not still planning to use my picture in the paper?"

Sam tilts his head to one side and fixes me with a glare.

"You really do like leaping to conclusions," he says. "Why would you make that assumption?"

"Housemate solidarity," I say genially. Is it not obvious? I think back to the number of occasions I've allowed Zara to get away with murder at work, purely because I didn't want to create difficulties in the household.

He rubs his hand against his stubbly cheek.

"No, I've still not got it. Can you explain more clearly?"

Is he being deliberately obtuse, or does he genuinely not understand?

"Now you know we live together, you won't want to

drop me in it, right?" I deliberately keep my tone light and friendly, despite the churning sensation which is growing in my stomach.

"We share a roof, Alexa, that's not the same as living together. As we've just demonstrated, I don't know you from Adam, and beyond the fact that you have my phone number, what proof can you offer that you do share a house with me?"

"Why would I lie about something like that?" I ask, my irritation growing by the second.

"Why wouldn't you? From our brief acquaintance, the only behaviour I've seen you demonstrating is violence, shortly followed by an attempt at manipulation. It doesn't exactly inspire confidence."

My answer comes in the form of a snorting harrumph, the only sound my complete sense of indignation will allow me to articulate.

Sam wrinkles his nose in disapproval.

"Let me put it another way. You claim to be a lawyer, correct?"

"I bloody am a lawyer," I retort, finally finding the words to start defending myself, although I'll admit I would probably have retained more credibility if I'd left the "bloody" out of it.

"Fine, you say you're a lawyer. Well, I wouldn't ask you to throw a case for me within five minutes of having met you. I'd like to think that you would extend the same professional courtesy towards me."

"It's not the same at all," I protest.

He pauses as he's about to put his phone back in his pocket.

"Care to elaborate for me? I give you advance warning to think very carefully before uttering phrases like 'fake news' or 'gutter press'."

I realise I'm on very delicate ground here.

"That's not what I'm saying."

But I can't think of another way of trying to get my point across. I attempt an appeal to his better nature, if he has one.

"Look, could you do me this massive favour, and I will owe you forever?"

His face tells me that he's not interested. I try a different tactic. As my grandma says, sometimes honesty is the best policy, even if it means confessing all to a man who's already demonstrated a worrying lack of trustworthiness.

"Have you ever woken up and felt like everything's too much? Like you've been running on a treadmill for ages, and you've suddenly realised that however much you try to up your pace to match the machine, it's just going to keep increasing the speed, and you're still not going to get anywhere?" My voice is choking up as I try to explain the weird feelings that led me to the position I'm in right now. It's hard to justify the choices I've made so far today when I don't even fully understand why I've been making them. My head is frazzled and everything seems unreal, like if I pinch myself hard, I'll find myself back in the office as normal, briefing a client, rather than here in the street, pleading with an indifferent journalist. I start talking more quickly in a bid to disguise my growing emotion. "This morning was just one of those days. Something felt wrong and weird from the second I woke up, and I made a foolhardy decision to take the day off."

I'm hoping that by couching it like that, it makes it sound less bad. Maybe he'll assume it's a legitimate day's leave, and won't judge me quite so harshly? Not that that would really make any difference, because the second he mentions this situation to Zara, then all my efforts to get back home before her return and keep her in the dark will be in vain anyway. But if I start worrying about that now, I'm going to get overwhelmed again.

"I had fully intended to spend it catching up on sleep, but I stupidly decided to answer the door and take in a parcel for you. In fact, I think it could be argued that it's your fault that I've found myself in this mess, and you owe me a favour in return."

"You really aren't having a great day, are you Alexa?" says Sam, demonstrating his journalistic ability by stating the bleeding obvious.

"Up to this point, no I certainly haven't," I snap back, then I take a deep breath. "But I'm really hoping that my luck is about to change now I've met you."

I don't know why I'm attempting anything even vaguely resembling flirtation. I'm crap at that kind of thing at the best of times, let alone when I'm dressed as a fluffy fantasy creature. And I don't want to give him the wrong impression.

His stance remains impassive, but I think I detect a slight flicker of something resembling amusement in his expression.

"I'm not a completely heartless beast, whatever you may think of the tabloid press," he says. "Shoot. In what way do you think I can improve your day?"

I decide to go for broke.

"Lend me your keys? And don't run the pictures of the protest which have me in them?" I beg, actually clasping my hands as if I'm praying, and fluttering my eyelashes half in parody, half serious.

"No," he says shortly.

"You absolute bastard," I say, enraged that he's lured me into pleading, when he had no intention of helping me in any way.

"Charming. To make sure you're properly informed before you curse me further, I don't have my keys on me. They're back on my desk at work. You're not the only one having a forgetful day. And you already know my stance on the other issue."

I decide to take his admission of forgetfulness as an indication that he might be softening slightly in his attitude.

"Can't you go back and get them?"

Sam checks his watch.

"Jeez, is that the time? No, I certainly cannot. I'm running late now, thanks to you, a delightful exchange though it has been. I've got another job to go to. Maybe I can meet you on the doorstep and let you back in when I get home from work later? It's been, um, interesting to have met you."

I'm instantly dismissed, and he starts striding away from me down the street. But I'm not going to let him get away that easily. I skip after him, struggling to keep up. My teddy slippers are no match for his Chelsea boots.

"Or you could give me your security pass and I could fetch the keys from your office? That way I wouldn't be stopping you getting your very important work done."

That's my final attempt at appealing to his reasonable side. But it would appear he doesn't have one.

"Security would take one look at you and send the building into lockdown," he says. "Especially after I file my story, which now I'm not going to be able to do until after my next job, because you've kept me hanging around with your ridiculous tale of just 'happening on a protest'."

I refuse to rise to his insults and instead focus on the tiny bubble of hope his words give me. If he's not sending the story in straightaway, then I still have a chance of stopping this disaster before it unravels further.

"It's not a ridiculous tale." I take a deep breath, my mind made up. "And if that's the way it's going to be, you leave me with no choice," I say.

Sam pulls a face. "Oh, I'm so scared," he says sarcastically. "What have you got planned, Bambi?"

I smile sweetly, doing my best to ignore another Disney jibe. "You claim you're not going to change your mind, do you? Well, as I said, you leave me with no choice. I'll have to stay with you until you do change your mind. You're going to hand those keys over to me and delete those photos by the end of the day, you just see."

I speak with as much confidence as I can muster. In reality, I have no idea how I'm going to make that happen, but sticking at his side and wearing him down is the best I can come up with right now. And if I don't succeed, then I'd better start making plans to move back home with my parents, because newspaper article or not, I'll be losing my job regardless if I don't get back to bed before Zara gets home from work this evening and discovers my absence.

Chapter Ten

12.21 p.m.

S am is clearly not going to take my threat seriously.

"Do whatever you like," he says, striding off again.

I'm now having to run to keep up with him, and I'm seriously regretting my lack of a bra beneath the unicorn gear. I fold my arms across my chest to try to keep the girls in place before they knock me out. I've never looked more undignified in my life. All this charging around is getting me out of breath, and I'm wheezing worse than a smoker with a fifty-a-day habit. I'm appalled at how unfit all this sitting behind a desk has made me. That's it, I'm joining a gym next week, if I still have a job to be able to afford it.

A bloke across the street openly laughs at the surreal sight of a man being pursued by a unicorn with a bouncing bosom.

"You look like you're well in there, mate," he calls out.

Sam and I experience a brief moment of common

purpose as we simultaneously send a two-finger salute in the heckler's direction. But whereas I cringe at the stream of abuse that is sent back at us, Sam is apparently impervious.

"I guess you're used to being sworn at as a journalist," I pant, trying to keep the lines of communication open between us. "Lawyers tend to prefer our hostility to be of the passive-aggressive variety. Sometimes I wish people would just come out and say what they really think. All the tiptoeing around each other keeps me constantly on edge."

"Well, in the spirit of openness and expressing what I really think, will you kindly bog off and leave me alone?" Sam retorts, then increases his pace, forcing me to put on another burst of speed to stop him getting away from me. It should be illegal for tall people to walk so quickly when there are shorter folk like me trying to keep up.

It's not just the running that I'm finding challenging. I'm also on edge, very much aware that Sam will want to get rid of me as soon as he's able to, so I'm trying to minimise the likelihood of that happening by attempting to anticipate his next movements. I have a horrible feeling he's heading to the Underground. Unless I stick to his side like glue, it'll be really easy for him to give me the slip in the maze of the Tube network. Just in case, I get my phone out and try to find the wallet function while on the move so I'm ready to pay.

Sam turns a final corner, and sure enough, there's the distinctive red and blue sign for Bank Underground Station. I take a parallel gate to him and swipe through without any problems, but then I realise he's still on the other side of the barrier apparently having an issue with using his flashy smart watch to get through. I resist the urge to make a comment about his defective technology. Then I start worrying that he might be bluffing, using it as a ploy to throw me off his trail. Facing a dilemma, I'm about to tap my way back out again, when finally, the gates swing open and he makes for the escalator. As soon as we stepped foot in the station, I knew this moment would come, but my heart still sinks.

Now, I have to confess that another reason I hate my daily commute by the Tube, aside from the feeling of being locked in a cattle truck, is that I'm rubbish with escalators. I have this pathological fear of falling down them, and the ones on the Tube are particularly bad as most of them are so ridiculously steep and long. It's not an unfounded fear. At the end of my first week at Richmond Woods, I saw an elderly gentleman stumble at the top of the escalator at my local station. I reached out to try to save him, but I was too late and he tumbled seemingly endlessly, until his fall was finally stopped by a portly Underground worker who literally flung himself forward to act as a barrier. The poor old man survived the experience, amazingly, but he was battered and blue, and since then, every time I step onto an escalator I hesitate, seeing his bruised face before me.

You would imagine that using the system a minimum of twice daily for the last two years would have built up my immunity somewhat, but the escalators still have the capacity to send a shiver down my spine, and even provoke the occasional panic attack, a weakness that makes me pretty disappointed with myself.

As it's after midday, the Underground is a lot quieter

than I'm used to and there are fewer people getting on the escalator to block the sight of the steep drop from my gaze. I can feel my breath catching in my throat and it's not all down to the two hundred metre sprint I've just involuntarily completed.

But there's a lot at stake, and I'll have to pull on my big girl pants and get over my fear if I'm going to stick to Sam and persuade him to change his mind. He leaps nonchalantly on the escalator with practised ease. Despite my determination, I still hesitate at the top before I jump on behind him, legs wobbly with nerves.

Unfortunately, I haven't allowed for the fact that today I am wearing fluffy teddy bear slippers, which introduces a whole new level of hazard. For a horrifying moment, the fluff gets caught in the brushes at the side of the escalator, keeping one foot trapped at the top while the rest of me slowly heads down the steps, my nightmare coming true. I'm gripping onto the handrail like my life depends on it, but that's travelling at a different pace to the steps, so now my arms are being twisted round too. My mouth is dry and my heart is going quick-time as I anticipate the terrible fate that is about to befall me. The elderly gentleman's face flashes before my eyes once again, and I brace myself for the horrible falling sensation.

Then, just as I'm convinced I'm about to get split in half, a great big chunk of fluff rips away from my slipper, freeing me from my predicament, but also sending me staggering forward. I yelp in sheer terror and put my arms out, stopping my fall at the expense of Sam, who grabs onto my waist, but only just manages to prevent himself tumbling to the very bottom of the escalator. I clutch the back of his shirt in a vain attempt to help, although it just makes things worse.

"What the hell are you doing? Trying to kill me so I don't publish the piece?" he barks, neatly sidestepping his way out of my grasp as if he's been burnt. We're both breathing heavily with the shock of the moment. "Nice try, but it'll take more than that to finish me off." He brushes his sleeves as if trying to get rid of the contamination from being touched by me.

I'm so thankful he stopped my fall, I'm impervious to his rudeness. When we reach the bottom of the escalator, I'm so relieved to have made it in one piece that I nearly kiss the ground in the manner of the Pope arriving in a new country. But there's no time for me to get carried away with my survival of the hazards of the escalator, as Sam is clearly on a mission to get rid of me. He feigns going one way, before doing a swift about-turn and heading in the opposite direction. But I didn't grow up as an annoying younger sister for nothing, and I recognise that tactic of old from my big brothers. When Sam sets off towards the Northern Line, I am there waiting for him, smiling smugly.

He shrugs as if in defeat, but the frown on his face tells me he won't give up that easily. Besides, I'm sure you can't work in the ruthless world of the tabloids without knowing how to get your own way. When he slows down so I can keep up with him, it confirms my suspicions that he's biding his time while he plots.

The train arrives in a cloud of hot dust, and travellers surge forward to get on board. Sam waits for a pregnant woman to take a seat, then, quiet as a lamb, he sits down at a double bench so there's space for me to sit next to him. Despite this apparent consideration, he gazes out of the window at the tunnel, pointedly ignoring my presence. I spend the whole journey on tenterhooks, preparing myself for leaping off at any moment, but then he starts calmly tapping on his phone, apparently in no hurry to go anywhere. I try to sneak a look at the screen in case he's starting work on the article, but he manages to shield it from my gaze, all the while acting as if he has no awareness of my presence.

Of course, when the train draws into London Bridge, it's a whole different story. Sam sets off like he's competing in the Olympics and only the good fortune of him having to slow down to avoid colliding with a man carrying a cello case enables me to catch him up.

I can't help gloating a bit when he gets on the Jubilee Line and I'm still right there at his side. He'd obviously thought that he'd get rid of me back there, so he visibly sulks for the duration of the journey. Although I attempt to make polite conversation, asking about his job and fishing for information about his plans for the rest of the day, he's having none of it. Never mind. I'll get it out of him eventually.

I squirm uncomfortably on my seat, feeling a bead of sweat tracing its way down the length of my spine. The furry onesie might be perfect for keeping me warm in my chilly house, but it's far from ideal running kit. I'm beginning to worry I might be about to marinate in my own juices. Feeling a little daring, I unzip the front a bit and roll the cuffs up past my elbows in the hope that it will allow some cool air to circulate. It can't make me look any more ridiculous than I already do.

I lean forward to examine the full extent of the damage to my beloved teddy bear slippers. I think they're going to have to go to the shoe shop in the sky if, or when, I finally get back home. I only hope they last for however long I end up having to chase Sam around the capital. As I inspect the soles, I hear a gasp from an elderly woman sitting by the doors, and realise with horror I've inadvertently flashed half the train carriage.

I hastily zip my onesie back up to my neck as Sam snorts into his phone.

"Don't you dare add that detail into your article," I say. "I know what you tabloid hacks are like. Any hint of flesh and you'll write in great detail about me 'flaunting my curves in front of a shocked captive audience'."

"Good line, I must remember that one," he responds. "This is our stop, by the way," he adds, to my great surprise. Is this another classic double-bluff? But he even waits to help me check my tail isn't going to get caught in the doors when we get off.

Waterloo Station is bustling, and I watch Sam closely for any signs that he's going to make a break for it, but he's clearly decided on another tactic. As we emerge from the concourse, he turns to face me.

"I'm going to level with you. I'm off to the National Theatre for a press call. They're launching a new production and they've got some big-name luvvies appearing in it who are graciously going to sacrifice their rehearsal time and parade for the press. That means there will be present a whole bunch of us 'tabloid hacks', as you so charmingly describe us." He keeps his voice very matter-of-fact, but his eyes narrow as he delivers his threat. "I'm normally loath to share a story with a competitor, but every so often, I'm happy to make an exception. I'm sure they'd love to hear all about the Unicorn Thug and her exploits. We so-called hacks are very keen on justice being done, and once we cover a story, the police can hardly turn a blind eye to it." He pauses to see what impact he is having on me. I determinedly keep my face as a neutral as I can, while inside I start to feel sick. "People love to read that kind of thing, great clickbait, sells lots of papers. Still fancy joining me for the ride?"

He smiles broadly, convinced that this move will make him win the game. He's a sneaky so-and-so, I'll give him that. There's only one way to play this, and that is to call his bluff.

"Bring it on," I say, with as much gusto and confidence as I can muster. "It will be a delightful experience for me to meet more ladies and gentlemen from Her Majesty's press."

Actually, I can't imagine anything worse. He won't follow through on his threat and shop me to them, will he? I've got no choice but to take the risk and find out for myself.

Chapter Eleven

12.53 p.m.

S am reports for duty at the National Theatre's box office, announcing his name and job title, and, to my confusion, introducing me as the work experience girl. I guess he had to come up with some way of explaining my presence and getting me in front of the enemy, but I see it's OK for him to make up stuff when it suits him. The man behind the counter frowns suspiciously. There can't be many people who'd turn up on work experience dressed like a walking rainbow, surely? Sam seems to realise this because he continues with his fiction.

"Outreach programme, you know," he says in a confidential tone. "Taking people with difficult backgrounds and helping them to reintegrate in the community. Isn't that right, Alexa? Maybe you could tell the nice man about your troubled past?"

What is Sam playing at? The receptionist is looking

seriously worried. Not only am I a freak in a unicorn onesie, I'm now apparently a freak with a dodgy history. I've clearly wound Sam up to the point that he's prepared to make himself look like a prat in order to drop me in it.

"That was a long time ago," I hasten to reassure the receptionist, thinking up my retaliation quickly before I get thrown out of the building. Sam is going to regret trying this tactic. "I'm a completely reformed character. I even think twice before picking up my cutlery, I'm so concerned about the dangers of knife crime. And it's all thanks to my hero, Sam. Anything he tells me to do, I'll do it. Anything," I finish breathily, trying to create the impression that he's been taking advantage of the vulnerable work experience girl. I put my arm around his waist and look up at him with faux worship in my eyes to really hammer home the charade. As he catches my gaze, I narrow my eyes to give him my best warning stare. If he's going to start telling stupid stories, then I'm going to give as good as I get.

Sam shuffles uncomfortably, and tries to remove himself from my reach, all while attempting to pretend that everything is completely normal. I tighten my grip and snuggle against him some more. Sam looks like he's just been forced to drink a mug of sour milk.

The man behind reception is completely flummoxed, looking between the two of us like we're participants in a horrifyingly bad tennis match. He shakes his head, as if trying to bring himself to his senses. Finally, when it becomes apparent that we're not going anywhere, he emits the sigh of a man who has reached his limit.

"Well, whoever you guys are, you're late. The press call

was twenty minutes ago and our actors are on tight schedules." He's looking triumphant now, certain that we won't be his problem for much longer.

Sam shoots me an angry glance and finally twitches himself free from my grasp. He leans forward on the desk and turns on the lads-together act with the receptionist.

"Look mate, I'm really sorry I'm late. Circumstances out of my control, you know what it's like in the world of news. Things change from one minute to the next. Do me a favour, and see if you can pull some strings for me?"

Oh, so it's OK for him to ask a complete stranger for a favour, but not me? He's such a hypocrite.

There's a queue gathering behind us now, members of the public keen to book tickets but finding their way inexplicably blocked by an angry giant with his unicorn sidekick. They're being polite at the moment, but some of them are starting to clear their throats in that frightfully British way of expressing imminent anger.

The receptionist pulls a face, clearly deciding it's best to go along with Sam's wishes if it'll get us out of the way.

"Fine," he says. "I'll ring the PR Manager to let her know you're here."

Sam claps him on the shoulder.

The receptionist does not share his optimism.

"I'm not sure she'll be able to accommodate you now..." *Especially given the disreputable appearance of the team* is the unspoken comment at the end of his little lecture.

He steps away from the desk to make the call, no doubt giving the PR Manager advance warning of the reprobates awaiting her. I'm half-expecting to see security descending to escort us off the premises.

Sam spins around and drags me to a nearby pillar so we're out of earshot of the crowd gathering behind us.

"This is getting beyond a joke, Alexa. Will you please quit bugging me? You're making me look massively unprofessional," he hisses, running his hand through his hair so that it stands up on end.

"Sure will, as soon as you hand over the memory card with those photos," I reply. "And I reckon you do a good enough job of making yourself appear unprofessional. Trying to pretend I'm the work experience? What planet are you living on? I know I look a state. I'm locked out in my pyjamas. But what's your excuse for looking like you just rolled out of bed? You wouldn't last two minutes at Richmond Woods."

"Says the woman who's so screwed up by the place, she pretends to be ill in order not to go in, and then weirdly spends the day doing anything she can to preserve her position there."

"What—? I—" My retaliation dies in my throat. Sam's words almost take my breath away. I'm so angry with the man I can hardly speak. How dare he twist things like that, making me out to be some kind of pathetic mass of contradictions, a woman who doesn't even know her own mind? He is utterly infuriating. Can't he see that there's a difference between being a little run-down and jaded and needing some time to myself, and deliberately throwing away everything I've poured my blood, sweat and tears into achieving? Just because I decided to take this day off, it doesn't mean I want every single day off in the future. I'll admit things have spiralled from my morning blues, making me impulsively plump for a duvet day. But I just need to get this situation back under my control, and then everything else will follow from there. Fine, I'll also concede that the situation at Richmond Woods has driven me almost to breaking point, and I know I need to make changes to my life, but that doesn't mean I want that change forced upon me, which it would be if I were to be rumbled today and lost my job because of it. Whatever I do next, I want to do it because it's *my* decision, not because I don't have any other options left to me.

I glare at Sam, hands clenched, breathing fast as all these thoughts race through my mind. Why can't I open my mouth and articulate all this in a coherent way? Anger and upset are stealing the words from my throat, and I have a horrible feeling that unless I get a grip on myself, the tears welling up in my eyes might be about to spill over. I want to shout at him, make him see where I'm coming from. But then again, why should I have to explain anything? The man's got a nerve, trying to manipulate me into justifying myself to him. I decide to keep quiet. Besides, he wouldn't understand.

But then again, I barely understand myself.

Sam raises an eyebrow, apparently amused at the effect his words have had on me.

Someone clears their throat. "Sorry, am I interrupting something?"

I suddenly become aware of a woman with a clipboard standing at our side looking between us in confusion. She holds out her hand to shake mine – I respond like an automaton – then she turns to do the same with Sam.

"I'm Lydia Browne, Head of Communications. Thanks for making it in the end. I've managed to persuade the actors to hang back for five minutes longer so you can get your pictures, but I'd really appreciate in future if you could arrive at the time specified on the release. Otherwise we may have to reconsider whether it's worth including your publication in our press calls." She manages to tick Sam off while retaining a perfect veneer of politeness. This kind of passive aggression is almost like being back at work.

Sam shoots me another angry glance, then hurries to smooth Lydia's ruffled feathers, turning on the charm and having her laughing in no time. He can obviously be pleasant when he wants to be. Their discussion continues as she leads us through the public areas of the building. I hang back, still keeping my quarry in sight, but lurking far enough away that I don't get caught up in the conversation. I'm not feeling quite up to pretending everything is fine at the moment, and I don't want to give Sam any excuse to tell her why I'm really here.

Despite the precarious nature of my position, the thrill of visiting the backstage area of the theatre soon starts to overtake my churning sense of uncertainty. I've always wanted to see a show at the National Theatre, but it's another thing on my long list of stuff I haven't got around to doing. At least now I'll be able to look at the picture of it on my bedroom wall without experiencing that pang of disappointment at never having set foot in the building. Behind the scenes, everything is a lot scruffier than I expected, nothing like the glitzy world of showbiz that the movies depict, but there is still a zing in the atmosphere from all the creative work that goes on. We're led through a maze of dark corridors until eventually we reach a room with a piece of paper on the door saying "Rehearsal Space". Before Lydia can knock and announce our presence, a slightly younger clone of herself rushes out into the corridor.

"Thank goodness you're here, Lyds. Tom is going ballistic about being kept back from his lunch. He's on a strict programme at the moment and has to eat at certain times and if he doesn't get food in the next five minutes, then I think he might explode."

Lydia shoots a worried look in Sam's direction, probably concerned that he'll be noting down this little gem of backstage gossip to use in his article, but Sam affects deafness and steps away to join me by the noticeboard. I raise my eyebrow in question, surprised at this apparent gesture of compassion.

"What? I do have some sense of tact and discretion you know," he whispers.

"Could have fooled me," I mutter, wishing he'd decide to use it in my situation.

The two PR women lower their voices and much hissing back and forth ensues, until eventually the younger one retreats into the room clutching a cereal bar which Lydia has magically produced from her handbag. I wonder if she's got a spare one in there that she wouldn't mind sharing with me.

"My apologies, they'll be ready for you in a couple of

minutes," says Lydia. "In the meantime, is there anything you'd like to ask about the production? I'm afraid I've run out of printed press releases, but I can email one to your newsdesk later if you like?"

Sam agrees, although I get the sense he's not best pleased that his newsdesk will be receiving that email, probably because it'll make it clear that he's messed up. Serves him right. If he hadn't kicked up such a fuss with me, he'd have been here in plenty of time. It's probably because of this that he plays his next card.

"Alexa, why don't you ask the questions? It will be great experience for you," he suggests sneakily.

He smiles broadly, knowing full well that he's dropping me in it, because I don't even know what the rehearsals are for. But I'm determined not to let Sam get one over on me. I've seen *Notting Hill* and felt for Hugh Grant's character when he accidentally gets swept up in a press junket and asks the star of a space movie if it features horses, so I'm not going to fall on that particular hurdle. My opening question needs to be neutral, but probing, something that will strengthen my position and undermine Sam's little game.

"What message are you hoping to get across to the audience with this production?" I settle on. I'm not a lawyer for nothing.

I see the look of irritation on Sam's face and feel pretty pumped with myself for demonstrating the danger of underestimating me. But before Lydia can answer, her assistant emerges and beckons us into the rehearsal space.

The first thing I notice is that we appear to be the only members of the press there. It's a massive relief. I'm not convinced Sam ever intended to tell his rivals about my adventures, but it's a lot better that temptation isn't in his way. I'm hopeful that he'll be too busy concentrating on doing his job to bother explaining to the cast and crew the real reason for my presence.

Once I've established that, I relax a little, and start to examine my surroundings more closely. After all, when will I get the opportunity again to spend time backstage at the National Theatre? I'm fascinated by the tape markings criss-crossed over the floor, and the mishmash of furniture creating a makeshift set. And then I do a double-take as I realise that the boxes and chairs are laid to resemble a courtroom. It's weirdly disconcerting. Even though my work is done in an office rather than in front of a judge, it feels like fate is conspiring to make sure there are reminders of my profession chasing me everywhere today. It also reminds me of the urgency of my situation. Unless I get hold of those photos of the protest, they could be used as evidence against me, and I have no wish to appear in the dock for assaulting a police officer.

I try to distract myself from the unsettling feeling which is squirming its way around my insides by seeing if I can recognise any of the actors in the room. I almost squeal with excitement when I realise that Tom is *the* Tom Whiston, who appeared in a film which was so controversial that even people in my office broke away from their tort law to discuss it. I watched it on Netflix over several nights (mostly because I was watching in bed and kept falling asleep ten minutes in – no shade on the quality of the movie, I was exhausted) and thought it was actually a pretty decent story, despite all the rather gory fighting. I wonder if I could ask him for an autograph? I'm sure I could invent some other scenario in which I met him so I could post about it on social media and finally have something upbeat to boast about to my old friends. He seems pretty ordinary and approachable with his casual rehearsal clothes on, stuffing his face with the cereal bar that was smuggled in earlier.

My stomach rumbles in envy. I'm starting to feel lightheaded with hunger. It feels like a very long time since I was enjoying spoons of Nutella. I sidle towards a table which is being set up with plates in preparation for the lunchbreak, but Sam summons me back to his side before I can check to see if any grub is going spare.

"Now, now young Alexa. Keep away from those knives."

Could the man be any more patronising?

If it was only us, I'd have grabbed one of the knives to spite him, but I can feel Lydia's gaze boring a hole in my back. She's probably preparing to bundle me out of the room at any second.

"Sorry Sam," I say, sounding anything but. "I was trying to scope out some camera angles for you, just like you taught me."

I sense Lydia relaxing again as Sam's levels of tension increase. I can see he's heartily wishing he hadn't introduced me as the work experience. Now he'll have to get me involved in the shoot.

He sighs. "Cheers, Alexa, but I've got it. Perhaps you can hold my bag while I gather up the actors."

It's obviously the most mundane task he can come up with, but my heart starts racing at the opportunity he has unwittingly handed me. Because in that bag is his camera, and if I'm really quick, I should be able to get the memory card with those incriminating photos out of it and safely into my possession.

I nod, trying to look as calm and innocent as possible.

"No problem, Sam," I say, fighting to keep my voice steady.

He hands the bag over to me and I nonchalantly put it on my shoulder. He's a few feet away from me when he turns back and taps his top pocket.

"I've got the memory cards by the way, in case you were thinking of trying anything funny," he says, crushing my fragile hope, and saunters over to speak to Tom, a smug expression on his face.

I let the bag slide off my shoulder and slam it noisily down onto the floor, not caring if the contents are damaged by my deliberately clumsy handling. Foiled again. How did he manage to sneak them away when I was watching him so closely all the time? Maybe it's worth checking anyway to be on the safe side. I wouldn't put it past him to tell a little white lie. Quickly glancing up to make sure he's not looking in my direction, I squat down and open up the leather bag. I gingerly pick my way through the reams of folded-up newspaper cuttings, tangles of charger wires and bits of orange peel. Sam really is a disgusting slob. No wonder our kitchen is in such a terrible state.

Eventually I find the camera case and I'm about to open it when I realise Sam is standing over me again.

"Thank you, Alexa, I'll take that if you don't mind."

I'm reluctant to hand it over, and clutch it to my chest in what I'll admit is a very childish manner.

He actually dares to click his fingers patronisingly, before he holds his hand out again.

"I'm warning you, Alexa. We've got a job to do, remember."

With a grimace of frustration, I grudgingly pass it across.

"Thank you."

He turns to the actors and raises his voice to address them all.

"Ladies and gentlemen, I very much appreciate you doing this extra press call for me—" he hesitates, "—and my colleague. We will keep you for as little time as possible. Tom, would you mind standing over there with your script. I know your character Atticus isn't in the courtroom for all of his scenes, but I'd like a few snaps with the cast in shot together and the courthouse is a good backdrop for that."

Atticus Finch. Of course, they must be doing *To Kill A Mockingbird*, another inspiring tale featuring a heroic lawyer. As I like to remind people, we're not all bad, although when was the last time I got to make a moral stand like Atticus? I promise myself that if I get through the rest of today unscathed, I will return to my normal life with renewed determination to get on a better path.

As Sam starts working, he transforms into a different man – charming and personable, putting the actors at their ease with humour as he hurries about getting the pictures he wants. Even the most camera-shy member of the crew is gently persuaded to take her turn posing. I'm discovering a whole new side of him. He's even relatively reasonable when he turns around mid-photo to ask me to fetch him a reflector, whatever the heck that is.

It gives me another perfect excuse to search his bag, and by the time I've finished, I'm satisfied that his keys are definitely not in there, and there aren't any memory cards lurking anywhere either. I've even sneaked a quick look at his diary – yes, despite his shiny Apple watch, he's old school enough to have a paper Filofax – to try to work out where he might be heading next, just in case. However, I'm still at a loss as to what a reflector is. Fortunately, Lydia's assistant sees I'm struggling and points out the circle of white fabric and demonstrates how it snaps open into a large disc to reflect the light in a more flattering angle against a subject's face.

"Thank you," I whisper. "He's horribly bossy and I'm scared he'll write me a bad reference if I don't do exactly what he says."

She pulls a face in sympathy.

"He seems to know what he's doing though, so I'm sure you'll not go far wrong shadowing him during your work experience."

I hurry back to Sam with the reflector, and he absent-mindedly gestures at me to hold it in position for him. It takes a bit of practice to get it at the right angle, but before long, I get the hang of it and even start to enjoy myself.

I would never have imagined when I got up this morning that a few hours later I'd be rubbing shoulders with people like Tom Whiston. It would be thrilling if I wasn't up against the clock to get back home.

"Can you move in a bit closer please, Alexa?" Again, Sam is addressing me in a reasonable tone of voice. It's so unexpected, I do exactly as bidden, realising too late that he's tricked me into getting into shot so he can snap a few extra photos to add to his collection of blackmail material.

Without thinking about it, I stick my tongue out at him, clearly regressing in my behaviour to match my childish outfit. The actors burst out laughing, and I can hear the shutter on Sam's camera going like crazy as he captures the moment.

He flicks back through the pictures, nodding in satisfaction.

"The last one is definitely the best. I guess I've got you to thank for that, Alexa," he admits, and I feel a warm glow of satisfaction, despite the grudging nature of the thanks.

Lydia asks to take a look and is so pleased by the images that she offers us both free tickets to the first night of the show. By the way she's cosying up to Sam, she's clearly forgiven him for his tardiness.

"I can't really accept freebies," protests Sam. "The bosses are cracking down on that kind of thing. Gives the tabloids a bad name, they say."

I snort. "I'm pretty sure you do a good enough job of arranging that for yourself without throwing freebies into the mix." I turn to Lydia. "He'll say yes eventually, he's only pretending to be polite."

Lydia looks between the two of us. "Perhaps I should arrange for the tickets to be in separate areas of the theatre," she says tentatively.

"Sounds like a plan," I say, as Sam shrugs his shoulders. I notice he doesn't protest any further about the free tickets.

"Let me take your email addresses and I'll get them sent over to you both," says Lydia.

I'm about to automatically recite my Richmond Woods address, before I catch myself just in time and instead spell out my old teenage email letter by letter, too embarrassed to admit that yes, my email address as a seventeen-year-old contained an extremely ill-advised "Sexy Lexie".

I catch Sam smiling as he works it out. "Not a onesie wearer all the time then, hey?" he mutters.

I roll my eyes. "You, for one, will never find out," I retort.

He laughs and returns to packing up his camera kit. I watch out of the corner of my eye to see where the memory cards get secreted, but once again he's too quick for me.

There's a clattering at the door as a guy in chef's whites wheels in a trolley of delicious-smelling food. I was hungry before, but now I've smelt those delectable spices, I'm absolutely ravenous.

"That's our cue to leave," says Sam, crushing my hopes of tucking into the yummy food, and casually chatting with Tom Whiston over lunch. "Come on, Bambi, I know when not to overstay my welcome, even if you don't."

Lydia escorts us downstairs and we part ways at the front desk. I hope she follows through with her offer of free tickets. *To Kill A Mockingbird* was always one of my favourite books when I was at school and I'd love to see how it translates on the stage, particularly with the lovely

Tom in the leading role. I'd much rather be stuck with him for the day than my current companion.

Sam checks his watch.

"Time for a very brief spot of lunch before my next task. I'm guessing you're planning on hanging around for this too?"

"In the face of such overwhelming hospitality, I'd be a fool to turn such a generous invitation down," I reply.

Sam sighs in resignation.

Chapter Twelve

1.41 p.m.

S am decides to grab some food at the theatre's café and so naturally I do the same. Despite his best efforts to pretend we're not together, I attempt to make polite conversation in the queue, but he's having none of it and keeps staring into the middle distance with a pained expression on his face. He's trying a new tactic of ignoring me completely, perhaps thinking I'll grow bored and leave him alone. I wish. Believe me, I can think of much better ways of spending my time than traipsing around after His Grumpiness, root canal work being one of them, but at the moment this is my only option. I really don't know what his problem is. He could make this whole situation go away, if he wanted to. I don't think I've met anyone more stubborn in my life. He's clearly spent far too long working as a lone wolf, doing everything his own way. Well, today he's going to regret forcing a situation whereby I have to become his sidekick.

The effort of my morning on the run forces my mind to more prosaic matters. My hunger has developed to the extent that I am now absolutely starving. It feels like there's an empty space in my torso where my stomach should be. I'm not really used to this kind of appetite. Sitting at a desk for hours at a time, up to my neck in complicated paperwork, it's easy to forget about little things like proper meals. I can't remember the last time I achieved the heady heights of 10,000 steps in a day, and I gave up wearing a Fitbit long ago as it kept buzzing at me in a worried manner, thinking I'd collapsed because I hadn't moved in such a while. Today, I'm sure I've easily surpassed the 10,000 steps mark already, and consequently, I could honestly devour the entire menu of this café.

I grab a tray and survey the range of delicious-looking dishes in front of me, my mouth watering. I'd love to go for a full-on sit-down hot meal, but out of the corner of my eye I can see Sam selecting a meagre sandwich. He's obviously sticking to his plans to keep this meal break quick, so I regretfully do the same, although I can't resist grabbing a bag of crisps and a selection of veggies and houmous, which I optimistically tell myself I can always eat on the move if necessary. I grab the largest bottle of water I can find to help me replenish all the liquid I've sweated out during my exploits this morning. I swear it steams as my toasty hands come into contact with the cool condensation on its surface. I briefly rest it against the side of my head, relishing the chill of the bottle.

"If you're trying your own version of a Diet Coke ad in some weird attempt to get me on side, then I'm sorry to disappoint you, but blatant displays of exhibitionism are really not my thing," Sam says, although I can't help noticing the way his eyes follow a bead of moisture as it trickles down towards my neck.

I'm about to protest I was doing no such thing, but then decide that if he's going to jump to that kind of conclusion, I might as well have some fun playing up to his assumptions.

I trace the length of the bottle, lick the accumulated condensation from my fingertip and attempt my best sultry expression.

"Aw sugar, you disappoint me," I say breathily, internally cringing at my own ridiculousness.

Sam holds my gaze and we stare at each other for an uncomfortable amount of time. Then he frowns as if to say "Really? Are you really going down this route?"

I try to keep a straight face, but fail miserably. I burst out laughing, the infectious kind of laughter where it makes your sides ache and you just can't control yourself. Sam turns away from me, doing his best to radiate disapproval at my silly behaviour, but I catch his lips twitching as he looks down at his lunch tray. Maybe he's starting to soften in his attitude towards me.

Unfortunately, my dreams of a full stomach are dashed when we get to the till and I discover they're having trouble with their internet connection.

"Sorry love, cash only," says the checkout assistant, gesturing at the blank screen of the card machine as I try to proffer my phone to pay. I could cry with the disappointment. It's the first time I've had an actual lunchbreak in weeks, and now I'm not going to be able to eat anything in it? Typical.

I do that thing where you slap your hands against your pockets to demonstrate your lack of ready money, and look hopefully across at Sam. Surely if he's got any sense of decency, he'll offer to sub me and pay for my food.

He makes a great point of picking out a piece of cake for himself, then turns to me in mock surprise.

"No dosh hidden away in that outfit of many colours? What a shame." His voice says it's anything but. He hands a ten-pound note over to the assistant. "I'll take a cup of coffee to go as well please," he says.

"Are you paying for this lady's sandwich?" she asks, and I mentally thank her for her sisterhood solidarity.

He looks like he's considering her question carefully. He turns to me.

"Are you going to stop pestering me?" he asks.

I shake my head, even though I can guess what's coming next.

He turns back to the assistant. "In which case, no, I'm not paying for this unicorn's food," he replies.

I roll my eyes at his predictability.

The assistant casts me a sympathetic look as I tramp back over to the fridge and put the tuna mayonnaise panini and other goodies back on the shelves. Thankfully, she waves at me that I can keep the water bottle. I'd feel rather guilty if some other person had to buy it after I'd been wiping my face with it. I'm annoyed at Sam's pettiness. I know I'm not exactly going to starve to death in the next few hours, but a girl needs her food if she's going to be able to cope with this level of anxiety all day.

I help myself to a couple of sachets of sugar from the cutlery table at the end of the counter, reckoning they'll come in handy as an emergency energy boost if things get really bad. I stow them away in my pocket and vaguely wonder if I'm desperate enough to help myself to some leftovers at a table which hasn't been cleared yet.

And then I look around in alarm. While I've been distracted obsessing about food, or rather my lack thereof, Sam has managed to disappear out of my immediate sight. I desperately scan the crowds enjoying their lunchbreaks in the theatre foyer, and eventually spot Sam partially obscured by a pillar, smugly settling down for his feast at a table for one.

I stride across in as dignified a manner as possible, and hope nobody notices when I stumble over my fluffy feet.

"Nice of you to wait for me," I say.

He pointedly ignores me, and pulls his laptop and some cables out of his bag.

"What are you doing?" I ask.

I'm starting to behave like an annoying toddler, and I know it, but I'm tired, hungry and stressed, so what do you expect?

He ignores me.

"Are you transferring your pictures from the camera to your laptop?"

Still no answer. My irritation levels are growing and I wonder if I could accidentally-on-purpose hit the delete button on his keyboard mid-transfer. I only hope that the lack of Wi-Fi in the café will make it more challenging for him to send the pictures back to base.

I fetch an extra chair and plonk myself down opposite Sam, cupping my chin in my hands and staring intently at him in what I hope is a really irritating way. Politeness clearly won't work with a tabloid-hardened hack like him, so I've got to be blatant with my behaviour. To be honest, it's a relief to be off my feet for a bit. I might as well have been walking barefoot for all the protection my slippers are providing me, and the soles of my feet are tender, with the tell-tale throbbing of imminent blisters adding an extra level of discomfort. I subtly massage my jaw which I realise I've been clenching in tension because of my constant awareness of the clock ticking down to my deadline to get back home.

I surreptitiously check Sam's watch. If this was an ordinary Tuesday, I'd be inhaling a mug of coffee while I frantically prepped for the weekly meeting with my line manager. I like to think I'm a strong, confident woman, but those encounters have the ability to reduce me to a quivering shell of a human being. I realised within minutes of my first one, that it wasn't so much about helping me positively develop as a lawyer and a human being, as about constantly checking up on me and driving me towards unrealistic corporate goals. For example, at the last one, I was told my billable hours weren't hitting the quota and that if I didn't get them up to scratch, then I could be put on a written warning. I did the sums and realised I'd have to work through every evening and weekend for the next three months to get them back up to target, a prospect which left me weeping silently in the toilets and cursing my weakness for reacting in such a pathetic way. I know that nobody is going to die as a result of me not hitting Richmond Woods' targets, but sometimes the powers-that-be can make it feel that way.

If I ever return to work, I'll try not to take things so to heart, I promise myself. But it feels like a big if at the moment. I try to distract myself from my spiralling thoughts by focusing on Sam, watching him take every mouthful of his BLT. It sets my stomach grumbling again. He's definitely making a big play of enjoying the meal, his tongue tracing his lips for stray crumbs after every bite. He's even making the occasional overzealous "Mmmm" sound, really going for it in a way which makes me fear he might be about to develop his performance into a *When Harry Met Sally* moment of exaggerated enjoyment. For a man who claims to despise exhibitionism, he's surprisingly comfortable engaging in it. But if he thinks he's going to embarrass me into leaving him alone, he's got another think coming.

"If it tastes so good, I'm sure you won't mind sharing a bite with me," I say, making a play to grab the second sandwich.

He picks it up and licks the bread and then proffers it in my direction. For a moment I can see the irritating teenager he must have been.

"Seriously?" I say. "You're really descending to that level of pettiness?"

He smiles, smugly pleased with himself, but what he hasn't yet spotted is that when he picked the sandwich up, half the contents fell out onto his plate, remaining wonderfully uncontaminated by Sam saliva.

Figuring it's fair game, I snatch up a chunk of lettuce and a stray bit of bacon, guzzling them like I'm starving. Sam rolls his eyes, but he does relent enough to push another untainted piece of lettuce in my direction. I gobble it down.

"Feeling better?" he asks.

I nod, surprised by his sudden apparent concern for my welfare. He must be up to something. I watch him carefully, and my suspicions grow still further when I manage to snaffle a chunk of cake without him complaining.

Sam leans back in his chair and puts his hands behind his head, making his shirt rise to reveal an inch of stomach and the surprisingly jazzy waistband of his boxers. I would never have put him down as the type to wear Mr Happy underwear. He'd be much more suited to Mr Grumpy or Mr Selfish, if you ask me.

He fixes me with a stern expression. "Give me one good reason why I should be bothered about whether your bosses see a picture of you in the paper," he says. "Put across a sufficiently convincing argument and I will consider it with the weight it's due."

Chapter Thirteen

1.47 p.m.

This is my chance. He's not promised that if I convince him, he won't go ahead and publish anyway, but it's worth a shot. I don't know why I'm feeling so nervous and exposed. I'm a lawyer. I present arguments for a living, so I should be good at this. But there's something about Sam's steady gaze which is making me feel trapped under a magnifying glass. I need to speak honestly with him, but it's hard when I'm struggling to be honest with myself about how I feel about my life.

I try to start listing bullet points in my head – clear, coherent reasons which will make my case and change his mind. Should I begin by appealing to his better nature, or dive in with an explanation of my long-term career ambitions and their altruistic aims? But they're so divorced from my current day-to-day reality that it feels almost deceitful to cite them. How can I say that I need him to take pity on me because I want to make a difference in the world, when I've spent the last two years making precisely no difference whatsoever? How can I explain to Sam why I've made no progress on my dreams when I can't really explain it to myself?

I always tell myself that tomorrow will be different, but how long am I going to be able to keep believing that lie? The sense of personal failure grips me with an almost physical ache, pressing down on my chest and tightening the skin across my forehead.

I've got to say something. I open my mouth, hoping that instinctively I'll find the right words. But my pesky emotions are getting the better of me. I can feel tears pricking at the back of my eyes, and I'm scared that if I start speaking now, I might lose what little grip I have on my emotions. When things get tough at work, I normally manage to plough on through by giving myself a pep talk, but even my usual mantra of "woman up" is failing to help me cope with the pressure of this moment. Why am I falling apart like this?

I'm now really worried that I'm just going to sit here and cry at him, a humiliating prospect at best, and at worst, a reaction which Sam could easily misinterpret as me trying to engage in emotional blackmail. When did I turn into such a pathetic creature?

I open my mouth to try again, fingers trembling now as my stress levels ramp up to overdrive, when the checkout assistant stops by and slips a cheese sandwich onto the table in front of me.

"It's a day past its sell-by, so eat it at your own risk, but it's yours if you want it. The world looks better on a full stomach," she whispers, before collecting Sam's empty sandwich plate and shaking her head at him as she lets a few crumbs accidentally-on-purpose fall onto his lap. "It's not my place, love, but that girlfriend of yours looks like she needs a proper meal. I know you think you're being all modern man and equal opportunities or whatever, but a proper gent would have paid for her lunch back then."

I feel like hugging her, touched by the simple act of kindness from a complete stranger. Her show of solidarity gives me a little injection of confidence, while her Yorkshire accent reminds me of my childhood. I feel a pang of longing, remembering the good old days when everything was much more clear-cut, and I was full of optimism and hope for my exciting future.

I wonder what teenage Alexa would make of me now? She'd probably have a right go about my terrible fashion sense. But worst of all, I have a horrible feeling she'd be disappointed in me, selling my soul to the corporate machine and allowing myself to be trampled into the ground by it. She'd have told me in no uncertain terms to get my act together. Don't get me wrong. I have no desire to go back to being a teenager, at the mercy of raging hormones and trapped in a tiny community where nothing happens, so the fact that you've gone up a bra size in just one month becomes a major topic of conversation. But at least back then I had a modicum of self-belief, despite my train-track braces and prematurely top-heavy figure. When the boys teased me, I'd stand up for myself and would even defend my actions to the teachers when they told me off for retaliating. Now whenever conflict presents itself at work, or things happen which I fundamentally don't agree with, I feel scared rather than empowered, and shrink back, avoiding the situation rather than confronting it face on. The stress of my surroundings is turning me into a shadow of my former self.

Maybe it's time to admit defeat, let Sam do what he likes with the pictures and return home? And by that I don't mean my grotty house-share, but back to the Dales, a place that still feels like my home, even though I've spent barely any time there since I started my career.

Behind Sam's back, the checkout assistant winks at me and shakes her head in disapproval at him once more, her broad grin boosting my spirits ever so slightly. What was it she said?

The world looks better on a full stomach.

I realise that I'm not ready to give up yet without a fight. If Sam wants a convincing argument, then he's going to get one, just as soon as I've revived my brain with food.

I tuck into the sandwich greedily. Despite the slightly stale bread, it tastes delicious. With every bite, I can feel my strength returning and my resolve growing stronger. I will not be defeated by this situation.

Sam taps his watch. "Are you going to convince me or not?" he says. "Only I'm setting off in the next thirty seconds, so you're running out of opportunities."

My mouth is too full of cheese to be able to reply immediately, and by the time I've chewed sufficiently, he's already packing his laptop away.

"Come on Sam, hear me out," I say, angry and frustrated

that he's not giving me the time he promised. Then I start choking as a chunk of cheese threatens to go down the wrong way. I can feel the tears forming in my eyes as I gasp for breath. I thump my chest, but the cheese is still in place, clogging up my windpipe and making the room spin. I'm starting to fear that this might be how it all ends, then suddenly Sam is right next to me. He whacks me hard in the centre of the back, and dislodges the cheese. I grab the table and lean forward, gasping in relief. Then I wince as Sam whacks me again.

"Just to be on the safe side," he says.

I'm going to be covered in bruises by the end of the day.

"Finished dying yet?" he asks, ever Mr Sympathetic.

I cough a bit more then nod.

"Thank you," I gasp, still rather befuddled by the whole nearly dying thing.

He steps crisply away as if he can't bear to spend a second longer in my presence than absolutely necessary and fixes me with a stern expression.

"In which case, Alexa, pay attention to what I'm about to say. You've had your fun now, but I really can't afford for you to come on this next assignment. If you're still having trouble getting back into the house, text me at close of play, and I'll have picked up my keys by then. But until that point, kindly stop stalking me and trying to make your problems mine. It's just selfish."

He's raising his voice by the end, and the noise in the café quietens as people turn to stare at the bunny boiler harassing the nice young man. If only they knew what a stubborn mule he is.

"Good to know who I can rely on in a crisis," I say, a little unfairly, seeing as he's just saved me from choking and all. "And what time exactly does close of play correspond to?" If he finishes at five, there's still a chance for me to get the keys and be back, tucked up safely in bed, before Zara's return. I've long since kissed goodbye to any remaining dreams of having a proper duvet day.

He shrugs. "7.30, 8 o'clock? Something like that. But the boss's secretary is leaving and I heard a rumour of free drinks for his goodbye bash, so to be honest it might be later than that. I wouldn't worry. The weather forecast is good and I'm sure you'll find enough free stuff to do in London to keep you occupied for the rest of the day."

His blasé attitude nearly tips me over the edge. He has no idea what I'm facing and 7.30 or 8 o'clock is way too late for me to be returning home. There was a period when I regularly didn't make it in until midnight, and when we were in the middle of a big deal, I could see the dawning of two days at work. But in the last few weeks, they've been trialling booting us out of the office doors early, i.e. before 8 p.m. They're still expecting us to work into the evening at home, you've got to understand, but sending us home to do it means they get to boast about their staff members' work–life balance in trade publications, and have the added bonus of saving a bit of dosh on the office electricity bills.

I can guarantee that Zara will be going straight back to the house to carry on with whatever tasks she's picked up to curry favour with the bosses, and the first place she'll visit is my sick bed to assess whether I'm still ill enough to improve her promotion chances. That's the trouble with living with someone who's at a similar level of seniority (i.e. very junior) in the firm. We are natural rivals for any promotion that might be on the cards in the future. I was keen not to let this get in the way of a prospective friendship, but from early on she made it clear that she'll do anything to better her chances of getting ahead, even if it comes at the cost of her housemate. I once made the mistake of confessing to her that I hadn't read a brief properly for a client meeting because I'd received it too late, and she made very sure that not only was the client aware of it, but my line manager and everyone else who mattered too. If she gets back home and I'm not there, she'll make it her business to tell everyone in the company about it before the front door has even closed properly.

"And what about the photos?" I ask. If he agrees to delete them, it would be a huge weight off my mind, and leave me free to leave him alone as requested, and think of another way of getting hold of the keys.

He snaps his laptop shut decisively. "I thought as a lawyer you were meant to be bright. I'm running out of ways to tell you that I have no intention of deleting the pictures. Can you imagine if politicians asked the press to delete compromising photos of themselves and what effect that could have on the free functioning of democracy? As a journalist, it is my job to hold people to account. How hypocritical would it be of me to delete photos of a climate change protest that turned violent, just because my housemate was involved? I'm really offended that you keep asking it of me."

I feel like chucking the bottle of water over him in

frustration. He is the most stubborn, infuriating man I have ever met. I channel full lawyer mode as I hit him with my response.

"To take your points individually, it's flattering that you imagine I'm that important, but I hardly think I, a junior lawyer, qualify on the same scale as a politician asking for pictures to be deleted. Democracy is not going to fall because you get rid of a couple of photos. As to holding people to account, why aren't you aiming your efforts at the big energy companies and those responsible for the worst pollution rather than coming down hard on a group of people who are trying to make a stand for what they believe in? I'm not asking you to delete all the protest pictures, just the ones with me in so I don't get arrested and fired. You don't understand what really happened, and those pictures are not an accurate reflection of my conduct during the protest."

I might as well be talking to a brick wall for all the attention he's paying to my argument. All he seems to care about is packing up his stuff and getting out of here as quickly as possible.

"Whatever," he says, like an ignorant teenager. He chucks a couple of quid on the table for the checkout assistant and strides away from me.

Naturally, I give chase and soon catch him up. Before he leaves the building, he swings to the right and comes to an abrupt halt.

"You can't follow me in here, Bambi," he says, a look of triumph on his face. "See you later."

He points at the sign above his head before he

disappears into the Gents' toilets, leaving me grimacing in frustration. Of course, he'd pick the non-gender-neutral facilities. Fortunately, it looks like there's only one entrance so I should be safe loitering out here until he emerges, and whatever Sam imagines, I'm not ashamed to lurk outside the men's bogs.

But come to think of it, I could do with going to the loo myself and the Ladies' toilets are right next door. I hop experimentally on the spot, wondering if I can wait a bit longer. But who knows where I'm going to end up in the next hour? I decide it's best to use the facilities now when I know I've got the option. Praying that there's not a queue, I dash in.

Fortunately, there are plenty of empty cubicles, but of course the thing I hadn't factored in was the faff of going to the toilet when wearing a onesie. First of all, the zip gets caught in the fluff and takes quite a bit of tugging to come free. Then when I'm about to lower myself to the seat, feeling rather exposed on the top half as all my clothing is bunched around my ankles, I realise there's no toilet paper in the holder, so I have to get dressed again and pop into the cubicle next door. Thank goodness I checked before I went. It takes me a few seconds to be able to relax enough to actually pee – there's nothing like pressure to cause wee-fright – but finally I'm done and feel a huge sense of relief. I hadn't realised how desperate I was. I wash my hands as quickly as possible and emerge from the cloakroom wiping them dry on my onesie, finally grateful for its furriness.

I take up my position outside the Gents' again, hoping that for once there was a queue in there which delayed Sam.

I wait, my heart jumping every time the door swings open, but still he doesn't emerge. I loiter some more, but I'm starting to get funny looks, and I can see a security man in the distance talking into his radio and watching my every move. I'm kicking myself for allowing it to happen, but I'm pretty sure Sam has given me the slip.

Just to be on the safe side, I decide to conduct a quick search. If in doubt, assume an air of confidence and walk around like you have every right to be in a place, or at least that's what Charlie always says when it comes to getting into places you're not meant to be. I stride into the men's toilets with my head held high, calling out Sam's name. A man at the urinals jumps in surprise, my sudden appearance unfortunately causing his aim to go off, judging by the cursing which follows.

"Sorry," I call in his direction, though that probably made the situation worse. I knock politely on each cubicle door, just in case, getting a range of gruff male responses, but none of them are Sam. With a sigh, I finally accept that he's long gone and hastily depart. As I leave the cloakroom, the security man is waiting for me at the door.

"I'm sorry, I got confused there and went in the wrong room," I say, but he's having none of it, and firmly grabs my elbow and escorts me off the premises. I'm really not having any luck with my encounters with authority figures today.

Chapter Fourteen

2.13 p.m.

I've just been deposited beyond the perimeter of the National Theatre with a firm exhortation not to return, when my phone rings. Optimistically hoping it's Sam calling to say he's changed his mind about the pictures and the keys, I answer quickly without checking the caller ID on the screen first. There's a muffled sound at the other end, and I initially can't make out what's being said.

"Hello?" I say, straining to try to work out who has rung. The rustling sound repeats itself. I move the phone away from my ear to do what I should have done in the first place, and check the caller ID facility. As soon as I see the name on the screen, an icy surge of sheer fear fills my body. It's Zara.

I put the phone back to my ear and try to shield the speaker by cupping my palm around it as best I can so she can't hear the background noise, but I'm not sure how effective my efforts will be against the din of the buskers who've just struck up with a lively rendition of a Motown classic.

"Zara, hi, thanks for calling. I'm trying to distract myself from feeling sick with some music," I say in my best slurred poorly-person voice, saying the first thing that occurs to me to try to explain the noise of my surroundings. There's no response at the other end. Then someone five yards away pipes up enthusiastically trying to sell the *Big Issue*.

"The music is featuring in a radio play about homelessness," I riff hastily, "and youth unemployment," I add desperately as a bunch of kids on a school trip launch into a particularly shrieky game of catch. It's like everyone around is conspiring to expose me.

I hold my breath, waiting for Zara's response, but there's still nothing from her. I put my finger in one ear to try to block out the ambient noise and try to concentrate on the sound coming from my phone. If I'm not very much mistaken, Zara has accidentally pocket-dialled me. I'm about to hang up in relief when I recognise my name being said. They say eavesdroppers never hear anything positive about themselves, but this is too good an opportunity to miss. I pull my hood up to create a cocoon of extra soundproofing around my ears and listen carefully.

"I'm not sure Alexa's head is really in the game at the moment," says Zara to an unknown person. "I didn't like to say before, but I've been having to support her an awful lot with the O'Reilly deal. There was a whole clause in the contract that she nearly didn't include which would have caused a big mess for us all."

I cover my mouth with my hand to stop myself from gasping out loud. The scenario she's describing did happen, but it was the other way around. I was the one who picked up on her mistake and saved her bacon. She begged me not to tell anyone as it was a big enough error to warrant a written warning if it hadn't been spotted, and I agreed to keep quiet because I didn't want to drop her in it. I needn't have bothered. She clearly has no compunction about twisting the truth to get ahead at my expense.

I strain my ears, trying to work out who she's speaking to. There's an indistinct buzzing, then Zara's voice comes through clearly again. There's definitely a gleeful tone to her voice.

"Sure Genevieve, no problem. I'll keep an eye on her and continue reporting back to you."

It confirms something I'd begun to fear but which I'd been trying to tell myself was just another manifestation of my growing paranoia. Zara has been spying on me and is reporting back to Genevieve via a video conference call. Who does that to a colleague and housemate? I wonder what else she's keeping a secret. I soon find out when she steers the conversation around to a very interesting topic.

"And I'd love to have a chat with you about that job coming up on the fifth floor. I know you said you were going to mention it to Alexa as well, but what with her illness and everything, it might be better to give her some recovery time."

The two-faced so-and-so. How dare she pretend to be acting in my best interests when she's only looking out for herself? She's never shown the least bit of interest in getting into the pro bono department, but if it means snatching my biggest dream from me, then suddenly she's keen. If I weren't "off sick", I'd march over there right now and give her a piece of my mind.

But then Zara's voice changes and I recognise the panic in it.

"Oh sorry, Genevieve, just realised I've accidentally dialled someone. Be back with you in a moment."

She's onto me. I quickly end the call and hope she doesn't realise I was listening in. Five seconds later, my phone rings again. Zara is calling back, no doubt to check how much of her exchange I might have been listening to. Fortunately, it coincides with the band stopping to have a drink and the *Big Issue* seller quietly chatting to someone buying a magazine. The schoolchildren meanwhile have been cowed into silence by a telling-off from their teacher.

I answer with a flurry of fake gagging and choke out the word, "Hello?"

"Hi lovely one, how are you feeling?" says Zara, her voice so full of insincerity it genuinely does make me feel a bit sick.

I let out a little groan. "Still absolutely rotten," I moan. "But I'm determined to be better by tomorrow," I add. No need for her to start thinking she's got ages to build on her web of manipulation.

"You're sounding a bit better," she says suspiciously. "Have you got the television on?"

The implication is that if I'm well enough to watch television, then I'm well enough to be at work. What would she do if I suddenly announced I was coming in this afternoon after all? But I'm too far into my deception to do that, even if it means that I can't yet correct Genevieve on the lies Zara has fed her.

"Just wanted some noise in the background to distract me from the sicky feeling."

I cup my hand around the phone and fake heave right into the microphone. I can hear Zara cringing at the other end.

"Eurgh, better go."

I end the call quickly before she hears anything else to ignite her suspicions still further.

How is it that not being at work is ending up twice as stressful as actually being there? I tuck my phone safely back in my pocket and run through the conversation in my head again. After two years of waiting and hoping, it sounds like there might finally be an opportunity in the pro bono department. But if Zara has set her sights on it and has spent the day briefing against me in my absence, then the battle for the position is well and truly on. I try to put aside my anger at her behaviour and examine the situation logically. If Zara feels she needs to try dirty tricks to get the role, then she must have some doubts about her ability to get it on her own merit. That must play to my advantage, surely? The answer comes quickly. In normal circumstances, yes, but these are far from normal circumstances. Given the precarious nature of my current situation, I think even a law student would have a better chance of getting the role than me. I've got to get my act together and come up with a plan to get myself back on track.

Chapter Fifteen

2.15 p.m.

Feeling emotionally drained with the effort of all the trouble I've got myself into, I settle myself down on a concrete bollard sufficiently far away from the National Theatre not to attract the attention of their security team again, and assess my options. I'm now several miles away from home and still no closer to being able to get back indoors. One housemate is conspiring against me, and I've made an enemy of my other housemate, who's going to file those compromising photos as soon as he's finished his next job.

Sam's next job. He did seem particularly het up about it, stressing how important it was that I left him to do it in peace. It's obviously a big deal for him. But those photographs are a big deal for me, and if I don't do something about them, and soon, then everything that I've worked so hard to achieve will be ripped away from me.

The whole being a lawyer thing has taken over my life, and not in a positive way, I'll admit, but without that, I have no idea who I am, and that's an even scarier prospect. I've been focused on this goal for so long, I'm not sure what I'd do without it. And now that I could potentially lose everything, it's made me realise just how much it all means to me. I know that I need to make changes to improve my quality of life, but I want to be able to make them at my own pace, rather than because it's been forced upon me because of my foolish decision to take a duvet day. Besides, if I can survive tramping around central London in a unicorn onesie, then I can survive anything. Yes, I've had a good few moments where I thought I was going to fall apart, but despite it all, I've kept on going and I've not completely lost hope. Maybe I'm stronger than I thought I was. Maybe when I return to the office, I will be able to find a way to make it work for me.

Of course, before returning to the office, there's the small matter of needing to find Sam, make him change his mind about publishing the photos, oh and nick his keys as well. Piece of cake. But London's a vast place and he could be anywhere. What are the chances of me being able to track him down among the several million people who inhabit this city? My stress levels begin to creep up yet again, but this time I force myself to ignore the disaster scenarios playing out in my head. Panicking is not going to help the situation.

I take a deep breath and tell myself to think about this logically. I need to systematically dismiss options until I settle on a sensible solution. Technology first. It's a slim chance, but I check the "Find my friend" function on my iPhone just in case Sam appears on that. Funnily enough, he's not enabled me to access that kind of information about him. I'm distracted for a few moments by looking at the locations of friends I've not spoken to in ages, but who are still active on my list. I really must make the effort to get in touch with them again. If I had something else to focus on outside of work, then maybe it would help me feel better. The others seem to have a healthier work–life balance than I do. Even though it's a Tuesday afternoon, it would appear that Laura's at the cinema, lucky her, and Michael's on the south coast. He must be on holiday. Maybe I should book a trip like that for myself some time? If I had taken more regular breaks in the first place, I wouldn't have felt the need for a duvet day and got myself into this mess.

I clock Zara at the Richmond Woods headquarters on Gray's Inn Road. To be honest, I'd be shocked if she was anywhere else. She's probably pacing up and down, plotting how she can take advantage of my absence to steal more of my clients. But if I can see where she is, what if she can see where I am? It's a horrifying idea. My efforts to save my reputation and return home will be completely pointless if Zara's been tracking my progress from the office all day long. My fingers tremble as I swipe through my phone settings, and I have to check three times before I'm able to reassure myself that I'm in the clear.

I try a bit of social media stalking next, but Sam and I have never become Facebook friends – if we had been, I would have realised he was a Samuel and not a Samantha, which would have saved on one bit of embarrassment – and although I send him an optimistic friend request, just in case, I imagine hell will freeze over before he accepts it.

It's always interesting to see what people share with strangers online. Sam's page is pretty locked down, and although I scroll back as far as possible to try to glean as much information as I can, I can only see a few pretentious photographs of him posing with his camera and staring into the middle distance. I can't find an Instagram account and if he's on Twitter, his handle isn't anything I can track down, although I try my best by looking up the official account for his newspaper and trawling through the reams of people it follows.

I rack my brains and think about the contents of his shoulder bag. Apart from outing him as a borderline hoarder of junk, there wasn't anything particularly revealing in there which gave away much about his personality or more importantly, his plans for the rest of the day. The only potential clue I can think of was the 2.40 p.m. appointment listed in his old-school Filofax, but the scrawled initials next to it didn't mean anything to me at the time, and I still can't think what they could stand for. But the timing alone is a clue, and on the plus side, if his job is due to start in the next few minutes, then he can't have gone too far. He only set off about five minutes ago and he didn't seem to be in that much of a rush, apart from being in a hurry to get rid of me, of course. But a twenty-minute Tube ride, or even a walk at his overzealous pace, could get him to a lot of places, so I need more information to narrow down the options.

I close my eyes and picture everything else that I had

seen in the bag. The one anomaly in among all the rest of the rubbish had been a school prospectus. Sam definitely doesn't strike me as the kind of guy who would be carrying around a brochure about a girls' private school for no reason. I google the name of the school and realise it's on the other side of the Thames, up near St Paul's Cathedral. I do a few quick calculations and realise it's somewhere he could easily get to by 2.40 p.m. Maybe that's the location of his next job? But I need to be sure. I can't just turn up at a random posh school and ask for Sam, especially not in my current guise. I have to find out the nature of the job, and use it to talk my way into the building. If I show up and quietly threaten to create a scene, then surely he'll admit defeat and agree to help me out? I feel a pang of guilt, knowing how I would feel if the situation were reversed and someone did that to me, but it's the only tactic I can come up with for now that I think will have any impact on him.

I do some more googling, typing in the name of the school and the name of the newspaper Sam works for. It's amazing and rather terrifying what you can find out on the internet. After some pretty basic online detective work on my part, I discover that it's the secondary school which his boss's daughter moved to back in September under circumstances which, reading between the lines, seem a little suspect. Perhaps this job is more personal than professional? If it's being done as a favour for the boss, it would explain why Sam is making such a big deal about it.

But all this is speculation, and as any good lawyer knows, circumstantial evidence is not enough to make a case. I can't afford to waste time by taking chances, so I need to reduce the odds in my favour and there's only one way I can think of to do that. Before I chicken out, I ring the newspaper switchboard and ask to be put through to the newsroom. I may be about to make a complete fool of myself and cause a lot of trouble for Sam, but I've got to sort out this mess I've got myself into, whatever the cost. I'll deal with the consequences later.

Chapter Sixteen

2.22 p.m.

A s the phone rings, seemingly endlessly, my mind wanders once more to the worst-case scenario. If I can't find Sam, and he goes ahead and publishes those pictures, then it's highly likely the authorities will see them and be able to track me down. I barely touched that police officer, but I can't imagine he'd easily forget the humiliation of being bested by a woman in a unicorn outfit. Besides, the police are always on the news talking about their zero-tolerance policy, and I have a horrible feeling mine would be exactly the kind of case they'd love to make an example of. The penalties for assaulting a police officer are tough, even if the assault consisted of slapping away an overly-friendly hand and accidentally breaking his radio.

Could I cope with prison? I've seen too many episodes of *Orange is the New Black* not to be terrified at the prospect. It would destroy me. But worst of all, it would destroy my parents. They'd be so disappointed in me. It's a long-running joke that Charlie is the black sheep of the family, but even he has always managed to avoid arrest, despite a few close calls I've been sworn to secrecy about. It doesn't bear thinking about. I've got to get hold of Sam, come what may.

My first hurdle in tracking him down is having to charm my way past the gatekeepers on switchboard. They don't sound convinced when I say I have the story of the decade for him, but finally, reluctantly, they put me through to a lady called Brenda, who apparently works at the neighbouring desk to Sam. She answers the phone with a curt, "Newsroom," and I can hear her tapping her nails impatiently on her desk as she waits for me to speak. I'm getting a strong impression that she doesn't suffer fools gladly. She probably takes a dozen time-wasting calls from members of the public every day, and if I'm not careful, she'll dismiss me straight away. I'm not stupid enough to tell her about the photos, but I also wimp out of telling her about the lost keys and foolishly go in a whole other direction.

"Hi, is Sam there? It's Zara."

Why did I say that? It'll take him about two seconds to work out who really called when he finds out about it. But somehow it feels easier to assume someone else's identity for this call, and it gives me the confidence boost I need not to end the conversation straight away. After all, Zara wouldn't think twice about doing what was necessary to achieve her own ends.

"And who might Zara be when she's at home?" asks Brenda, her voice showing a complete lack of interest.

I reckon I've got about ten seconds to get her attention or she'll ring off. I have a feeling that a housemate calling for information won't really cut it with this woman.

"I'm his girlfriend," I say, then immediately kick myself. What if Sam really does have a girlfriend, but she's called something completely different? I hurry on with my falsehood before Brenda has the chance to hang up on me. "I've got out of work early, and I was hoping to surprise Sam when he's finished his job at the school. Do you know how long it's going to take him? It's for the boss, isn't it?"

I'm quite pleased at how easily all this is tripping off my tongue. Clearly faking a sick day was just a gateway falsehood and I'm now turning into a hardened liar.

Brenda takes a noisy gulp of a drink. Unfortunately, she doesn't rise to the bait to fill in the gaps in information I deliberately left.

"He will have other jobs to do after that, Zara, or whatever your name is. He can't just be dropping everything because you've taken a fancy to him entertaining you for the rest of the day."

I can hear her shuffling papers around and I can imagine her hand hovering over the end call button. This conversation is not going well. I try one last-ditch attempt to extract the information I need.

"But it's really important that I speak to him as soon as possible. I've got some big news for him," I say vaguely, hoping it's enough to excite her journalistic instinct.

"Look darling, unless you're pregnant, there isn't news

big enough for you to go along distracting him when he's at work, especially when he's on a personal assignment for Sir Clive. It's more than his job's worth, trust me."

"But I am," I find myself saying desperately, knowing this is my only shot.

"You're what?" she says.

"I-I am pregnant," I stutter, shocked at the depths I'm prepared to plunge to. I am behaving in a truly shameful way, but I tell myself it will be worth it if it brings out the result I need. It's this, or face the loving disappointment of my family, and a lifetime of trying to live today down. Besides, if Sam had been decent enough to agree to help me in the first place, I wouldn't have had to resort to such underhand means. I know I'm trying to justify the unjustifiable, but I'm desperate. "I wanted to let him know as soon as possible."

It has the desired effect, because suddenly Brenda is all ears and I find myself on the receiving end of another journalistic grilling. She lowers her voice confidentially, presumably so she doesn't share her scoop with her colleagues until she's ready.

"Pregnant? Congratulations, that's such exciting news. And to think, none of us had any idea Sam even had a girlfriend. He always plays his cards close to his chest, but even for him this is quite something. So, tell me all about it. How did you meet? And how long have you guys been together?"

"Since December," I say, naming the date he moved into the house. Someone needs to pass me a shovel for the size of hole I am digging for myself.

"And you're how far gone?" says Brenda with obvious excitement at this rollercoaster relationship she's finding out about.

"Sorry, did you say when Sam will be finished?" I say. I'm too far into the pretence now, but I need to stop making things worse. Also, the more complicated I make this deception, the more likely I am to trip myself up with getting something wrong. Normally I'm quite good at keeping myself on message, but my head is all over the place today, so I'm not going to take the risk.

Brenda sighs with disappointment. She waits a while, no doubt hoping I'll relent and tell her more, but I stand firm. Eventually I hear the tapping of a computer keyboard as she looks up the information.

"He's down for a political job late this afternoon at Millbank, but up until then, his time's his own, once he's helped the boss out by photographing the girls doing their charity *Bake Off*-inspired competition. And he's got to file on that demo job from this morning too, of course. Taking his time with that one. The desk will be chasing him for it before long. The deadline for the website is always five minutes ago, or so they say when they're having a go at us."

Her last words harden my resolve. If the newsroom is going to start chasing Sam for the protest pictures, I need to get to him first. And at least now I know my deductions were correct. I ring off, trying to quell the guilt I'm experiencing for dropping Sam into it like that with his colleagues. Hopefully he'll be able to explain me away as a crazy ex or something. He's going to get an awful shock when Brenda rings up to congratulate him on becoming a father.

I'll worry about making amends for that one later. Now I just need to work out how I'm going to get to the school in time for the start of the baking competition.

I'm about to get up and head for the Tube station when a man stops in front of me.

"How much?" he asks, gesturing vaguely in my direction.

"Pardon?" I say, completely thrown by his question.

"For the *Big Issue*, how much?" he says.

Just great. I'm apparently so bedraggled now that I look like I'm a rough sleeper. I draw myself up to my full height and try to explain with as much dignity as I can muster that I'm not homeless, and point him in the direction of the genuine *Big Issue* seller down the boulevard. He doesn't look convinced, but I leave with a twitch of my tail before he can thrust the fiver on me anyway. There are far more deserving people in need of that.

Although I need to hurry in order to make it to the school in time to meet Sam, I find myself loitering on the South Bank, longing to spend more time exploring the quirky collection of street food vans and craft stands. It's strange seeing that there is a whole world of interest and excitement happening out here while I'm normally closeted away trying to keep up with the ruthless demands of the corporate machine. Was it only twenty-four hours ago that I was getting caffeine shakes as I attempted to power my way through the paperwork of the infamous O'Reilly merger? But roll back six months, a year, and beyond, I was probably doing pretty much the same thing, trapped in the hamster wheel, and unable to see a way of making it stop.

I force my thoughts away from that destructive path. I am taking back control. Instead, I concentrate on my surroundings. There's a group of skateboarders leaping their way around, using the street furniture as hurdles and props to show off their skills. They're full of enthusiasm and laughter, and I feel a pang of envy at the apparent ease with which they are enjoying life. Next to the river there's a seat with a sign on it explaining that it's a "friendship bench", there to encourage conversations between lonely strangers. If I wasn't up against a deadline, I'd go and sit down for a few minutes. It makes me feel a bit better to see acknowledged in public the idea that I'm not the only lonely person in the city. I watch the people wandering up and down, reminding myself how easy it is to pretend to be OK to everyone else. I wonder what stories are hidden behind the faces they present to the world.

I'm relieved people can't discern my truth from a mere glance. I take a deep breath, and savour the moment, making the most of my liberty while I still can. A weird part of me is actually enjoying the freedom of exploring London like this. I mean, so far today I've ticked off the Bank of England, the National Theatre and South Bank, all places I've managed not to see in the whole duration of my time in the city. South Bank is my favourite so far, quirky and vibrant. It would be a fun place to come on a date, I decide, although there is as much chance of me growing a unicorn horn for real as being asked out any time soon. That's another thing I really must change in the future.

I check the time and realise I need to stop daydreaming and get a move on. I walk back to the station with my head held high, feeling a growing sense of optimism that I'm taking the right course to sort out my mess. And with all the colourful characters surrounding me, the buskers, street performers and living statues, the girl unicorn is not completely the odd one out for once.

I arrive back at Waterloo and tap into the Underground system once again, bracing myself for the usual Tube chaos. As I quickly check the best route to take, I realise that my phone is already at fifty percent battery. I'm going to have to go steady using it from now on. It's my only means of paying my passage around London, unless I dash back and ask that man if he wouldn't mind giving me that fiver after all. And I'll probably also need it to navigate my way back home once I've sorted this mess out. It would be just my luck to get lost in the city and end up bumping into Zara or one of the bosses. If I'd known I was going to end up on an epic adventure around London, I'd have charged it up properly. My work phone is normally permanently plugged in to charge to prevent the disastrous scenario of it running out of battery mid-important conference call, but my personal mobile doesn't get quite such solicitous treatment. Maybe Sam will lend me one of his chargers when I arrive at the school.

I'm being foolishly optimistic. I have a feeling he's going to be anything but welcoming when I rock up.

Chapter Seventeen

2.46 p.m.

I t's quite a walk from the Tube stop at St Paul's to the actual entrance of the school, which it takes me a good few minutes to track down, given the size of the building. St Paul's Girls' High School is an absolute fortress of a place, slap bang on the banks of the Thames. I don't know why, but I find it astonishing that among all the office blocks and trappings of corporate life, there is a school right in the middle of it. I suppose it's because it couldn't be more different from the rolling hills and winding farm tracks which surrounded my school.

Being educated in the centre of the capital must give the girls a strong sense of being right in the seat of power. I wonder if it imbues them with a greater confidence and self-belief than I managed to leave my Dales country high school with? The last time I returned, I was held up as an example of an alumna who had gone on to achieve great things. My parents beamed proudly from the audience as I handed out the prizes at speech day and nodded their heads in agreement at the words of praise, but all the while, inside, I was feeling like a complete fraud. If my school finds out about what I've got up to today, they'll definitely strike my name off their list of former pupils.

I'm feeling pangs of that imposter syndrome now, although in this instance it is well founded. I gaze up at the imposing brick building with its ugly, but impressive, brutalist architecture, telling myself that I am Alexa Humphries, lawyer at Richmond Woods, and I have every right to be here. As well as lying to everyone around me, I'm clearly becoming good at lying to myself today.

I quickly run through my plan of action, take a deep breath, then march confidently to the buzzer at the front door. I have no doubt that a school this illustrious will have an extensive CCTV system, so they will be watching my every move and judging whether I am safe to allow in. I need to persuade them that despite the surface appearance, I am a perfectly respectable individual.

I hold the buzzer down and wait an inordinate amount of time for a response, the nerves growing in my stomach. If they won't even talk to me, then I really don't know what I'm going to do. There are probably half a dozen ways of getting out of this school, and Sam could very easily give me the slip again. The only way I'm going to achieve success is if I get in the building alongside him.

Just as I'm about to buzz again, a crackly voice comes out of the speaker.

"Can I help you?"

I lean close to where I think the microphone is.

"Yes, hello, I'm Alexa Humphries. I'm working with Sam Harris. I'm here to help out with the *Bake Off* photoshoot."

My voice is brimming with confidence, and it sounds like a reasonable enough explanation; I just hope they buy it.

There's another pause.

"I'm afraid you're not on the list of expected guests, Ms Humphries."

I should have expected a school in central London would have a very strict approach to security. I rack my brains and quickly improvise.

"That's a surprise. Sir Clive did say he was letting you know we'd both be coming. I know he's keen that Katherine's efforts in the competition are properly recorded."

I'm shamelessly name-dropping now, but I've got to throw everything at this. Fake it until you make it, and all that. The silence is longer this time. I start praying that the CCTV cameras are in black and white in the vague hope that my outfit looks less startling in monochrome. If they go and check my story with Sam, then I'm screwed and he'll probably publish the pictures instantly just to spite me.

Eventually, the door clicks, and the disembodied voice tells me to wait in reception until someone can come and fetch me. Calling the room a reception feels like overstating it a bit, as it's more of a holding pen, a glass box keeping me trapped in a hinterland between the outside world and the protected environment of the school itself. Only the lists of exam successes and league table ratings give away the real purpose of this building. I settle on a hard plastic chair, feeling like I'm waiting to be signed in for visiting time at a prison. If I don't succeed in my mission, I could have to get used to spending time in this kind of institutionalised environment.

The uncomfortable feeling it gives me also reminds me of my office, which is similarly exposed to stares. I never realised before I started work how basic stuff you'd take for granted, such as windows looking onto the outside world, would become highly sought after, and a very visual means of demonstrating exactly where you are in the pecking order. At Richmond Woods, they've done away with open-plan workspaces, pairing people up to share rooms in which the amount of floor space and access to natural light you are granted are dictated by the company hierarchy. I'm on the lowly second floor, in the row of offices which have been created in the middle of what was once a big open-plan working area. It's essentially a glass box with zero privacy, so when I'm working, I feel like an exhibit in a case at a museum. The soundproofing is one thing they have put effort into, but while it means I can have telephone conversations with a modicum of privacy, I can never hear people sneaking up from behind. I therefore assume at all times that there is someone standing behind me scrutinising my every move. It doesn't make for a relaxing working environment.

The other principle they enforce in the shared office environment is that each glass box contains a senior and a junior member of staff. Even though we might be working in completely different areas of law, I am still answerable to my senior officemate, and woe betide me if I leave before they do. My day finishes when theirs does. And because the senior person is a step closer to promotion, they're more likely to stay as long as possible to impress the partner who works in an individual office with their own actual window to the outside world and supervises us all with a fiery stare from the end of the corridor. The whole set-up creates a pressure cooker environment, but perhaps I'm just weak for not being great at handling it.

The bell rings and a bevy of girls charge past the glass box on the way to their next lesson, apparently unmoved by the strange woman waiting in reception. I wonder how many of these bright young things have aspirations to become lawyers? I hope the road to achieve their dreams is easier than mine has been. But then again, without the struggle, would anyone know the value of what they've got?

I jump to my feet as a teacher unlocks the door and enters my holding pen. Sam is trailing behind her, a look of thunder on his face. I hold my breath. The next few seconds are going to go in one of two ways. He'll either deny all knowledge of me, thereby inviting further questions about the security breach of a complete stranger knowing the details of his assignment, or he'll vouch for my identity and punish me later. The situation I've engineered hasn't really left him with much choice. But whichever option he goes for, I know that by turning up here, I am showing how serious I am in my intention to make him admit defeat and back down. There is a time and a place for being holierthan-thou and I need him to be a bit more flexible in his principles when it comes to my circumstances.

The teacher is staring at me with interest, half-appalled and half-amused by my unusual get-up. She's dressed in an outfit similar to my normal work attire – dark trouser suit and plain white shirt – and I wonder if she ever has moments of wanting to sack off being sensible and indulge in a duvet day. She checks the piece of paper in her hand and turns to Sam.

"I apologise for dragging you away when you were in the middle of setting up, Mr Harris, but is this young woman also on the assignment, as she claims to be? She says she's called Alexa Humphries, but I have no such person on our list of visitors today and we're normally very accurate about that kind of thing. Of course, it is unusual for us to be inviting a member of the press onto the premises, but I would expect our admin team to be more accurate in these circumstances, rather than less."

Sam shoots me a glance laden with disappointment. Somehow, it's much worse than if he just looked angry with me. The silence stretches out between us, and my feelings of shame and guilt do battle with my desperate need to sort this situation out and get back home. I try to tell myself he brought this on himself, but I know I'm behaving really badly, and it would serve me right if he asked the school to call the police and had me escorted off the premises. I try to signal my contriteness with my eyes, but he's not having any of it. He looks hunted, and I know it's my fault for backing him into an impossible corner.

Eventually, and very reluctantly, he nods his head, a

movement which seems to cost him greatly. When he speaks, his voice is slow and steady, but completely lacking in emotion, which I find rather disturbing. His face is guarded, and it's clearly costing him a lot not to fight back and give as good as he's getting.

"Yes, this is Alexa Humphries. She is shadowing me today."

I've got to hand it to him. He is, after all, telling the truth.

"Did you manage to get rid of those pictures?" I ask, giving him a final opportunity to say yes and get me off his case.

He folds his arms. "What do you think?" he challenges, his face full of defiance. Why is he so darn stubborn? I glare at him, willing him to admit defeat, but he merely smiles back at me, a challenge if ever I saw one.

The teacher looks between the pair of us in confusion. It's obvious to her that something is going on here, but she can't quite work it out.

It's time to press home my advantage. Steeling myself to behave in a way which goes against everything in my normal nature, I start pushing back, demonstrating that I'm prepared to go to any lengths to make Sam back down. I twirl on the spot and swish my unicorn tail.

"That's a shame. I guess I'll have to stick around and help you do that. By the way, is this outfit suitable, Sam? You did want something bright and upbeat to entertain the kiddliwinks, didn't you? Help you get the best out of them?"

I'm deliberately being brash, putting my hands on my

waist and wiggling my hips so that the tail continues flicking from side to side. I know full well that the photography job is with Year 11s, who are well beyond the stage of being patronised as "kiddliwinks". There's no way any professional would consider bringing along a sidekick dressed in a silly costume in order to get decent pictures. It's even more inappropriate at this school where clearly a lot of emphasis is put on maturity and sensible conduct.

The teacher looks suitably horrified. I pull up my hood, dying a little inside, and make sure she gets a proper view of the ridiculous starry eyes of the unicorn.

I think I hear a noise along the lines of "Harrumph" escape from Sam's lips, but when I glance back at him, he's still stony-faced and showing no sign of relenting.

"I must say this is highly unusual," says the teacher eventually. "But who am I to question your methods, Mr Harris?" She holds out her hand to shake mine. "I'm Mrs Choudhary. If you'd like to follow me, Ms Humphries, I will take you both to the Home Economics department where the competition is taking place."

I'm in. But what lengths will I have to go to now in order to get out of the mess I've created for myself?

Chapter Eighteen

3.01 p.m.

Once we're beyond the perimeter of the reception, the school environment becomes a lot more homely and welcoming. In any other circumstance, I would have enjoyed getting the opportunity to look around such a famous institution and discover the inside track on a place I know several of my colleagues attended and now send their offspring to. But as that thought idly crosses my mind, it's replaced by a much more worrying idea. It's a slim chance, but what if one of my colleagues' daughters recognises me? A few of the senior partners brought their teenage children along to the year-end party so they could indulge in some networking and get an advantage when they apply for summer internships. Most of them weren't bothered about making my acquaintance, but I did speak to one or two, doing my best to convince them to go down the altruistic legal route, rather than the corporate one, not that I'm really a shining example of that. I try to tell myself I'm being ridiculously paranoid, but the way this day is going, it would be just my luck that little Ophelia or Constanza would make the connection and mention it to their parents. I pull my hoody tighter around my face and rack my brains for a further way of disguising my identity.

As we climb the stairs past walls decorated with tasteful landscapes painted by members of the Upper Sixth, Sam seizes my elbow and pulls me near so he can hiss in my ear without Mrs Choudhary hearing what he has to say. His closeness is disconcerting.

"I thought you were bonkers when I first clapped eyes on you, and now you've proved it. What the hell do you think you're doing here?"

I twist slightly and try to fix him with a steely glare, but we're so close to each other, it doesn't quite have the effect I desired, and my words don't come out with the strength of conviction I intended.

"You know exactly what I'm after."

I push away from him, refusing to be manhandled. He might be used to bossing people around in tabloid land, but I'm having none of it. My sudden movement sends him off balance and he stumbles forward, only catching himself at the last moment. But before I've got a chance to feel guilty and check he's alright, he sticks his foot out, tripping me up in a classic move last used on me by my brothers during my teenage years. I hurtle forwards and only Sam's hand grabbing the back of my baggy onesie prevents my shins coming into painful contact with the stone steps. He lets go so quickly that I'm not entirely sure that he was even responsible for stopping my fall in the first place.

"That's so mature," I hiss at him.

He narrows his eyes. "Pot, meet kettle," he retorts, the ghost of a smirk crossing his face before he settles into his default expression of grumpiness.

Mrs Choudhary turns around, eyes narrowing at the scuffle.

"Is everything alright?" she asks, teacher code for warning us to start behaving ourselves.

"Yes, Mrs Choudhary," we chorus in the manner of the unruly children we're behaving like.

I flash another glare at Sam. He smiles in mock sweetness and I fight the urge to send a rude gesture back at him. His irritating nature is definitely bringing out the worst in me.

Mrs Choudhary tuts disapprovingly and fixes us with a stare honed over many years to cow even the most recalcitrant teenager into submission. I find myself standing up straighter, and trying to brush the dust off my onesie, while Sam moves as if to straighten a tie he's not actually wearing.

We step apart, hands at our sides, our faces the picture of innocence to demonstrate our intention to behave ourselves. Mrs Choudhary still isn't convinced. Our invitation to head further into the building hangs in the balance. I'm torn between wanting to get thrown out so I can have an undisturbed conversation with Sam about my situation, and feeling uncomfortable about getting him into any further bother. But then I remind myself that he's shown no compunction about getting me into trouble, and I stiffen my resolve.

Sam senses the teacher's dilemma and steps in with a smile, all sweetness and light.

"Many apologies for my colleague's unconventional approach to this assignment. She's new, but very enthusiastic about her work." He gives me a sideward glance and I try to embody the spirit of a passionate photographer. I suspect I just look like I've got indigestion because he gives a slight sigh, then turns back to the teacher to continue his charm offensive.

"When did you say the competition was starting?" he asks.

Mrs Choudhary checks her watch and tuts in annoyance, only just managing to restrain herself from hustling us forward.

"Ten minutes ago," she says. "And if we don't get a move on, it'll be the end of the school day and the girls will have to leave to catch their transport home. I'm afraid I'm going to have to ask you to hurry up."

She rushes up the stairs, taking them two at a time. Sam waits until she's a little way ahead of us before continuing our conversation.

"Look Alexa, I'm sure you're having a whale of a time trying to ruin my life, but enough's enough. I'm not sure how I can make myself any clearer, but those photos are not being deleted, and it's physically impossible for me to give you my keys because I don't have them on me. Why won't you bog off and leave me alone? You are irritatingly persistent, and your stubbornness is, quite frankly, annoying."

"My stubbornness? Coming from the King of Stubborn, that's pretty rich," I hiss back. "Would it really cost you anything to delete those photos? No. I've given you every opportunity to do the decent thing, and yet you refuse to help, even though you've got dozens of other perfectly good pictures you could use instead of the ones of me. If you're going to keep digging your heels in, then I'm afraid I'm going to have to resort to dirty tactics to get this situation resolved."

He quirks an eyebrow at me and lets out a snort of laughter. "Dirty tactics? How utterly terrifying."

He's grinning now, and it's really getting on my nerves. Why won't he take me seriously?

"Bring it on, Bambi. Do your worst."

If he's going to lay down the gauntlet, then I'm more than happy to take up the challenge.

Chapter Nineteen

3.05 p.m.

I thought the atmosphere at Richmond Woods was competitive, but when I walk into the Home Economics department, I soon realise it's got nothing on St Paul's Girls' High School. Sam and I are ushered into a big L-shaped room which is equipped with banks of state-of-the-art ovens and gleaming hobs. Behind each workstation is standing a gaggle of sixteen-year-old girls, each team eyeing up the others while pulling a range of equipment out of the cupboards and setting it up on the work surfaces in the gleeful manner of torturers preparing their instruments. Between the Waitrose Bags for Life stuffed with ingredients I don't even recognise, and the wicker baskets full of artisan produce, it's clear these girls mean business. I do a quick scan of the faces, and am greatly relieved that none of them look familiar from the year-end party.

Mrs Choudhary clears her throat.

"Ladies, this is Ms Humphries. She's working with Mr Harris today."

The girls turn away from clattering their catering implements and stare at me. For a moment there's shocked silence in the room as they take in the full startling rainbow effect of my scruffy attire, and then the sniggering starts. I imagine it's the first time they've encountered an adult on these premises who's been anything but perfectly turned out and exuding authority.

"Dress Down Tuesday, is it?" says one bright spark. Her friends titter gleefully. Silly as it sounds, given that I'm the grown woman in this situation and they're only teenagers, their superior attitude instantly makes me feel about two inches tall. I tell myself to get a grip. These girls are not mini-Zaras. Besides, I survived cycling through the East End like this. Navigating my way through a bunch of giggling schoolgirls is small fry in comparison to that feat. I force myself to stare defiantly back, daring them to do their worst. They don't even flinch. I really need to work on my imposing presence.

"Now girls, what was it we were saying the other day about the importance of not judging by appearances?" says Mrs Choudhary.

I shoot her a grateful glance, surprised and pleased that she's standing up for me despite her own misgivings about my respectability.

"Sorry Mrs Choudhary," says the clever clogs, and then reluctantly repeats the apology in my vague direction after being on the receiving end of another of her teacher's disapproving stares.

As soon as Mrs Choudhary's back is turned, the girl's look of contrition turns into a glare of annoyance that I'm the cause of her telling-off. Sam smiles sweetly at her. He's either automatically taking the side of anyone who is offensive towards me, or he's already begun his mission to impress his boss's daughter. From what I could glean reading between the lines of a couple of newspaper articles online, Katherine Headington-Rodgers, the only offspring of the infamous Sir Clive, has inherited many of her father's talents, including his ruthlessness and his lack of respect for authority.

I'd had a half-baked notion that I could appeal to her better side, and ask her to use her influence to persuade Sam to cut me some slack, but now I've encountered her in person, I realise I need to reassess. It doesn't matter. I've already got another idea forming, and this one is more robust. It should put me in a strong enough position to turn the tables on Sam, thereby allowing me to take control. Let's get one thing straight – I don't want to outright sabotage Sam's entire assignment, but if I could convince him that I'll put it in jeopardy unless he's prepared to help me, then that could work in my favour.

My plan is predicated on the fact that this is a girls' school, a place designed to train the next generation of female leaders. They'll be used to seeing powerful women, perhaps even more accustomed within the school walls to seeing women in positions of authority than men. If I assert myself, and am convincing enough in the charade, perhaps I can get Mrs Choudhary and her pupils to take the lead from me, rather than Sam. And once Sam realises he's lost control of the shoot, then he'll have to turn to me to get it back, and there we go, I'll have my bargaining chip.

Speaking of the man himself, he's watching me now, eyes narrowed, a dozen suspicious thoughts forming in his mind. It's time to show my hand.

I march across so I'm standing next to Mrs Choudhary.

"It's great to see the girls working so hard on this charitable endeavour," I say, channelling the behaviour of a senior partner at my firm so that everything about me exudes authority. "How did they decide which charity to assist? Perhaps you could fill me in as I get set up? Sam, pass the camera bag across, could you?" I deliver the final sentence as a casual aside, barely acknowledging his presence while I keep Mrs Choudhary focused on me by continuing my stream of confident chatter. It's a subtle power move, one I've seen executed by male lawyers at work countless times when they want to assert themselves in a situation and put a female colleague in the position of subordinate.

"Sam, the bag?" I don't wait for him to hand it over, but instead pluck it out of his hands, and then ignore him completely.

Out of the corner of my eye, I see Sam do a double-take. He clears his throat, but I refuse to give him a chance to interrupt. I carry on talking animatedly to Mrs Choudhary, all the while carefully and subtly manoeuvring myself so that the teacher's back is turned on Sam, leaving him hovering redundantly, a look of thunder on his face. And now the girls unwittingly come to my aid, gathering around Sam, flicking their hair and practising their poses, enjoying the novelty of having a press photographer in their midst. They're moving in, working as a pack to back him into a corner, all desperate to attract his attention and become his muse. They're clamouring to be noticed, and I start to feel a little sorry for him as he shuffles uneasily, looking around for someone to save him. It must be intimidating becoming the focus of so much juvenile female attention. But he shouldn't let it go to his head. If it's anything like the all-girls school my friend Laura went to, men are probably very much the minority here, so any new, moderately good-looking male is bound to become an object of great interest. And while they corner him, I've got complete control of the camera.

The trouble is, I'm having to work hard to keep up the conversation with Mrs Choudhary, getting into a debate about the current state of the media, and the blight of fake news, so that she doesn't spot Sam's situation. If she runs to his rescue, then I'll miss my opportunity to relieve the camera of its memory card. I'm now multi-tasking to my best ability – talking to Mrs Choudhary, trying to feel for the eject button on the camera, and also tuning into Sam's predicament.

"What are you doing, sir?" asks the girl I'm now ninety-nine percent certain is Sir Clive's daughter Katherine.

"Well, I was hoping to get some photos of your competition," says Sam, a slight edge in his voice which I know is directed at me.

Katherine twirls her hair around her finger and peers up at him through her deliberately lowered eyelashes.

"Make sure you get a picture of my buns, sir. They're rising beautifully."

The girls all giggle at her suggestive comment. I glance across and see Sam's face has turned pink with embarrassment. For a man who's over six foot tall, he's doing a pretty good job at making himself as small as possible as he backs away warily, looking around for someone to save him from this incredibly uncomfortable situation. I'm starting to feel guilty that he's at the mercy of Katherine and her gang.

Sensing my distraction, Mrs Choudhary claps her hands, and the girls hurry away from Sam, quickly forgetting the delights of attempting to flirt with him as the heat of competition takes over. He strides over in my direction and I dart away, pretending to be occupied taking photos of the girls' intricate cake stands, all the while still hunting for that eject button. Sam can't exactly snatch the camera off me with such a big audience, but he makes sure he follows me closely, glowering in an off-putting way.

"Will you give me the camera back?" he hisses, all the while keeping a rictus grin fixed on his face.

"Absolutely not," I reply, with equally forced politeness.

"You're not going to get great pictures with it set up like that. The lens cap is still on, for a start."

I shoot him a quick glance.

"Maybe I don't want to get great pictures," I say under my breath.

Perhaps it's because I'm so hyperaware of the tense undercurrents in the room, but my attention is drawn past him to Katherine, who is looking shiftily around her, eyeing up her *Bake Off* rivals and assessing the competition. She obviously doesn't like what she sees, because she quickly checks no one nearby is watching, then surreptitiously pours a load of salt into the sugar jar on the other girl's workbench. Not content at just the one attempt at sabotage, she quickly turns up the oven, before casually sauntering back to her own work. I hear her hissing, "That'll serve Briony right" to her gaggle of acolytes, then they all stare across at the workbench opposite and giggle.

Katherine's rival Briony has the gangly appearance of someone who hasn't quite got used to the height they've suddenly achieved. Her glasses are slightly lopsided, with lenses so thick they distort the shape of her eyes, and she moves with the small, nervous actions of someone whose spirit has been systematically beaten down. I can empathise with that feeling. Katherine is clearly the Queen Bee of this classroom, and I'm pretty sure I know exactly how Briony is feeling at being the object of her bullying behaviour. Nobody should be made to feel small and insignificant like that. I find myself rooting for her and determine to intercede.

Unfortunately, Briony pours the salty sugar into her mixture before I can warn her. There is, however, still time for me to do something about her super-heated oven. If I'm quick, I can turn it down before it turns her bread into charred toast. I'm so fixed on my goal that I absent-mindedly tuck the camera down the front of my onesie and set off on my mercy mission. It's only when I start moving across the room that I realise I've failed to secure the camera around my neck with the strap. It starts sliding down from stomach level to my groin and then lower, making my onesie hang down like I'm wearing an overfull nappy. It's fallen too far for me to be able to reach down and grab it, not without having to do some serious unzipping, so I'm forced to waddle rather than walk, trying to clamp the camera between my thighs so it doesn't fall to the ground. Much as I need Sam to delete the pictures, I'm not quite at the stage of wanting to smash his camera in order to achieve it, tempting though it might be.

"Please tell me you've not got my camera stuck down there," says Sam, continuing to stick to my side like glue.

"OK, I won't tell you," I say, clenching hard as the camera threatens to fall down my right leg. I'm giving a very good impression of someone who's desperate for the toilet as I cross my legs to hold the camera in place.

Sam narrows his eyes and fixes me with one of his disapproving stares.

"Just hand it over, Alexa."

"And how do you think I'm going to be able to do that?" I respond sweetly.

I see his expression change as he glances down, and realises just how precarious his camera's position is. Now he looks even more uncomfortable than he did when the girls were taunting him. For a few seconds, I successfully fight the urge to laugh, but then the ridiculousness of the situation wins out. It starts as a giggle in the bottom of my stomach, then grows into a great big, side-splitting guffaw which makes my ribs ache. It feels liberating to laugh like this, and although I know I've picked a really bad moment to let go, it feels good to do so.

Sam is utterly mortified. He addresses me through gritted teeth, a grimacing grin fixed on his face as he desperately tries to pretend that everything is OK and that he's got the situation under control.

"Perhaps if you went out of the room, you might be able to extricate it?" he says, enunciating every word very slowly and fighting to control his anger.

Actually, at this particular moment in time, nothing would please me more. My muscles are aching with the effort of holding the camera in position, but I'm not convinced I can make it out of the room without the camera falling down still lower. I gesture helplessly. I'll worry about that in a second, but before I do anything else, I want to save Briony's bread.

"Katherine, I think you got confused." I raise my voice over the melee of schoolgirl chatter. "You seem to have accidentally turned up Briony's oven rather than your own. And muddled up her sugar and salt. Perhaps you could exchange your own mixture for hers to sort it out?"

Katherine's face is a picture. She can't believe that someone is daring to call her out, and I can tell she's itching to tell me to get stuffed. But she can't really admit she sabotaged her rival's efforts deliberately, so very reluctantly she switches her bowl with Briony and turns the oven back down to a normal temperature. Briony shoots a grateful look in my direction, and I feel a surge of pride that after all the mess-ups of today, I have actually done one good deed at least.

But while it's worked out for Briony, I suspect my intervention isn't going to bode well for Sam, judging by the shadow of sheer rage clouding Katherine's features. I get the impression there haven't been many times in her short life when someone has dared to challenge her on her behaviour. She is not a happy bunny and someone is going to suffer for it. I only hope it's not Briony or any of her cohort. Sam can take care of himself, I have no doubt.

Mrs Choudhary claps her hands again and orders the girls to get back to work. While she recaps the rules of the competition, I take advantage of their momentary distraction to duck out of sight behind a bench and fish the camera out of my clothing.

I still can't work out how to remove the memory card, and with my options now greatly reduced, I admit defeat in this particular battle, and reluctantly hand the camera over to Sam, my better nature winning over my own selfish needs.

"Guess you'd better have this back. I promise you, it's undamaged."

He gingerly accepts it. "It had bloody better be," he says, turning it over in his hands and inspecting it carefully. "It's a bit warm." He pulls a face. "God knows what it'll have picked up being stuffed down your nightwear like that."

"Cheers for that. What are you implying?" I retort. "Has anyone told you that you can be really quite rude sometimes?"

"Frequently," he replies, without contrition. "And has anyone told you that you can be a royal pain in the arse?"

"Royal, I'm flattered. Much better than being a bog-standard pain in the arse," I hit back.

He rolls his eyes. "It's all water off a duck's back to you, isn't it? You really don't care who you damage in your bid to get your own way."

I cross my arms defensively. He's hardly in a position to preach. I'm pretty sure my expression says as much because Sam tuts at me, then turns his attention to checking the camera's memory card.

"This isn't over," I say.

Sam sighs. "Much as I'm enjoying our oh-so-hilarious banter, I need to take some photographs now, provided this thing hasn't steamed up thanks to its proximity to your royal arse. And judging by the expression on Katherine's face, I'd better make these photos pretty damn decent, otherwise she'll tell her daddy all about it. And if he starts making my life a misery, I shall know who to blame."

He begins ushering the girls into a group around one of the display stands, encouraging them to raise their hands in the air to demonstrate their enthusiasm for the competition.

Realising that I've pushed my luck as far as I can go for now, I feign professionalism once again, and trot over to fetch the reflector from Sam's bag. If nothing else comes out of today, at least I will have some improved photography skills to fall back on.

As soon as Sam starts shooting, Katherine cheers up, posing like a pro with her friends and their baked goods. Sam calls out encouraging comments, praising them as if they were professional models. It's weird seeing him cast aside the persona of hardened hack and turn into sycophantic snapper, charming even the most awkward adolescents into smiling for the camera.

Everyone, that is, except Briony, who I notice shrinks away whenever the camera comes in her direction. She's produced the widest range of baking of anyone in the room, and she's decorating it to perfection, but she's doing her level best to shield it all from view and fade into the background.

While Sam is focusing on getting some close-ups of Katherine's bread, praising it to high heaven and glossing over the fact that it's nearly as flat as a pancake, I wander over to speak to her much quieter rival.

"Not a fan of being the centre of attention?" I ask her softly.

Briony pushes her glasses back up her nose, leaving a smear of flour on her face.

"It doesn't bother me," she says, "but some other people get really upset if it's not all about them, so I'm happy to leave them to it."

She frowns in concentration as she pipes an elaborate swirl onto the side of her cake. When it's finished to her satisfaction, she turns towards me.

"Thanks for saving my bake, by the way. I've been working on the recipe for ages and I'd have been gutted if it all got burnt."

She pushes the warm loaf in my direction with quiet pride in her work, and urges me to tear off some of the thick, nutty crust. It's the best thing I've tasted all day and I tell her so.

"Sensible attitude to have," I add. "Sometimes it's best to let your work do the talking rather than acting in a look-at-me manner."

163

She looks rather surprised to receive this kind of advice from the woman in the garish unicorn outfit.

"Not my usual style, I promise," I hasten to reassure her. "Trust me when I say how mortified I am to be walking around like a real-life cartoon character. It's a long story."

Briony puts her head on one side and gives me a considered look.

"Actually, I was thinking I wished I had your confidence," she says. "It must be nice to walk around wearing whatever you like and not care about what people think about you." She gestures at her bobbly jumper and slightly faded skirt. "My mum scrimped and saved to get me these from the second-hand uniform shop. I was so proud to have got into this school that I didn't care that they're a bit old and worn. Most of the other girls don't care either, but there's a group who like to make a big issue about it and make sarky comments about me smelling of dead people, because obviously all second-hand clothes come from dead bodies. I wish I didn't care what they say, but I do, and I know that makes me a weak person, but that's the way it is."

My heart goes out to her. I'm moved that she's been admiring my outfit as if it was an expression of my supreme self-assurance. I feel ashamed that I'm not the person she has taken me to be.

I tear off another chunk of bread. "It's not weak to care. You have talent, Briony. I'm sure you could turn your hand to anything you put your mind to. Some other people aren't so lucky, and that makes them feel insecure. That kind of insecurity can make people lash out, and it's crap being on the receiving end, but don't let it get to you. You are better than that, I promise you. Be kinder to yourself," I tell her.

I'm quite proud of my motivational pep talk. I mean every word I'm saying and I really hope Briony goes on to great things, in spite of her tormenters.

She stares back at me and then smiles. "You should take your own advice too," she says, then turns back to start a new batch of baking.

Chapter Twenty

3.42 p.m.

Briony's words startle me. I'd been getting carried away with the wise, grown-up act, because Briony reminds me of my teenage self, and fondly patting myself on the back about how much I've developed and changed from that person in the intervening years. But while I thought I was imparting pearls of wisdom from a position of self-knowledge and maturity, Briony has seen right past that façade, echoing my advice right back to me.

I'm suddenly very aware of my position, trapped in an impossible situation completely of my own making, and digging a deeper hole for myself by the second. I may have a decade of experience, give or take, on Briony, but I'm not really all that much different from the insecure adolescent that I used to be. How hypocritical am I to be counselling a teenager to speak out about her struggles, when I can't even allow myself that same luxury?

A steel band of stress tightens its grip around my head. I pinch the bridge of my nose to try to ease the pain, and as I do so, I realise it's the first time I've made this particular gesture today. On an average day at work, I'd be constantly massaging my temple in a bid to relieve the headaches that plague me. Somehow, despite the many problems and stressful situations I've encountered today, they still haven't affected me in the same visceral way as the uneasy anxiety which is usually my constant companion in the office. It feels like weakness to be admitting this, even to myself, but maybe it's time to acknowledge the problem and think about how I can resolve it, if I'm ever in the fortunate position of getting through the rest of this day unscathed and having a job to return to.

I think back to a conversation I had this time last week with Beth, the fiercely intelligent senior lawyer I share my office with. It was just another ordinary day, full of client reports, meetings about meetings, and endless stacks of paperwork.

"Are you happy?" she asked, breaking the silence of the room.

Confused by her out-of-the-blue comment, I stopped typing, my fingers still hovering over the keyboard as I considered what felt like a very personal question. I lowered my laptop lid out of habit, and shoved a pile of papers to one side so I could actually see her face and try to glean the intention behind her words. My instinct, honed by two years of service in the cut-throat world of the second floor at Richmond Woods, was to be suspicious. Why was she asking me this? Although we'd shared an office for six months, we'd barely spoken about anything other than work. It was just not the done thing to go around asking other colleagues about the state of their emotions. And given my experiences with Zara, I instantly assumed that Beth was also up to something and had her own agenda for asking after my wellbeing.

I watched her expression carefully, as my brain went into protection mode, overanalysing Beth's words and worrying about what they meant. Then I took a deep breath and forced myself to don my dispassionate lawyer head and think about this logically. There was nothing to say this was not a genuine question. Beth's face was open and kind, and everything about her body language screamed non-confrontational and trustworthy. Maybe she'd asked me about my level of happiness because she herself had experienced the stress and pressure that I was struggling with. For a brief moment, I found myself wanting to confide in her, to admit that I felt lost and miserable and like an imposter. But then I fiercely reminded myself of where I was. The goldfish-bowl office was no place to be pouring my heart out with the constant stream of nosy, gossipy lawyers striding past and peering in. And could I even trust Beth to keep quiet if I admitted to the insecurities racking my mind?

"I'm fine, thanks," I said, deliberately choosing to dismiss it as a casual question of the same depth as asking the time, or checking if I wanted a coffee from the machine in the kitchen.

She pursed her lips and leaned back in her chair.

"Fine. Interesting word, that."

Trust a lawyer to start picking throwaway vocabulary apart.

I should have stayed quiet, but being an idiot, I took the bait and spoke up again. "What do you mean by that?" I asked.

She examined her fingernails. "I once heard someone say that 'fine' stood for 'fed up, irritated, nauseous and exhausted'."

"Oh," I said, privately thinking it sounded like a pretty good acronym to me. I was growing increasingly worried at the direction this conversation was taking and the effect it was having on my already fragile emotions.

I shook my hair forwards to try to shield my face, and pulled my laptop screen back up, hoping she couldn't see the pathetic tears pricking at the back of my eyes. I wasn't used to people on the second floor being kind at work, and it was having a disturbing effect on my usually unassailable guard.

"I didn't mean it like that," I said quietly, although I'm not sure I managed to get enough confidence in there to make it sound convincing.

Beth cleared her throat and turned back to her emails. There was a long pause, and I began to think we'd moved away from dangerous territory. I tried to concentrate on the document in front of me, but the letters were turning blurry and swimming around the page. Much to my mortification, a single tear fell and smudged a section of type. I dug my fingers into my nails, angrily telling myself to get it together. There was no way I was going to cry in the glass box for all to see.

"If you're ever not fine, it's OK to admit it," said Beth quietly. She let the words hang in the air for a moment, resonating with their power. Then the tone of her voice changed as if we'd never had this conversation. "I'm going to get a coffee from the kitchen. Black or latte?"

I stammered out a request for a black coffee with extra sugar, and then heaved a big sigh of relief as she left the office. The anxious questions were buzzing around my brain like annoying little gnats. Why had Beth asked me that particular question? And why now? Had my colleagues been talking about me behind my back? Did they think I was struggling? What if they'd been saying my work wasn't up to scratch?

I gave myself a stern talking to. There was only one solution to my weakness. I obviously needed to put more effort in and nip any rumours in the bud before they caused me serious trouble. That night, I didn't stop work until 11 p.m. and I stayed awake worrying until 3 a.m.

Now, I swallow. Despite the happy chatter of the teenagers in the room, I feel as though I've been whisked right back into that tense workplace situation, feeling hunted and speculated about. My mouth has gone dry and the pounding of my head can only be matched by the thudding of my heart against my ribs. The laughter of the girls and the clicking of the shutter on Sam's camera morph into a dull background roar and all I can focus on is the effort it takes to draw one shuddering breath in after another. I clutch the edge of the worktop, gripping it so tightly in a bid to remain upright that my nails graze the surface. My stomach is churning with anxiety and I can feel the panic building within me, starting to race around my veins with frightening speed. I fight the sensation, brain trying to tell body that everything is OK, that I'm safe, that nothing bad is going to happen, but it's one of those situations where logic can't win out and I surrender to the feeling of helplessness. Rationally, I know that I'm not dying, that this is just a panic attack, and it too shall pass. But rationality is no match to this.

I know what's happening to me because it's not the first time I've experienced this terrible, drowning sensation. It started catching me out every so often during the last six months, crippling me in the moment, confirming my sense of failure, and increasing my fear of suffering another attack in a Catch 22 situation of the most vicious kind. The most recent occasion was about ten seconds after Beth left our office to get the coffee. Has just thinking about that incident triggered another one? I'm so angry at myself for letting things get this bad.

But calling it "just a panic attack" is to underestimate how truly terrible I'm feeling. I may have faked one kind of sickness in order to have my duvet day, but maybe there was another genuine problem bubbling in the background all along. Was that what I was too scared to admit to myself earlier when I croaked my excuses to Zara? Maybe I was too cowardly to call it by its actual name.

Stress. It's a word that is used a lot at work, especially in the frequent missives we're sent by HR about how to identify the signs and what we need to do if we're concerned about someone. But instead of feeling supported by their apparent care for their employees, I've always felt threatened by it. Because every time I get one of those emails, dripping as they are with their subtle undertones of threat, it feels like they could replace the word "stress" with "failure". If I'm stressed, it's because I'm failing to handle my workload effectively. If I'm upset by a colleague's bullying attitude, it's because I'm not emotionally strong enough to stand up to them and deal with it appropriately. And if I'm tired from staying up all night worrying, it's because I'm not good enough at compartmentalising the different parts of my life. It's all on me, nobody else.

I read those emails then look around me and wonder how everyone else is managing to cope with such effortless ease. I gaze through the windows of my glass cage and see them all working away. Nobody else has their head in their hands. No one else looks upon a trip to the toilet as being a highlight of the day because it actually allows them to get away from their desk. How come they are so sorted and I'm just a mess?

I wonder what would happen if I did go to HR and confess that sometimes it feels like my head is about to explode with the tension of trying to do everything that is required of me, that I'm so tense all the time that I've forgotten what normal feels like. But I always stop myself before I expose my weakness to anyone. What good would it achieve? To admit my vulnerability would be akin to putting a great big target on myself. The head of HR doesn't have the nickname of "Damon the Dementor" for nothing. You can feel his presence before you actually see him. He's there sucking the enjoyment out of any rare moment of levity, always watching, judging and making notes for your next review interview.

My dad says that when workplaces changed the name of the Personnel Department to Human Resources, that's where things started to go wrong. Because now, we people are viewed on the same level as the computers and the photocopier and the air conditioning unit. We are merely another resource to facilitate the workings of the business. And much like machinery, if we're not working properly, we'll get updated or replaced. And I really don't want that to happen. Despite it all, I still love the law as a profession. It's the politics and the competitiveness surrounding it which get to me. I'm not going to pretend that my dream role in the pro bono department would transplant me into a place full of shiny, happy people who spend their days untouched by stress – far from it. But the lawyers there do have the knowledge that what they're doing is helping to make a difference and they are generally driven by more important things than who's going to get the biggest bonus or pull one over on a colleague.

I know this all sounds deeply pathetic and like I'm wallowing in self-pity. But it's hard to explain it properly without sounding like a Moaning Minnie. On the rare occasion I've tried to talk to my family about the stress I'm feeling, they just don't get it.

"Why don't you get another job?" says my eldest brother Thomas. "A woman with a skillset like yours, they'll be snapping you up."

He makes it sound so simple. I try to explain it's not as easy as he thinks, that the competition for every job in

Magic Circle law firms is more ruthless than anything he would ever have encountered, even in the equally stressful profession of teaching. I try to tell him that having spent the last two years devoting my blood, sweat and tears towards the goal of making the pro bono department and doing some good in this world, jacking it in now would mean the last two years have been a complete waste of my time. And I point out that I am only qualified to do jobs similar to my own, and that even if I were to move to another firm, I'd have to start at the bottom and go through all this pain all over again in order to get to the same position. But still he repeats his suggestion that I find another job.

My grandma listens sympathetically, and urges me to take good care of myself, saying that no job is worth sacrificing everything for. And then she changes the subject and starts dropping heavy questions along the lines of have I found a nice young man yet, and did I know that Sylvia next door is a great-grandmother three times over already? And although I know she's very well intentioned, it doesn't stop it becoming yet another anxiety which plays through my head on repeat in the middle of the night; that one day I'll wake up and the prime of my life will have passed me by, and I'll still be trapped in the glass office cage, a dried-up old husk of a human being, alone and forgotten. I don't even know if I want children, but it feels like my grandma is leading the pressure from the rest of society, telling me they should be my ultimate ambition. I swear she doesn't have the same kind of conversations with Charlie, who's just as unattached as I am. There are still a lot of battles to be won in the war for feminism.

Mind you, sometimes I look with envy upon colleagues who are going off on maternity leave because at least it means they're going to get a few months of freedom out of the office. Now, before anyone says anything, I know they're probably going to have it ten times harder than me, suddenly having the terrifying responsibility of keeping a baby alive and all that, but they do at least have a tangible reason for being so tired all the time, one that is considered acceptable by the rest of the world. No one's going to think twice if they complain about being up all night and being short on sleep. But I don't think getting pregnant just to have a sabbatical from work is really a good enough reason to add that extra edge of complication into my life.

"Earth to Alexa, are you receiving me?"

I feel like I'm moving through treacle as I slowly raise my head and fight to focus on the man standing in front of me. I'm expecting to see the usual mixture of disdain and irritation which fills Sam's face whenever he's looking at me, but there's something else in his features, something which I would have interpreted as a look of concern in any other person. But this is Sam we're talking about, and I've been the thorn in his side all day, so the panic attack must still be distorting my judgement.

I blink at him in confusion, not trusting that my voice will be strong enough to reply yet.

Over on the other side of the room, Mrs Choudhary calls on the girls to be quiet so that the winner of the competition can be announced.

Sam glances across at the teacher. "Can I leave you for thirty seconds more?" he asks.

I nod in slow motion. If I didn't know better, I would think he was actually worried about me.

He hesitates, then pats my hand awkwardly.

"Thirty seconds," he repeats, before dashing across to capture the moment when Briony is crowned the winner of the competition. I muster the strength to applaud her victory, then I collapse onto a stool and focus on slowly counting my breath in and out until finally I start to feel some semblance of control over my body again.

I'm angry with myself for getting in such a state for no good reason, and I feel as exhausted as if I've been competing in a race. Never has the thought of curling up in my bed seemed so inviting. If I wasn't so desperate not to draw further attention to myself, I would rest my head on the work surface for a few minutes until the pounding finally subsides. I compromise by resting my chin on my hands and staring into the middle distance, trying to make my mind glaze over and calm itself down. Not for the first time, I wish I'd had time to read and digest the mindfulness book that my mum bought me for Christmas.

Sam is now quietly chatting with Mrs Choudhary. I have a horrible feeling that I'm the topic of conversation, because they both keep glancing across at me. I try to muster the strength to care, but I don't have enough energy left to worry about what they're saying. I need to accept once and for all that I am not in control of my situation today, and that I haven't been since I shut the front door and locked myself out. My fate is in their hands.

The ear-piercing ring of the school bell nearly sets my heart racing again. There's a stampede for the exit as the girls scoop up their baking and barge their way out, chattering merrily on their way to after-school clubs or to catch their public transport home. Only the discarded washing-up and crumbs on the benches give any sign that they were ever here, and the room immediately feels eerie in its emptiness. Mrs Choudhary waves and sends a warm smile in my direction, before she then bows out too, leaving Sam and I in the room. I wonder what he's said to persuade her to leave us alone.

He carefully and methodically packs up his kit, checking around the workbenches to make sure he's left nothing behind. There's something quite calming about watching his slow and steady movements. When he's finished, he comes and sits opposite me at the workbench.

"Feeling up to moving yet?" he asks.

Again, I'm surprised by the lack of sarcasm in his voice.

I'm not entirely sure how bad I was during my panic attack, but it wasn't dramatic enough to attract the attention of the girls, so it can't have been too awful. But I was clearly behaving oddly enough to come to Sam's attention and to make him soften his attitude towards me. The thought of being pitied by him makes me cringe inwardly. I nearly tell him I'm fine, but then I hear Beth's acronym in my head and swallow back the words.

"Sure, no problem," I say, trying to sound hearty and strong, like I've suddenly assumed the jolly hockey sticks persona of one of the teachers at this school. The thought of appearing feeble in front of Sam is somehow mortifying and this apparently genuine concern he's showing towards me is rather unsettling. I'd almost prefer he went back to acting like a despot again.

I leap up from my stool with as much enthusiasm as I can muster and try to ignore the feeling of heaviness in my limbs.

Sam eyes me warily. "You're not going to keel over, are you?"

He moves his camera equipment so it's out of range and hovers nearby, looking like he's ready to dive in and catch me if I start to fall. He's probably worried about me causing another scene.

"I'm perfectly alright," I insist, annoyed that he can recognise my weakness. I don't want to hand another weapon to him.

"Sure you are," he says. "And I'm the Pope. But if you feel up to moving, Mrs Choudhary would be grateful if we got going. And then we're going to find somewhere quiet to sit down and I'm going to buy you a strong cup of tea."

He's speaking in a tone which allows for no argument. I pull a face, but allow myself to go along with his plans. I can't help feeling a little warm glow that someone's paying attention to my welfare for a change.

It's probably that, combined with my still-wobbly feeling from the panic attack, which makes me consent to Sam looping his arm through mine as we are escorted off the premises. While we follow Mrs Choudhary and trek down the many flights of steep stairs and negotiate our way through the winding corridors, I find I'm grateful for the solid feel of Sam's presence. He may be as irritating as hell, but at least he's come good in this mini crisis of mine.

Chapter Twenty-One

4.01 p.m.

S am passes over a handful of change to the man in the
coffee van, then picks up the two steaming mugs of tea
and comes to sit down on the bench next to me. While he's
been ordering the drinks, I've been staring at the swirling
waters of the Thames, focusing on the boats buzzing up and
down the river, and watching the cans, twigs and other bits
of detritus lapping up on the shoreline. Even though we're
in the heart of the city, there is a certain peace that comes
with being right by the water, a sense of continuity that only
a river which has been flowing through this spot for
hundreds of years can bring. I remind myself that many
disasters and conflicts have come and gone, but the Thames
has kept its steady course, bringing life to the city.

I prop my feet up on the stone balustrade which
separates the river from the bank, and lean back, cupping
the warm mug in my hands. It's one of those giant Sports

Direct ones, probably big enough to hold a pint of tea. It's not my usual hot drink of choice, but there's something frightfully British about having a cup of tea in a crisis, and just holding the mug brings a strange kind of comfort with it.

I take a sip and nearly choke.

"That's a bit sweet," I protest. "There's meant to be room for actual tea and milk in among all this sugar."

Sam pulls a face. "Thought it might do you some good, having a bit of extra sweetness."

"I think you'll find I'm sweet enough," I say lightly. Sam nearly smiles at my bad joke. "This much could send a girl onto a serious sugar high, and I've had enough excitement already for one day, thank you very much."

"Well, they say sugar is good for shock and stuff."

Sam shrugs, and adds an extra packet to his own mug, which is emblazoned with the words *Best teacher in the world*. I wonder how it's ended up as a communal mug at a hot drink van. Maybe Mrs Choudhary got rid of it after being presented with it by a particularly irksome pupil.

"The only shock I've had today is you being nice to me just now," I retort, then instantly feel guilty for being an ungrateful so-and-so. "Sorry. Thank you for the drink."

Sam nods his head in acknowledgement. "And I suppose I should say thank you for giving me my camera back undamaged, if not unsullied."

I can't help smiling at this.

"I'm still determined to stop you sending those pictures of me," I reply.

Sam smiles back, and I notice the way the skin around

his eyes crinkles with the fullness of his grin.

"We'll see about that," he says. He stirs his tea with a wooden stick, and then sets it carefully down on the bench between us. "You see, the thing that's confusing me is that you're really desperate for your bosses not to find out that you've been skiving, which speaks to a love of the job at some level, yet you've faked a sicky in order to have the day off, which suggests that you're fed up with the place. So, which is it? How do you really feel about where you work?"

What I should sensibly do is remain politely neutral and fob him off with my usual set piece about the delights and challenges of working for an elite and highly competitive law firm in the centre of London. After all, I don't need to give him any more ammunition against me than I already have. But when I open my mouth, I find instead I'm admitting to the confusion I feel, torn between aiming for better things, and feeling crushed by the reality of my current circumstances. I know I shouldn't be confiding in someone I barely know, a tabloid journalist at a paper with a dodgy reputation of screwing people over to boot, but once I start speaking, I find I can't stop myself. Blame it on me still feeling vulnerable and not having yet got my guard up again after my panic attack, but there's also something about the quiet way he listens which encourages confidences, and it all comes pouring out. It actually feels liberating to be getting everything off my chest like this, even if it's to someone I probably shouldn't be trusting with it.

Sam stares at me in astonishment.

"It sounds more like you're in an abusive relationship with your job than just having an employee–employer vibe going on. Don't you think you'd be better off letting me publish the pictures and being free of the toxic place once and for all?"

I consider what he's saying. I suppose from an outsider's perspective, it does look like I'm suffering from a serious case of Stockholm Syndrome. I could probably list the negatives of working for Richmond Woods far more readily than the positives. But then I think back to the naïve but enthusiastic person I was when I first joined the company, and I long to recapture that feeling of hope for the future. Because I know that once I've served my time wading through the crap and the stress, then I will eventually get to a place where I can affect real change, where I can use the power of the vast corporate machine for good. And yes, I'll admit that my work–life balance is dire, and that the amount of stress I'm trying to juggle is probably not good for my health. But if I give up without even trying to reach my goal, or if my departure from the company is forced upon me rather than being on my own terms, then I will always regret it. And regret can be as unhealthy as stress. Or so I'm told. Besides, if he publishes those pictures, losing my job is just one worry. The spectre of that police officer still hovers over me.

The silence draws out, and I realise that Sam is still waiting for my response. I take a deep breath.

"No. It's complicated, I know, but trust me on this, it would be much, much better for me if you didn't publish the pictures."

Sam purses his lips. "After that display in there, and from what you've said, it sounds to me like you could claim this as a legitimate sick day," he says. "Friends of mine have been off with stress and it is OK, you know."

There's only kindness in his voice.

"And give Zara another reason to spread rumours about me being crazy? No thanks," I say, trying to keep my voice light. "I'm just tired, honestly."

"Whatever you say," replies Sam. "Stress doesn't mean failure, you know. Although I maintain you're definitely not quite right in the head, following me around like this."

I should have known there'd be a sting in his apparent offer of support.

"Besides," I continue, "Richmond Woods has a very narrow definition of a sick day and chasing around London getting into all kinds of scrapes would definitely not fall within their guidelines. I'd have thought that as an employee of the notorious Sir Clive you'd understand exactly where I'm coming from."

Sam shrugs and takes another slurp of tea. I wonder if there's a reason he's trying to hide his expression from me.

"Sir Clive doesn't bother himself with the day-to-day running of the paper. As long as it's flying off the newsstands and the website's ad revenue is sending those pound signs spinning, he really doesn't give a damn."

I pick up the wooden stirrer and twizzle it in my fingers as I consider my response.

"But he obviously keeps a close enough eye on things to know which photojournalist he'd like to send to cover his only daughter's school event. There must have been a reason he chose you over everyone else. And there must be a reason why you're so desperate to please him with the snaps you produce."

Sam looks as though he's about to answer, then suddenly turns away. "Oh, you lawyer types are all the same. You're not going to catch me out that easily. I'm not going to give you any information which you could use against me. I plead the Fifth. And yes, I know that's not a thing in the UK."

He's definitely excited my curiosity now, but he holds back from any further revelations. We appear to have reached an impasse. We stare each other out for a few moments. But where there was hostility between us, there's now something else humming in the air. I'm the first to break into a smile, then Sam grins back and we settle in companionable silence. It's weird how much better I feel having spoken out loud about the extent of my confused feelings about work. Sam is an unlikely confidant, but to give him his due, he did listen very effectively and even managed to restrain himself from tutting and disagreeing with me too much.

A police boat speeds past, setting the debris on the shore dancing in its wake. A few droplets of mucky river water splash up, soaking into the grimy fluff of my formerly-pristine slippers. I shiver slightly. Although it's a warm spring day, there's a cool clamminess in the air from the Thames which is starting to seep through the furry fabric of my onesie. Without really thinking about it, I shuffle closer to Sam, until I can feel the warmth emanating from his body millimetres away from mine. For a few moments, we're both tense, holding ourselves stiffly upright to maintain that delicate gap. But then, gradually, we relax, until my right-hand side is flush with his left. I can feel the warm strength of his muscles through my clothing and something flips in my lower belly. Sam clears his throat and I wonder what he's thinking about, and if his thoughts are running in the same strange direction as mine.

When Sam's phone starts buzzing, I'm irritated that our quiet moment is being interrupted. At first, he ignores it, but when it vibrates again, he picks it up and idly checks the screen. Then he sits upright, and starts scrolling through his messages, his features clouding over. There's a coldness along my side where he was sitting.

"What the hell?" he mutters, frowning in confusion.

The phone bleeps again to warn it's got a voicemail message. I'm starting to get a bad feeling about this. I strain to listen in, but can only make out the cheery tone of whoever is at the other end of the line. If they're that upbeat, it can't be bad news, I try to tell myself.

But the expression on Sam's face warns me that something is terribly wrong. He deletes the message with an angry swipe and turns to glare at me. He's directed more than a few disgruntled looks in my direction today, but this is hands down the worst. There's a disappointment in his face which is somehow so much worse than pure anger. I brace myself.

"That was a voicemail from my colleagues in the newsroom, ringing to congratulate me on my impending parenthood with a woman named Zara. Is there something you'd like to tell me?"

Chapter Twenty-Two

4.17 p.m.

"Don't worry, I'm not pregnant," I say, somewhat facetiously, hoping to inject some levity into the situation.

He's not going to let me get away with it.

"That doesn't surprise me. I can't imagine anyone would want to go near enough to you to make that a possibility," says Sam.

That's a low blow, and I flinch as if he had physically lashed out at me with his cruel words. I spring up from the bench to put greater distance between us and fold my arms defensively, smarting from the insult. Sam opens his mouth as if to say something, and for the briefest moment I think I see a flicker of apology in his features, before the shutters go down on his face again and he can't meet my gaze.

"I needed to find out where you'd gone." I shrug, trying

to maintain an air of unruffled calm to disguise how much I'm hurting from the sting in his speech. "It was a stupid, impulsive thing to do, but needs must."

I don't know why I'm trying to defend the indefensible, but I can't let him see that I'm upset.

Sam shakes his head in disgust. "Needs must? Are you bloody kidding me? You've been pouring your heart out about your sad little life as a put-upon lawyer, and I was actually starting to feel sorry for you, more fool me. Now I know it was all an act. You're a queen manipulator, completely selfish, and a liar. I think while you've been cloistered away in those glass bubbles you profess to hate so much, you've forgotten what it's like in the real world." He takes a deep breath and runs his hand through his hair, making it stand on end even more than usual. "Do you have any idea how much trouble you've caused for me? You think the gossip is bad in your law firm? Try working in a newsroom. You sneeze and someone two floors up texts to say 'Bless you.'" He laughs bitterly. "Journalists live for gossip, and the gossip with the greatest currency value is newsroom gossip. It's their main entertainment. I can guarantee that right now there's not a single person in that building who isn't aware of my impending fake fatherhood. Even the work experience person who's barely stepped foot in the door will know about Sam and his secret, pregnant girlfriend."

It would be better if he was shouting at me. This overly calm, steady tone makes him seem all the more angry. I feel terrible about this whole situation. It's all my fault for being so thoughtless. I rack my brains for something to say which will make things better.

"But you're Mr Knows His Own Mind. I wouldn't have thought you're the type of person to be bothered about what other people think about you," I say, meaning it as a compliment, but realising too late that there's a danger he'll interpret it as sarcasm.

"Trust me, I don't give a toss about what most people think about me," he retorts. "But if there's one thing I hate, it's my private life being talked about rather than my professional prowess. And when I tell my colleagues that this situation is all a big lie perpetrated by an irrational housemate I'd never even spoken to before today, they'll gossip even more." His expression is stern yet troubled. "I've worked hard to build a reputation, one which is based on being diligent and fundamentally good at my job. Now, whenever anyone in the newsroom thinks about me, they'll associate me with this story. Do you really expect them to be able to take me seriously after this?"

I'm cringing so badly right now. No, it's more than cringing. I'm really upset that I'm the cause of his troubles and I'm genuinely repentant. I've made some spectacularly bad choices today. Most of them have come back to bite me on the backside. But while I can cope with suffering personal injury and getting myself into scrapes, I really hate being the cause of problems for someone else. It was never my intention for my thoughtlessness to be a source of this much distress for Sam.

I don't know what to say. I'm pretty sure that whatever words come out of my mouth will make things worse, so I remain silent, hoping that he'll cool down and we can sort things out. But Sam interprets that silence as a lack of remorse. He throws his arms up in the air and turns his back on me, striding off at speed, determined to try to pick up the pieces of his ruined day.

"Sam, I'm so sorry," I call after his retreating form, but the wind is whipping up and he gives no sign of having heard my words.

For a few seconds I hesitate. Trailing after Sam is only going to anger him still further, but what alternative do I have? I need to make things right.

I hurry to catch him up, but my slipper catches on the uneven paving and I nearly tumble to the ground, my fall only stopped by the arm of the bench. I wince as my wrist takes the brunt of the stumble. But I don't have time to check the damage, and set off running again.

"Oi, don't you go leaving those mugs there!" yells the man from the hot drink van. I dash back and hand them over with a quick thanks. I can't afford to add anyone else to the list of people I've upset today.

Sam is already halfway up the stairs under Millennium Bridge, his long legs making easy work of striding up the steps two at a time.

"Sam, wait for me, I can explain," I call after him, so beyond caring about making a spectacle of myself that I'm happy to bellow like a banshee.

The Londoners in this part of the city are obviously a supremely calm and collected bunch, because barely any of them even bat an eyelid at the sight of the unicorn charging up the stairs. However, when I nearly do another ridiculous pratfall thanks to my increasingly decrepit slippers, a few tourists turn away from their Thames-side selfies and start videoing my antics. I lower my head and shade the sides of my face with my hands like a celebrity emerging from court after being done for being drunk and disorderly. I don't think I'd really appreciated until today to what extent people feel the need to record everything on their phones. I feel as though my every move is being logged and recorded for posterity, an extra body of evidence for the prosecution.

I let out a shout of excitement and point at something imaginary behind me, and as one, they all spin around to take a look. I didn't believe that tactic would work in real life as well as it does in cartoons. At least one little thing is going my way. Taking advantage of their temporary distraction, I weave through the tour group and carry on charging up the steps. St Paul's Cathedral is looming ahead of me, but there's no time to stop and stare at the historic landmark. I need to spot where Sam has got to.

The area is crowded, schoolchildren rushing towards the Tube and workers with their heads down hurrying about their business. It's bustling London at its finest, and for a brief moment I'm reminded of how small a fish I am in this giant, overwhelming pond. My breath catches in my throat again and that horrible sense of rising panic starts creeping back into my body. Then out of the corner of my eye I spot a flash of Sam's pale blue shirt and I feel a tiny burst of hope, although it's soon dashed. He's climbing into a taxi, and I have no idea where he's going. How can I make amends if he's vanishing into the distance?

Without stopping to think properly, I stick my index

finger and thumb between my lips and let out a piercing whistle, one which I haven't utilised since helping my dad herd the sheep into the barn back at home. I wave at another passing taxi, and to my surprise, it smartly pulls up at my feet.

Chapter Twenty-Three

4.31 p.m.

I jump in the taxi and manage to stammer out the words
which are a cliché even in movies.

"Follow that cab."

The driver turns and stares at me through the Perspex
partition.

"You what?"

His face is a picture. He can't decide whether I'm taking
the piss, or being deadly serious.

"I need you to follow that taxi. Please, it's really
important."

He scrutinises me carefully. I dread to think what he's
making of the wild-eyed, grubby individual looking back at
him. The last time I checked myself in a mirror back in the
toilets at the National Theatre, I looked pretty bedraggled.
Since then, I've gone through a great deal more trauma,

both emotional and physical. I'm pretty sure I don't look anything like the average fare a taxi driver would expect to pick up in this part of London at this time of day.

His hand is hovering over the phone attached to his dashboard. I'm certain he's seconds away from telling me to leave and calling backup, and I try to make myself appear as non-threatening as possible by flashing my most dazzling smile.

It doesn't impress him, but it does at least stop him from dialling.

"And where precisely is your destination? I'm a businessman you know, darlin', and if you're going to commandeer me for a job that's fifty yards away, then it isn't a sound financial decision for me to be taking. This is prime job territory with all the bankers and lawyers around."

"I am a lawyer," I say.

He bursts out laughing. "And I'm the Queen's private chauffeur. Pull the other one. Now, tell me your destination, or I'm afraid I'm going to have to ask you to leave my cab."

If nothing else, today is really emphasising to me how much of society is based on judging other people by their appearances. I'm sure if I'd got in the taxi in my usual lawyer get-up, then he would have accepted my instructions without a quibble, but now I'm looking less than respectable, I'm a person to be suspicious of. Mind you, given what I've done to Sam and my involvement with the scuffle at the climate change protest, the taxi driver is probably right to be wary of me.

I open up the bank card app on my phone and wave it towards him to prove I have the means to pay. The battery is hovering on a worrying twenty percent, and I pray it'll last the length of this journey to wherever it is we're going.

The taxi driver still doesn't look convinced. I would have blurted out a fake sob story in order to try to get his sympathy, but I've learnt my lesson on that one. Instead I take a deep breath and give him the potted history of my day, not holding back on a single sorry detail. I'm gambling that he'll be intrigued enough to want to play his part, rather than appalled enough to throw me straight onto the pavement. Thankfully, my move pays off. When he's finally stopped laughing, he wipes the tears from his eyes and puts the engine into gear.

"That's the best tale I've heard all week, and let me tell you, I get some corkers in the back of my cab. My name's Nige. Nice to meet you. Cheer up, love, I'll do my best to catch up with the other taxi. I've always wanted to get involved in a chase across London."

He demonstrates his commitment to the cause by immediately accelerating with a vengeance, flinging me back in my seat. I hastily fasten my seatbelt and grip onto the door handle for dear life as my new best friend starts weaving his way through the traffic as if his taxi were no bigger than a bicycle, leaving me wincing at the number of near misses we have. I soon realise there is no more ruthless driver than a London cabbie on a mission. Nige could give James Bond a run for his money.

Fortunately, Sam's taxi driver seems to be less adept than mine at avoiding the congestion, because I soon catch a glimpse of his vehicle up ahead. I shuffle down on my seat so my head is barely poking up above the window. I wouldn't put it past Sam to catch a glimpse of me and hit send on those photos in immediate retaliation – if he hasn't already sent them, that is. After the amount of trouble I've caused for him, he would be perfectly within his rights to do just that, but call me a foolish optimist, there's still a sneaky hope at the back of my mind that he's not yet hit the button which will seal my fate.

My stomach flips over as we zip around a tight bend. The trouble is, now I'm in stealth-mode, I can't properly see where we're going, and the motion of the taxi is making me feel queasy. Normally I have an iron stomach when it comes to travel, but it would unfortunately appear that all the stress and drama of today has rather reduced my levels of immunity. I swallow nervously and try taking a few deep breaths to calm my churning insides.

My mind is going as fast as the vehicle. I've no idea what I'm going to say to Sam when I finally catch up with him, but I need to make amends. And if he chooses to publish the photos and refuses to lend me his key in retaliation for my foolish actions, then I've probably deserved it. I need to accept that, for now, I am not in control of my destiny. I will worry about what happens when it happens, and not before. Well, that's what I keep telling myself, anyway.

We skid around yet another corner at sickening speed, and I pull myself upright, deciding it's better to be spotted by Sam than to throw up all over Nige's cab. Frustratingly, while I've been hiding, our quarry has once again disappeared out of view.

I'm not sure who's more upset by this turn of events, me or Nige. He's certainly thrown himself wholeheartedly into the pursuit, his grin getting broader with every inch of ground we're covering. I suspect the girl in the unicorn onesie is going to become one of his all-time favourite mad passenger tales. He's so invested in the outcome, he keeps taking his eyes off the road to turn around and address me, throwing suggestions of potential destinations in my direction, using his encyclopaedic knowledge of London's streets to narrow down the possibilities of where we're going.

Half the places he names, I've never even heard of and I'm growing increasingly ashamed about how little I know of the city I've called my home for the past two years. It's pretty sad that my life has mostly revolved around a triangle of work, home and the occasional visit to the supermarket near the Tube stop. But when Nige says Millbank, it sparks a memory at the back of my mind.

"That could be right. I'm sure his colleague mentioned he had an assignment there at some point this afternoon." Shortly after I'd bribed her with my fake pregnancy announcement. Another pang of guilt attacks my insides.

"Hold on tight," Nige calls over his shoulder. "Let's take this fight to the heart of Westminster."

At this point, I'm not sure how much tighter I can actually hold. My knuckles have turned white with the effort and I'm starting to lose sensation in my fingers.

I swallow a squeak in my throat as Nige speeds through

a set of traffic lights as they turn from amber to red. If there are any police officers around, they'll pull him over for sure. Knowing my luck, they'll probably add aiding and abetting Nige's crazy driving to my charge sheet.

And then, suddenly, Nige slams on the brakes, and cranks the vehicle back down to a normal speed.

"Got him. I'll pull in behind them."

He punches the air with glee. My delight is tempered by a fervent wish that Nige would hold onto the wheel with both hands.

Sam is right ahead of us, sitting bolt upright in the back of the cab. I lean forward and peer through the windscreen, trying to ascertain his mood, but there's not really much you can glean about a person's state of mind from the back of their head. I try to telegraph subliminal messages towards him that he should forgive me and allow me to make amends; anything to keep my mind off its current state of panic.

The traffic has snarled up again and we're now crawling along the Embankment, past monuments to the Royal Air Force and the Battle of Britain, inching our way towards the heart of Westminster. Our progress is frustratingly slow and I briefly consider getting out and walking to catch up with Sam's cab. I quickly dismiss the idea. There's no way he'd let me get in the vehicle with him, and I can guarantee the second my slippers hit the pavement, the traffic would miraculously clear again and I'd be left back at square one.

I gaze out of the window at the Thames and try to recapture the earlier feeling of calm I had from watching it. The sight of the stately war monuments on the embankment is a salutary reminder that I should have a little perspective on the gravity of my situation. Whatever else has happened today, nobody has died because of my actions.

Last time I was in this part of London, I was in the back of a client's chauffeur-driven car, trying to complete a stack of paperwork while she conducted a conference call, effortlessly slipping between three separate languages in a way which I found impressive and slightly intimidating. I was rather surprised that I'd been assigned to work for Cordelia Cheng, as she was a fairly new client for Richmond Woods, and one with an extremely high-profile and net worth. I was pretty new to the company myself back then, and wondered if this was some secret initiation test that I was being set. I'd overheard some of the more unreconstructed male partners describe her as "difficult", but then again, they tend to apply that description to most women with opinions. So far, I'd found Cordelia a hard but fair taskmaster, someone who knew what she wanted, and wasn't afraid to go after it.

Cordelia snapped her flip phone shut with a decisive click.

"The battery life is much more efficient," she explained as she caught me looking at the old-fashioned device. "No need to spend half your life tethered to a charging point. When you get to my age, you've much better things to do than worry about whether people think you're lame for not having the latest iPhone whatsit."

She tucked the phone away in her handbag and clasped her hands neatly on her lap.

"I must apologise for making you accompany me in the

car. This week is so busy, I was struggling to find time to come into your office for an appointment to discuss and sign off those initial documents. I suppose I could have done another virtual hangout, or whatever it is they call it, but when I'm going to work with people over a period of time, I like to meet them face-to-face to start with. I hope you don't mind?"

I shook my head. I was paid not to mind unreasonable demands from clients, but actually this request to meet in motion seemed particularly civilised. The Rolls Royce glided through the traffic so silkily that I was barely aware we were moving, and its plush and comfortable interior made a welcome change to the stark surroundings of the office. I could get used to meetings like this.

I double-checked the last few lines of my paperwork, then handed it over to Cordelia to read, feeling a pang of nerves while I waited for approval.

She pulled on her glasses and started scanning through the documents, occasionally stopping to ask me to explain details of the fine print. Without the added pressure which comes from being surrounded by my competitive colleagues, I felt myself starting to relax. I was in control of this situation. Maybe I was OK at my job after all. It was good to be working with someone who thought my opinion was worth asking and taking note of.

Cordelia took a gold-nibbed fountain pen out of her handbag. I held my breath as she re-read the last few lines, and then heaved a sigh of relief as she signed the documents with a flourish.

"Excellent, a good job, well done," she said. "And thank

you once again for going out of your way to pander to my demands. May I offer you a cup of coffee before you return to the office?"

Without waiting for an answer, she rummaged around in her bag again and pulled out a flask.

"Always be prepared, or so they told me when I was a Girl Guide."

She poured the coffee and added milk from a little bottle, all without spilling a drop on her immaculate suit.

I accepted the drink gratefully, and we clinked mugs, as if toasting our working relationship.

"Now, is that a slight Yorkshire accent I detect there?" asked Cordelia. "I know I'm right," she continued, without waiting for my answer. "I can hear it in your voice. I did a year in a North Yorkshire boarding school as an exchange student in the sixth form and got very accomplished at distinguishing a Hull accent from a Bradford one. I'd say you're more Dales-way, like many of my school compatriots. I think it's true to say that in England, the further north you get, the colder the weather, but the warmer the people."

I laughed. "Sounds about right. In my village, everyone always nods at each other and passes the time of day, even if they've never met. It's second nature. I got a shock when I first moved to London, smiled at someone on the Tube and they thought I was propositioning them. I kind of miss that sense of friendliness."

Cordelia patted my arm. "Well, the important thing to do is keep on smiling and pursue the things which really matter to you. Forgive the interview-style question, but where do you see yourself in a few years' time?"

And so, I found myself confessing my airy aspirations to do some good in the world and to fight for those without a voice.

"Sorry, I probably sound hopelessly naïve," I said after some time, realising that I'd been droning on a bit too long in response to what had probably just been a polite question.

"Not at all, my dear," said Cordelia. "It's refreshing to hear your thoughts. That kind of positive attitude is just what is needed in a stuffy old firm like Richmond Woods." Her phone bleeped to remind her that she was due on another conference call, but before she answered it, she threw one final comment in my direction. "Maybe at our next meeting, we can talk about the new charity project I'm looking to set up."

I nodded enthusiastically, excited about the possibilities of working on something important with such a go-getter as Cordelia. When I returned to the office, I drew a little smiley face on a Post-it note and stuck it onto the corner of my desk as a reminder to follow her advice to keep a positive attitude. However, as with most of my experience at Richmond Woods, my lofty dreams didn't last long. Somehow, Zara manipulated things so that she took the next meeting with Cordelia, and the opportunity to discuss the charitable plans never materialised. I'd vicariously followed the progress of the project for a short while through reading articles in the newspapers, then Cordelia moved her business to another firm, and that Post-it note got lost, along with my motivation.

I've not thought about that meeting in a while. I'm disappointed in myself for not making more of an opportunity that was handed to me on a plate. But then I remind myself that it's so easy to look back with the perfect clarity of hindsight and think, "If only..." There's nothing I can change about the past, but if I get through this day and still have a job by the end of it, then there is nothing to stop me contacting Cordelia and seeing if it's too late for me to pursue the project. I promise myself silently that whatever happens, I will return to the office with a new determination to find a way of working which allows me to keep on smiling.

We've now come to a complete halt, and Nige has even turned his engine off as the traffic shows no sign of moving anywhere. There's a minibus load of schoolkids in the lane parallel to ours and they're entertaining themselves during their boring journey by banging on the windows and trying to shock me with the variety of rude gestures and weird faces they can pull. My usual instinct would be to hide away, or at least pretend that I couldn't see what they were doing, but I'm starting to gain a bit of confidence in my unicorn skin, or maybe it's just giving me a devil-may-care attitude, and I can't resist sticking my tongue out and waggling my fingers in my ears in retaliation. It feels extraordinarily liberating, and I make myself laugh, even if the kids look rather bemused.

Inevitably, with typical Alexa luck, I time my best ugly face for the moment when the teacher turns around to tell off his pupils, and he gets the full brunt of my gurning. He frowns and shakes his head in disapproval as I feel my cheeks turn pink with embarrassment. Yet another person I've managed to make a fool of myself in front of today.

Just as I'm praying that the traffic will move forward so I can escape the condemnation of the teacher, I spot movement in the taxi up ahead of us. If I'm not very much mistaken, Sam is leaning forward to pay the driver.

"Looks like I might have to bail on you, Nige," I say. "My quarry is on the move."

I'm in such a hurry to pay, that I fumble moving my phone across to the card reader. For a second, I think I'll be able to hold onto it, but the inevitable happens, and seemingly in slow motion, I watch it slip out of my fingers and fall face downwards onto the solid floor of the taxi.

"No, no, no," I wail, "please don't let this be happening to me."

I dive to the floor and tenderly pick up my mobile, turning it over to survey the damage. The screen is shattered into a gazillion pieces but there is still light emitting from it. I gingerly run my finger over the surface, trying to open up my bank card app, but the touchscreen appears to have stopped responding. It flashes a few times, then goes completely blank. I press and hold the on/off switch, but to no avail. My phone appears to have given up the ghost. If today is going to be a marathon, then I think I've just hit the wall. I've no idea where to go from here. I'm now stranded in central London with no way of navigating, no way of communicating, and worst of all, no way of paying for anything. The taxi meter has risen to a small fortune, and I have no idea what to do. I jab the phone one final time, in case a miracle occurs and it is resurrected, but the screen remains stubbornly blank.

"Oh Nige, I'm so sorry, I promise you it was a complete accident," I say, desperately trying to think of a solution. He's been such a star helping me to chase my quarry, and I don't want his initial misgivings to prove correct. I have nothing to offer him except an IOU, and if he won't accept that, then I'll either have to throw myself on Sam's mercy again – fat chance of that coming to anything – or probably be dropped off ignominiously at the nearest police station, and accept whatever punishment is inflicted on passengers who don't deliver on their fares. Why do I keep on letting people down?

I hover anxiously in the cab, waiting to hear my fate.

Nige frowns, fixing me with a stern look. He would be perfectly within his rights to have me arrested as I have effectively stolen this journey from him. And after all of his kindness to me, too. I really am a terrible person. My heart is starting to beat faster and hot guilt is flooding through my veins. I seem destined to be on the wrong side of the law today.

Then all of a sudden, Nige grins broadly.

"Nearly got you there, darlin'. Don't you worry about it. You win the award for the most interesting passenger I've had in my cab for weeks. Take my details, and you can pay me later. I reckon I can trust you. You go get that young man of yours and let me know how you get on."

I accept the business card he gives me with profuse thanks and tuck it away carefully in my pocket. I also make a point of memorising his number plate and cab licence number, just in case. Knowing my luck today I'll lose the card, and I'd hate not to be able to pay my debts. I'm hugely grateful for his generosity. It's nice to be reminded that there are some genuinely decent people in the world.

Chapter Twenty-Four

4.57 p.m.

Nige hoots the horn cheerily as I tumble out of the cab, and set off in pursuit of Sam once again. Fortunately, there is such a cacophony of noise from impatient drivers stuck in the traffic that it doesn't cause Sam to turn around.

He's walking purposefully, his phone glued to his ear. I only hope that whoever is at the other end of the line will distract him sufficiently from my presence. I need to think of a strategy, a way to make amends for my thoughtlessness and to persuade him to go easy on me. But the only thing I can think to do is to apologise again and throw myself on his mercy, and it didn't exactly work too well last time.

I'm now about ten feet behind Sam and trying desperately to appear inconspicuous. In spy dramas, they always have a team of at least three trailing their quarry, plus they normally have a range of hats, scarves and other such clothing items to help disguise their profile and superficially change their appearance. I have no gang of friends at my beck and call, and I couldn't stand out more if I tried. There's no cover around here, well, nothing other than lamp-posts, and I'm not skinny enough to hide behind them, especially not in my voluminous onesie.

Sam finishes his call and I hold my breath, half-fearing, half-hoping he'll turn around and spot me. But he taps out a quick message and then tucks his phone away in his pocket and abruptly changes direction.

I dive behind a portly passer-by and engage in a weird game of Grandmother's Footsteps, copying my unwitting protector's gait and freezing every time it looks like he'll turn around and catch me in his wake. Ahead of me, I see Sam approaching a pedestrian crossing leading over Westminster Bridge to the perimeter of the Houses of Parliament. There's a heavy police presence in the area which doesn't do anything for my nerves. Even if they're not looking out for me after the trouble at the protest, in these days of heightened alert for terrorism, any kind of odd behaviour is liable to attract the attention of the authorities, and I really don't fancy my chances against a police officer with a gun.

A gaggle of tourists coo with excitement as a senior cabinet member whizzes past on her bicycle. For a brief second, I'm envious of how calm and collected she appears to be, then I firmly remind myself to stop assuming everyone else in the world is on top of their game while I'm the only one struggling. For all I know, she could be worrying about her political position and agonising over her next speech, and feeling envious of the hippy freedom of the girl standing on the pavement dressed in a unicorn onesie.

The distinctive clang of Big Ben starts striking out the time. It's five o'clock, close of play for workers in Dolly Parton's song. Thankfully I've got another few hours until Zara is likely to leave the hallowed corridors of Richmond Woods. At this time of day, she'll probably have at least another two client meetings to go. Fingers crossed they keep her too busy to check up on me. But I can't afford to get complacent. There's a lot I need to sort out in order to make sure I'm home and innocently tucked up in bed before she returns.

I dodge between a group of students staring up at the seat of power, and clock Sam's likely route. He's heading towards the road and the countdown on the crossing lights is indicating that there are only two seconds left until the traffic will be allowed through again. I silently will Sam to hold back and wait for the next green man to appear, but naturally he puts on a burst of speed and makes it over the crossing as the traffic lights switch away from red. I run forwards, but by the time I get to the road, there's a sea of cars, bicycles and lorries pouring through and there's not a single gap for me to make it across.

Despairing, I look across the road and that's when I realise I've been made. Sam is standing on the opposite pavement, a smug smile on his face. When he sees me looking at him, he salutes and sends a farewell wave in my direction, before turning around smartly and disappearing into the crowd.

The cheeky so-and-so. He knew I was following him all

the time and deliberately engineered this situation to throw me off his trail. I bet he's enjoying watching me suffer. I can't let him get away. I repeatedly jab the button on the pedestrian crossing in the hope it triggers it early. Of course, it doesn't work. I hop anxiously on the spot, trying to keep an eye on Sam's vanishing form, while also attempting to spot a gap in the traffic. The vehicles keep thundering through, and it seems impossible that I'll be going anywhere for quite some time, but suddenly there's a log jam in the first lane and I seize my opportunity. I take a deep breath and impulsively dart out into the road, throwing myself into the tiniest gap between vehicles and praying to make it to the other side in one piece. I reach the second lane of traffic, but the vehicles are still flowing through there. I take a step forwards and then huddle back as brakes screech and drivers curse. A cyclist swishes past so close to me I can smell their aftershave. Spotting another gap, I scoot around a van and then flinch as I misjudge the distance and nearly collide with a wing mirror. I'm three-quarters of the way across when my adrenalin-induced confidence/stupidity fails me, and I almost freeze to the spot. The noise of the traffic increases to deafening volume and the exhaust fumes nearly choke me with their thick, chemical taste. What the hell am I doing? What kind of a fool am I to be risking my life like this? And for what? Whatever challenges are ahead of me, it's much better to be alive to face them, rather than coming to an ignominious end squished by a politician's chauffeur-driven limo in Westminster.

I can feel the terrifying spectre of another panic attack

start tightening its hold on me, and my limbs are turning wobbly and clumsy with fear. Normally I'm careful and considered in everything I do, almost to the point of being overly cautious, but today I've been impulsive and reckless. Perhaps in the future I should find a middle ground. If I actually survive getting across this road, of course.

Then, suddenly, I feel strong hands gripping my arms and I'm pulled into motion once more. In the dim distance I can hear the beeping of the crossing, and other pedestrians start piling over the road. Despite the crowds surrounding me, there's a wonderful feeling of lightness and space now the vehicles aren't bearing down on me. And then, at last, I'm stepping onto the pavement at the other side. I take a deep shuddering breath and clench my fists at my side as I fight to get control back over myself.

"You've done some stupid things today, Alexa, but that has to be hands down the most foolish of the lot," says Sam. "I can't believe you were so silly to risk the crossing without waiting for the signal."

But it's fear I hear in his voice rather than anger, and I'm so grateful to him for being my knight in shining armour that I fling my arms around him and hold tight. He stands rigid for moment, then he manages to prise his own arms free from my embrace and pats me awkwardly on the back.

"I'm so sorry," I choke. I'm not just apologising for my idiotic lack of road sense, but for the whole appalling mess of today.

Sam's hand falters against me and then settles on the small of my back. I can feel the warmth emanating from his palm, and I feel safe, yet strangely off-kilter at his closeness.

I focus on his eyes, trying to read in his gaze whether I've been forgiven. There's a slight smudge on the right lens of his glasses and I can detect the faint whiff of peppermint from a recently consumed sweet.

Sam clears his throat, and gently removes himself from my grasp. I can still feel his hand burning an imprint on my back.

"Fine, apology accepted," he says gruffly, stepping another couple of feet away from me, "but only if you promise me never to throw a stunt like that again." He pauses, and then adds quietly, "I think I saw my life flashing before my eyes when you froze on the spot like that." For a moment, I think he's going to take hold of my hand again, then he appears to snap back into normal Sam-mode. "Did you see the size of the lorry that was approaching you at great speed?"

I force a laugh, as it seems necessary to lighten the mood.

"Thankfully no, but I could feel its presence. I thought I had enough time to get across, but like so many things today, I misjudged it."

Sam purses his lips and I can imagine the choice words running through his brain. But before he can lay into me again, his phone rings.

"Sam speaking," he answers gruffly. "Hold on, I can't hear you properly over the noise of the traffic. Give me five minutes and I'll call you back from College Green. I might be able to hear myself think there."

He strides off and I'm instantly forgotten. This time, I don't make the same mistake misjudging the traffic, but I have the advantage in that I at least know where he's heading. I catch him up on the patch of grass, recognisable as the backdrop of most live broadcasts from outside Parliament. I spot a news anchor being miked up by his camera operator, while another journalist appears to be performing both roles by herself. I weave my way between them, checking carefully to make sure I don't inadvertently get myself in the back of a shot. Reception at work is known to have a rolling news channel playing in the background and it would be just my luck for a senior partner to be strolling through and spot me on the screen.

Sam is pacing up and down, a familiar look of irritation on his face. I hope that this isn't something else I'm responsible for.

"Today? But why?" he asks the unknown person at the other end of the phone. "That can't be legal. And where do they expect the residents to sleep tonight if not there? Back out on the street? It's preposterous."

The other person continues their speech, and Sam's brow grows furrowed with concern.

"No, that's not on. Look, I'm coming over now. Can you hold them off until I arrive?" Another pause while he listens. "The desk will have to wait for their pictures. And I'm sure someone from the political team is perfectly capable of coming out here to do their own doorstep. This is far more important."

Chapter Twenty-Five

5.05 p.m.

S am fumbles as he puts his phone away in his pocket and looks around. He has the glazed expression of a man who is not really taking in his surroundings.

"Is everything OK?" I ask, tentatively reaching out and touching his forearm in a gesture of support. I'd have to be an idiot not to realise he's just been on the receiving end of some bad news.

Sam shakes his head as if to clear it.

"What's that?" he says, confirming my suspicions that his thoughts are miles away.

"Are you OK, Sam? Is there anything I can help you with?" I repeat.

"What? Oh, no, not really. Look Alexa, without wishing to be rude, I don't have time for this right now."

He scrabbles in his rucksack, pulls out a business card, and scribbles a few notes on the back of it.

"Look, this is where you can find my house keys on my desk. If you ask at reception, they'll send someone from security to go and get them for you. I'll message Brenda to make sure it happens. I'm giving you this on the understanding that there'll be no repeat of the earlier tales about surprise pregnancies, OK?"

He doesn't even wait for my answer, but hurries to the roadside and starts waving at taxis. I stare at the business card in my hands. This is my opportunity to get back home before Zara's return and avoid one very big problem. But it doesn't solve the issue of the incriminating photographs, and my conscience reminds me that I still haven't made amends with Sam for my thoughtless behaviour. I don't want him to think that I'm the type of person to walk away from problems I have created. Besides, there was something in his tone of voice on the phone just now that got me worried on his behalf. I can't abandon him to deal with whatever drama it is that's occurred. He sounded genuinely distressed and it was the first time today where I've seen him look properly flustered and unsure of himself.

Sam is now leaning out across the carriageway waving frantically at cabs. It's only a matter of time before he succeeds in persuading one of them to stop and disappears off into the distance, so I take a gamble and hurry to his side.

"Can I help with whatever the problem is? I wasn't deliberately eavesdropping, but you said something was happening that wasn't legal," I shout, trying to make myself heard over the noise of the traffic.

Sam tuts in frustration as another taxi driver ignores his

desperate summons and stops for a different passenger instead.

"Look Alexa, can you go away? You're putting off the taxis. None of them are going to pull up while you're hanging around me."

"Charming," I retort. "But like a bad smell, you're not going to get rid of me that easily. If something dodgy is happening that you think isn't legal, please let me see if I can help." I hurry on with my offer before Sam can laugh it off completely. "Despite current appearances, I am a fairly decent lawyer, you know, and I do occasionally perform good deeds. At least fill me in on what's going on, and I'll do my best to assist, if it's possible."

He shrugs his shoulders, only half listening to my offer of support. Just when I'm about to repeat myself, a taxi pulls up in front of us.

"Please Sam, give me a chance to make amends," I say as he clambers into the cab.

He hesitates, doing battle between his instinct to tell me to get packing, and his need to solve whatever problem he's just been presented with.

I embrace my newly-found assertiveness and start clambering into the cab without waiting for him to give the go-ahead.

"Fine, come on then, seeing as I'm clearly not going to get a choice in this," he says in a tone of resignation, although the optimistic part of me tries to read a look of relief on his face.

He undoes his seatbelt, and shuffles across, so I have space to sit down.

"Don't make me regret this," he adds, in a characteristically Sam tone of grumpiness. He gives the driver an address in Lincoln's Inn Fields, and then gets his phone out once again, engrossing himself in the screen, his fingers tapping away frantically.

I try to read over his shoulder, but he hunches his body away from me, protecting most of the screen from view. I decide not to take it too personally.

I gaze out of the window. In this rush-hour traffic, we're not going anywhere quickly. We'd probably have been better off hiring bicycles, although I'm in no hurry to repeat my ride across town from earlier today.

"So how can I help?" I ask. "Why don't you fill me in on what's happening before we get to whatever awaits us in Lincoln's Inn Fields?"

Sam continues concentrating on his phone.

"Look, it was a mistake to let you in the cab. I'm really not sure I should be trusting you with this," he says eventually.

I wait. I'm not going to beg him to let me help. It needs to be his own decision, otherwise I'm once again riding roughshod over him, and I've learnt my lesson about that. Somehow my continued silence reassures him.

He stares at me, as if memorising my features in case he needs to describe them to an E-fit artist in the event of me dropping him in it and going on the run. I resist the urge to squirm under his scrutiny and calmly stare back.

"Fine, I'll tell you. Desperate times call for desperate measures, I guess," he says with a sigh, the need to go against his own instincts for the greater good finally winning out. "Though it's probably a waste of time. If you spend most of your time handling big corporate clients, assisting a tiny charity in a crisis isn't going to be your area of expertise at all."

I shrug nonchalantly, even though his comment plays on every insecurity I have. I take a deep breath and remind myself that I am a good lawyer, with the ability to rise to any challenge that I face, if I only trust my own skills. If I don't believe in myself, how will anyone else?

"Well, we won't know until you try me," I reply in the most confident tone I can muster. "The corporate world may be my current official workload, but I've done my fair share of work for charities on a voluntary basis, and I do my best to keep refreshing my knowledge of areas of law other than the ones I practise on a daily basis. I'm probably not as clueless as you think I am, despite appearances."

Sam frowns. "No, you're definitely a lot shrewder than the fluffy unicorn outfit gives you credit for. Behind the silver horn, there's a ruthless streak going on there."

I purse my lips. I'm not particularly flattered at being referred to as "ruthless". But then again, I suppose I've not given him the opportunity to see much of a better side of me.

Sam holds his phone up so I can see a website on its screen. It's so different from the glossy, all-singing, all-dancing websites possessed by my corporate clients. This one is simple, with all the focus on the one word, "Help".

Sam clicks on the link and it slowly loads, showing a picture of a group of men gathered around a dining table. The smiles on their faces immediately leap out at me. It's not a posed picture, but instead is one which has managed to capture a spontaneous moment of pure joy and happiness. It's only after I look away from their grins to the worn lines of their faces, the hollowness of their cheeks, and the shabby mishmash of clothing they're wearing that I begin to understand that these are men whose futures are probably very precarious.

Sam nods as he sees the realisation dawning on my face.

"Yes, they're all homeless. I took the photo at their Christmas dinner. For many of them, it was the first time in ages they'd been able to relax and have fun in the moment without worrying about where their next meal was coming from."

"It's a good picture," I say, then hope he doesn't interpret my comment as patronising. He's a professional photographer. Of course his pictures will be good. However, he seems pleased by my praise.

"Thanks," he says. "I do what I can. So, this place is the Phoenix Homeless Shelter. It's a drop-in centre for people who find themselves on the streets with nowhere to go. The staff and volunteers provide advice, support, hot meals, and basically a helping hand when people find themselves at their darkest moments. It's called 'Phoenix' because the charity wants to give people the hope of a fresh start, of having the chance to change their future and move on from their current circumstances. Yes, the service-users are getting their short-term needs met – somewhere to have a shower, get warm, have a bite to eat – but they can also speak to supportive people about developing a long-term plan. They get help to wade through the bureaucracy that so many of them face. How can you apply for a job if you don't have a fixed address? How can you even open a bank account? These things are so basic, stuff which the rest of us all take for granted, but they can seem like an insurmountable hurdle if you're on the streets."

I nod. I may have been existing in a work-shaped tunnel for the last few years, but I haven't failed to notice how many more people are curled up in shop doorways, or asking for change outside the entrance to the Tube.

"It sounds like a really valuable service."

"A valuable service it most definitely is, and one which should be protected at all costs. The location is particularly important because it's so central, and near where a lot of the homeless lads and lasses spend their days selling magazines or begging for spare change. But that might also prove to be our downfall. Because it's such a desirable location, the landlord is trying to evict the charity from the building. If you ask me, he's got plans for the place to be converted into high-revenue office space. He took over day-to-day management of the lettings business when his dad retired. His father was always very supportive of our work, but the son definitely has his eyes on the pound signs. It's been rumbling on for a while, and today, things are coming to a head."

"Sounds like a proper David versus Goliath situation," I say, starting to dust off what I can remember about how to challenge evictions from the back of my brain.

"That's one way of putting it," says Sam. "Please try to remember that in this situation you're meant to be on the David side rather than your usual Goliath."

"Trust me, I never feel very Goliath-like," I say, although it does start me wondering. Richmond Woods represents lots of clients who have vast property portfolios. What happens if I arrive at the shelter and realise that it's one of my employer's clients who is behind this whole situation?

I quickly decide not to mention my fears to Sam. With any luck, they'll be completely unfounded, and I don't want to make him trust me any less than he already does. If I had my work phone with me, I could do a quick check through the shared files drive, just to put my mind at rest. And if I hadn't smashed my own phone, I could do a bit of my own research to reassure myself. But as I've told myself a thousand times today, there's no point in fixating on the "what ifs". If my position is compromised, I'll deal with it as and when. A vision of the solicitor who helped save my grandma from eviction swims in front of my eyes. This kind of situation is one of the reasons why I joined the legal profession in the first place. There's no doubt in my mind that if it comes to having to make a choice, my loyalties will lie with helping Sam's charity mates.

"So, how did you first get involved with the charity? If you don't mind me asking, that is. It obviously means a lot to you."

His enthusiasm for it is definitely showing a different side to him. Given his aversion to the climate change protest I'd been involved in, I'd originally had him down as a self-involved grump who was oblivious to the idea of the greater good. But as I've got to know him better over the course of the day, he's shown unexpected streaks of kindness, and somehow it doesn't seem so out of character that he spends his spare time volunteering at a homeless shelter.

Sam glances out of the window and does a mini fist pump as the traffic finally starts moving.

"I was beginning to fear we were going to be stuck here forever. How did I get involved with the charity? When I first moved to London, I didn't really know anyone. Sure, I made friends within the newsroom, but I soon got sick of my entire social life consisting of going to the pub and talking nothing but shop. Then I got sent out to take some pictures of Phoenix as part of a story on homelessness in general, and I got chatting with the volunteers. You may have noticed, but I always try and talk to people when I'm taking their photos. I always get a much better result as it puts them at their ease, and I'm bound to get more out of them. Unless it's a developing news situation, of course, and then I just snap away to get that powerful moment of a unicorn charging through a police line." He winks at me and I fight the urge to stick my tongue out at the gentle teasing. I'm surprised to realise I'm almost at the stage of being able to laugh about it with him, although I'd still be greatly relieved if he got rid of the pictures. "Anyway, their enthusiasm was completely infectious, and by the time I was meant to be heading back to the newsroom to file, I instead found myself hanging around and asking if they needed a willing pair of hands every so often to dish up meals, or to help with forms. They're always short of volunteers, so they were pleased to get me involved. I started out doing the washing-up for them, and it's gone from there."

He scrolls through his phone and shows me some more snaps of the team doing their thing, and points out a couple of guys who are at the heart of the action in every picture.

"In the time I've been volunteering, some of the lads have gone from service-users to volunteers in their own right. Take Nelson and Harry, for example – they used to sleep rough under Waterloo Bridge, and now they run the kitchen at Phoenix and are talking about setting up their own catering business. The centre is an extraordinary place. If it loses its home, I can't see how the charity will survive."

Chapter Twenty-Six

5.32 p.m.

S am's words are ringing in my ears as the cab finally turns into Lincoln's Inn Fields. After the busy traffic of Holborn, the peace of the square with its stately buildings set around the central plot of parkland is welcome. There's an exercise class happening by one of the gates, an enthusiastic instructor bellowing at participants to lift their knees higher as they leap up and down in a pounding rhythm which makes me tired just to watch. In another corner of the park, a small girl is chewing her lip in concentration as she wobbly pedals her bike, her dad hovering anxiously a couple of metres behind her in case she tumbles to the ground. Elsewhere, a couple are sitting on their coats on the grass, sharing a coffee and catching up on how each other's day has gone. It's like arriving in a small village in the middle of the city.

Examining the surroundings with my corporate head on, I can see why the landlord wants to make more of this location. It's exactly the kind of place clients at Richmond Woods would be interested in snapping up. Phoenix Homeless Shelter is based in a stately old Victorian building. It's at least four floors of prime real estate, a little run-down and tired looking, but the big elegant windows soon distract from that. The giant front door is dramatic and imposing and I can imagine it being adorned with a brass plaque engraved with the name of some elite hedge fund. But whereas hedge fund managers have the money to pick and choose exactly where they base their headquarters, and wouldn't care if they didn't get to occupy this building, the charity does not have that luxury. Without their central London base, would they even be able to continue helping their clients?

"I'll admit it looks shabby on the outside," says Sam, gesturing at the peeling paint and scuffed stonework as if he feels the need to apologise for them, "but that's only because the charity prioritises spending their funds on the service-users."

I hurry to reassure him.

"As is only right. Surface appearances don't always tell you everything about a building... or a person, come to think of it. The work that's done within those doors means that this is an amazing place," I reply. "And I suspect the air of tired grandeur isn't entirely down to the charity. The landlord holds a great deal of responsibility when it comes to the maintenance and upkeep of his own building. Have you thought he might be deliberately running it down as another tactic to force you guys out?"

Sam sighs. "Trust me, that thought has definitely crossed our minds. Yet the man has the cheek to say that our service-users are bringing down the area." He glances across at me, as if deciding how much information he can trust me with. "Someone has been making anonymous phone calls to the police, falsely claiming there's trouble in the building, and every time they respond, they blame us for the fake callout. They're threatening to stop attending calls to the place now, which would cause us huge problems from a health and safety point of view."

"Sounds like a pleasant guy. I can't wait to meet him," I say, once again praying that I'm not about to encounter one of my firm's clients. It sounds like just the kind of underhand tactics that Zara would encourage.

"I doubt he'll be sullying his hands by making a personal appearance." Sam narrows his eyes. "Although it looks like he has sent around representatives to make their presence felt."

The driver finally finds a place to pull over between the bicycle racks and the expensive vehicles which seem to be using the square as their own personal car park. Sam leans forward and hands him a couple of notes. "Keep the change, thanks, mate," he says, his attention already on the crowd gathering outside the front door of the building. He leaps out of the cab and hurries across to join them, without a backward glance to see if I'm coming too.

I clamber out of the cab, and hang back near the park

fence for a couple of minutes to take in the scene in front of me. I don't want to rush in and make things worse. There's definitely a tension in the air and I can see people from the neighbouring buildings lurking by the windows, like an audience awaiting a title fight.

I scan the faces of the crowd and recognise a few people from the photograph on the website. But today the men look far from cheery. One has an expression of thunder, while another is railing loudly about the situation as the tears drip unchecked down his face, his angry words undermined by the grief he is showing. Another guy is pacing up and down, too on edge to stand still. His dog loyally tracks his progress, twitching his tail whenever his master glances his way. They all appear utterly dejected and it's not surprising. If they're using the services of a homeless shelter, then they're going through some pretty tough times already. I can't imagine how devastating it must be to have the one beacon of hope in your life unceremoniously snatched away from you. It steels my determination to do whatever I can to help these men. This is about more than just making amends to Sam.

I turn my attention to the staff and volunteers who are hovering in the background. They're whispering among themselves, looking as shell-shocked as the service-users. No one turns up to work and expects to find themselves evicted from the building. They keep glancing nervously across at two blokes who are standing to the left of the front door. I instantly clock them as the enforcers, sent to deliver the landlord's message to his tenants. They look like they've walked straight from their other jobs as bouncers on the door of a dodgy pub. They're giants, built like proverbial brick houses, and they seem to be taking an unhealthy delight in the distress they're inflicting on the people around them. Every time someone looks their way, they scowl back and flex their muscles in a threatening manner.

At the moment, nobody is daring to go near them, but there's a tension bubbling in the air, and I have a horrible feeling that these two chancers are spoiling to throw their weight around and bang some heads together, quite possibly literally. One of them is ostentatiously fiddling with a key. I follow his gaze and see the shiny, new padlock which has been fastened onto the front door of the building. I'm prepared to bet good money that that hasn't been voluntarily installed by the charity.

I decide to go have a closer look at the lock. As soon as the bouncer blokes spot me, they nudge each other and start smirking like immature teenagers trapped in the bodies of grown men on steroids. I'm beginning to get used to having that effect on people. I send a sweet smile in their direction, their attitude steeling my determination to do what I can. It doesn't bother me if they underestimate me because I'm dressed in a ridiculous onesie. With any luck, they'll soon be laughing on the other side of their faces. One of them responds with an obscene gesture, which is noticed by the homeless guys, who start muttering angrily about it being no way to treat a lady.

"Do you want me to have a word with that tosser, love?" asks one of them.

"Thank you but don't worry about it. There's no need to lower ourselves to his level," I reply, touched by his gesture of kindness. I hold my hand out to shake his. "I'm Alexa by the way. I'm a lawyer, and I'm hoping to see if I can get you all back into your building."

My new friend pumps my hand enthusiastically. "Helpers come in many forms. Great to meet you, Alexa. And you're a mate of Sam, right? I'm Frank and this is my best friend Hercules." He whistles, and his dog scurries across from the bush he's been examining. "This place means so much to both of us. The best thing about Phoenix is that they don't make me leave Hercules outside like most of the other shelters do. He may be a big, hairy mutt, but he's a right old softie at heart, and he pines if he's separated from his dad."

Hercules sniffs my slippers with interest and then plonks himself down at my feet, leaning against my leg in a gesture of quiet trust.

I reach down to scratch his head and he grunts in appreciation. "What a gorgeous boy you are, Hercules. Frank, you're a lucky man."

He beams in pleasure. "Best thing that ever happened to me, being chosen by Hercules to be his dad. He was from a litter of street puppies, load of scrappy little things. They were all busy messing around, play-fighting, you know the score, but when I showed up, Hercules broke away from his brothers and sisters, and came across to introduce himself immediately. He's been keeping me on the straight and narrow ever since, him and the guys at the drop-in centre. Between them, they've pretty much saved my life, given me something to live for at any rate. One of the volunteers was going to help me update my CV today. But that ain't going to happen. Don't know why I'm bothering still hanging around here. It's clearly all over. Who cares about blokes like me when there's profit to be made?"

His eyes are growing moist and he's clenching his fists in frustration. Hercules whimpers, sensing Frank's distress. The dog gives me a quick look of apology, then pads over to his owner and wags his tail, gazing up at Frank with adoration in his eyes.

"Don't worry matey, I'll be alright." Frank tries to reassure him, but Hercules doesn't look convinced.

I wish there was something I could say that would make things better. I've promised him that I'm going to do my best to sort out the situation, but have I raised his hopes unfairly?

I can hear Sam calling me over to join him, but I don't want to leave Frank by himself. I dither in place, but Frank gestures at me to go.

"It's alright, love, you head off to Sam. We can talk all day, but we need someone to take action. If you guys have got something planned, that's the important thing."

"Thanks for putting your faith in us, Frank."

I squeeze his hand and give Hercules one final pat before I head over to join Sam, who is deep in conversation with the other volunteers and staff.

They're so in shock at the situation they're facing that they don't even flinch when he introduces me as a legal expert he's enlisted to help the cause. I try to look as responsible as I can, given my current state of attire.

"Alexa works for one of the top firms in the city. If anyone can help us, she can," Sam says.

I know he's only putting on a show of confidence to reassure his fellow volunteers, but I can't help feeling a warm glow of appreciation at the praise. It increases to something more when Sam smiles at me. It's the first time I've been on the receiving end of his smile on full beam and its effect is surprisingly startling.

"Alexa, what's your plan?"

I give my rebellious body a mental shake for getting distracted by a mere smile, and remind myself what is at stake here. I take a deep breath and rack my brains for a course of action, trying to ignore the little niggling voice which keeps telling me that I'm way out of my depth. This is not the time to fold under pressure, I sternly tell myself. Frank, Hercules and their friends need Sam and I to come up with a decent plan. I've got the skills and the drive, I just need to believe in myself.

"First things first, who are those chancers over there?" I ask.

The centre manager, hastily introduced to me as Fiona, looks across at them and shudders.

"A pair of bully boys, that's who they are," she says, brushing her hands together as if she wishes she could sweep the disreputable pair away in a similarly perfunctory manner. "And their language is appalling. Working at a shelter I hear some pretty fruity stuff, and that's just from the volunteers," she attempts a half-hearted grin, "but trust me when I say that every word that comes from the mouths of those two is nasty."

"They certainly look like extras in a gangster movie," I say, hoping to lighten the situation, but then I worry that

I'm making everyone even more scared of them, and so quickly hurry on. "But just because they've got brawn, it doesn't mean they've got brains. They're probably used to relying on strength and intimidation to get their own way. Trust me, we've got better weapons at our disposal. I presume they're the ones who've locked you out?"

Fiona nods. "I was in a heated discussion with one of them, and the other one set the fire alarm off so we all had to leave the building, and of course, that's when they slapped the lock on the door. It all happened so quickly."

I expected them to have used underhand tactics, but sounding the fire alarm? That was way out of order. That kind of unreasonable action could help our case in the long term, but we need to find something now which will resolve the immediate crisis of the charity being locked out.

"And did they serve proper notice to you and a reason for ending the tenancy? Where's the paperwork trail?"

In law, so much relies on a good paperwork trail. It's one of the things that was drummed into me when I first joined Richmond Woods. They're sticklers for it, even down to having systems for how you should name documents when you save them on the computer. It seemed ridiculous to all us trainees when we were first introduced to it, but two years down the line, I don't think there's any of us whose bacon hasn't been saved on at least one occasion by the logic of the system.

I'm hoping that the type of landlord who hires thugs to enforce his wishes probably isn't such a one for paperwork. This is the kind of case where attention to detail could make all the difference. If the landlord has failed to give the charity proper notice and hasn't dotted every "i" and crossed every "t", then it would give us the grounds to stop him in his tracks. But going through things with a fine-tooth comb will take me some time, and time clearly isn't what we've got right now. Then Fiona delivers another blow.

"The paperwork is all in the office inside and of course..." Her words tail off.

"And of course, you're locked out," I finish her sentence. "I don't suppose there's an electronic copy of it all?"

Fiona shakes her head. "That's on the iPad..."

"Let me guess, the iPad is also in the office."

"Bloody hell," says Sam. "What are we meant to do now?" He looks crushed by the revelation.

"Don't worry, there is more than one way to solve this problem," I say with as much confidence as I can muster. I can feel the gazes of Frank and the other service-users on my back, and I'm desperate not to become yet another person to let them down. Sam sighs, the expression on his face telling me he fears the battle has already been lost.

Muttering a quick apology to Fiona, I grab Sam's arm and drag him around the corner out of earshot of everyone. Then I fix him with a stern stare.

"Sorry Sam, but this is time to take a pep talk from me, so pay attention." He starts to interrupt but I hold my hand up to stop him. "If there's one thing I've learnt as a lawyer, it's the importance of remaining calm, whatever the situation. Yes, I know this sounds hugely hypocritical of me, given my tendency towards panic attacks and my complete lack of ability to act in a calm, rational manner today. But believe it or not, most of the time, I'm pretty good at remaining like a serene swan on the surface, while all the time I'm paddling frantically underneath. My clients will never trust me if they can see me flapping around when I receive their instructions. Likewise, these people here need to see that we're relaxed and in control of the situation. They're panicking right now, and that's not going to help anyone. So, we're going to take some deep breaths, and together we'll come up with a solution, I promise. They're all relying on us to take control and make this situation better. We can do it, we just need to approach things logically and calmly."

Now I need to live up to my word.

Sam looks like he's going to argue back, but then his shoulders slump and he nods, acknowledging that for once in our brief acquaintance, I'm speaking some sense.

"Sorry. I've covered far too many stories like this one, and I know how they normally turn out. The odds are stacked massively against us. Sir Clive promised a donation to Phoenix for doing the photo shoot at the school earlier. How can he donate to a charity which doesn't have a home any more?"

I squeeze his arm.

"Sir Clive's donation will be used by them, because we'll do everything in our power to retain this building for Phoenix. The bigger the challenge, the better the feeling when we've overcome it. Let's take things one step at a time and see what happens then." It's clear that Sam remains unconvinced. To be fair to him, it's not like I've given him many opportunities today to feel like he can trust me with something so important. Time to prove him wrong. "First things first. Is there a café nearby? I'm not asking for me, but for those guys – the volunteers, staff and service-users. Maybe a round of teas and coffees would warm people up and help dial back the tension around here?"

"How very British," replies Sam, but before I can blink, he's hurried across to hand his wallet over to one of the volunteers and persuaded her to take as many service-users as possible to collect takeaway hot drinks from the café in the centre of the square's gardens.

The guys are reluctant to leave, but we use our charm and drop a few quiet hints that this will help the situation in the long run, and finally they drift away, throwing a couple of curses in the direction of the heavies, who flex their muscles threateningly. But as the crowd diminishes, the tension in the atmosphere lightens slightly, and I'm less worried about the immediate threat of fisticuffs.

"And now perhaps you and I can put our heads together and come up with a plan?" I say to Sam. "I think I've got an idea which could help us to buy some time."

"I thought the key to resolving this issue was you checking their paperwork – which we're all hoping is dodgy – but we've already established that we have no access to that."

I jab my finger in the air. "That is but a tiny, insignificant detail. We have the right to demand they provide us with fresh copies of documentation, and that will also buy us some more time. And in the meantime, I think it's time you used your talents to help us get back into the building."

"What can I do? Despite your low opinion of tabloid

journalists, I've never descended to the level of breaking and entering. I'm afraid picking locks is not in my skillset."

I roll my eyes. "If it was, that would have been much handier to help me get back home. You said two key words there – tabloid journalist. These guys might not be scared of a fight, but perhaps bad publicity might have an impact on them."

The realisation dawns on Sam's face. "Damn, I don't know why I didn't think of that before."

"Sometimes it helps to have a person examine a situation with fresh eyes. How about you start making a few phone calls in the vicinity of those two? Maybe get them a little worried that they're going to be negatively portrayed in the press, go viral online, you get the idea, and in the meantime, I'll see if Fiona can help me find an alternative way into the building so I can check out that paperwork."

An alternative way into the building? I sound like I'm a wannabe James Bond. I'm half-expecting Sam to laugh at me, but he just smiles that devastating smile again, and to my surprise, gives me a high five.

"Sounds like a plan. Let's see if I can come across as suitably threatening."

"Oh, I wouldn't worry about that. You've had me terrified all day with your threats to publish those photos of me at the climate change protest."

And that's when he does laugh. "I should think so, although for someone who was allegedly terrified, you've done a good job at giving as good as you got. I'll admit one thing, Alexa, there's never a dull moment when you're around."

He nudges my shoulder in what I can only interpret as an affectionate manner, and then heads off to put the plan into action, humming to himself as he goes.

Chapter Twenty-Seven

5.46 p.m.

I stand back and watch Sam in action for a moment. As he approaches the heavies, he whips his camera out and takes a few snaps, ostentatiously getting as many different angles as possible and urging them to pose for their picture. I've got to admire his confidence. The heavies look like they'd happily smash the camera over his head. My stomach turns over at the thought of him getting hurt. Or anyone else for that matter. Now that most of the service-users have gone to get their hot drinks, there's no one around who looks tough enough to defeat the two bruisers. I hope Sam doesn't push things too far, because I'm pretty sure it will end painfully.

Sam, however, seems unmoved by their bristling, and I swear he sends an amused wink in my direction. He's such a show-off, but I can't help admiring his bravery. There's a definite swagger in his movements as he slings the camera over his shoulder and then uses his tabloid silver tongue to try to trick the heavies into giving up their names.

"Is Sam going to be OK?" asks Fiona, looking worried that one of her key volunteers might be about to be crushed between two thuggish giants. Sam darts backwards out of their reach and begins his trick of transcribing their every word into his notebook, which I have no doubt will prove productively irritating.

I glance across to reassure myself, and once again he sends a sneaky grin of enjoyment in my direction.

"I think he's got it under control," I say, only half-believing my own words. "Let's hope he can keep them distracted long enough while we try to get into the building another way. Tell me, did you leave any windows open when you left?"

Fiona thinks carefully. "Only on the fourth floor, and no offence, but I don't think either of us are capable of clambering up there. Not unless your unicorn ensemble happens to have wings?"

"Alas no. Probably a good thing. I've had enough grief for the outfit as it is."

Fiona continues to ponder. "However, there is a fire escape with a dodgy catch which we might be able to use to our advantage. We've been badgering the landlord to fix it for weeks but he's not got around to it. Of course, if it had been stopping the escape window from opening properly, I'd have done it myself," she adds hastily. "You can't mess around with fire safety. But given that there's not much worth stealing in the building, I figured we'd wait for the proper authority to arrange a fix. It'll serve him right if his shoddy upkeep of the place helps us put a stop to his dastardly plans. Sorry, that makes him sound like a cartoon villain, but he kind of is, really."

"Cartoon villains always get defeated," I reply. "So, let's show him what happens to the baddies when the goodies get involved."

I fist pump the air, feeling elated at the task ahead. My determination is growing with every second, and along with it my confidence. It seems extraordinary that running around London dressed as a unicorn could have such a profound effect on me, but away from the constraints of my usual routine, I have finally had the chance to examine my life with a fresh perspective, and it's made me even more certain about what I want in my future. Slowly, my self-belief is catching up with that ambition. I know that where I am right now is exactly where I'm meant to be, in a position to help. Admittedly, I'd prefer it if this realisation had come via a slightly easier route, but I'm prepared to admit that my duvet day hasn't been a complete disaster.

Fiona leads me around to the side of the building, checking carefully that our departure isn't noticed by the heavies. She points out the fire escape on the second floor. I swallow. Was I just saying how confident I felt? I definitely spoke too soon. It looks like a long way up and the fact that it is accessible only by pulling down a precarious-looking retractable ladder increases my feelings of concern about how practical this plan is. To add to our problems, the ladder is designed to be activated from inside the building and is way out of our reach down here at ground-floor level. I'm going to have to channel Charlie's fearlessness to get through this challenge.

"OK, let's not panic. We just need to find something to help us lower the ladder," I say, having flashbacks to using Sam's parcel to try to prise open his bedroom window first thing this morning. I still haven't found out what was in it. I must ask him at some point. I maintain it's entirely responsible for me getting locked out.

We look around, but funnily enough there isn't a handy pole lying around.

"I wonder if there's a branch in the park?" I think aloud.

"I'll go and look," volunteers Fiona. "I'll probably blend more into the background as I'm not dressed as a rainbow, no offence. If all this works out OK, you must let me know where you got that onesie from. It's fancy dress at my daughter's primary school next week, and she'd love to wear something like that."

Thanks Fiona.

She slinks back towards the park, while I skulk in the shadows at the side of the building, making one last vain attempt to see if I can revive my phone. It would be so good to be able to remind myself of any obvious loopholes that would help Phoenix get out of this mess. I press and hold the home button and jab the on/off switch a few times. I even try sweet-talking the thing. At one point, I think I see a flash of something on the screen, but realise it was all in my imagination and finally accept that I am deluding myself. I remind myself that there is no point in getting carried away with concern. I need to focus on tackling one problem at a time. If I can pass the first major hurdle of actually getting into the building and finding the paperwork, then I can always use their internet connection to double-check anything I'm unsure of, providing the landlord hasn't arranged to have that cut off too.

Fiona quickly returns, triumphantly bearing what looks like half a tree aloft. It's certainly long enough to reach the ladder, although we're going to have to be very careful not to scratch ourselves on the twigs which are sticking out from the stem at all sorts of crazy angles.

"I hope there isn't some hole left in the ground from wherever you ripped it out," I joke. "If I was Macbeth, I'd be getting very jumpy now."

"Fear not, it was lying around in the park. Look, there are some tooth marks on the trunk, so I think it may have fallen foul of a dog. The root bundle is still attached, so we can try replanting it as soon as we're done, and no one will be any the wiser."

The situation is getting more surreal by the second. We take it in turns to wave the tree above our heads, little bits of soil showering down on our faces, until eventually I succeed in hooking the bottom rung of the ladder and carefully lowering it to the ground.

"Victory is mine," I say, delighted at my success. This day is definitely making me realise I'm more resourceful than I thought.

Fiona carefully places the tree down, ready for replanting, while I dither for a bit about whether to remove my slippers and brave the ladder barefoot. The soles are torn to shreds from all the action they've been seeing, and I'm not sure I trust their grip. But then again, the ladder looks distinctly rusty, and I don't want to add tetanus to my list of problems. I decide to stick with the status quo.

"Wish me luck."

My voice is a little squeakier than normal. I clear my throat nervously and roll my sleeves up in what I hope appears to be a nonchalant manner.

Fiona gives me a double thumbs up, then gets into position at the bottom of the ladder so she can hold it in place.

I hold my breath, and start heaving myself up. The ladder creaks ominously with every move. If the landlord has been so careless about the maintenance of the actual escape window, then who's to say he's bothered to keep this contraption in working condition? My head starts spinning, then I realise that I'm still holding my breath, and so I take in another gulp of air. I must not look down, I remind myself firmly.

I'm doing alright, making slow but steady progress, and gradually getting closer to my goal. But as I'm reaching up to grasp the penultimate rung, and starting to think I'm nearly safe, my right foot slips off and my slipper goes tumbling to the ground. I hold the sides of the ladder with an absolute death grip, my fingers turning white with the strain.

"Are you OK?" calls up Fiona softly.

I feel like I'm frozen in position. My head starts playing on repeat the image of me tumbling to the earth like the slipper and landing with a great big splat. I'm not exactly miles up, but I know I'm certainly high enough to do myself some serious damage if I fall. The escalators on the Tube are going to be a doddle after this.

"Alexa?" calls Fiona again. "Everything alright?"

I'm still hugging the ladder like my life depends on it.

"Yes, I'm fine," I lie, that squeaky voice making another unwelcome appearance. "Just pausing for breath."

I really need to get a move on. I experimentally loosen my grip with my left hand and move my fingers to allow the circulation to start flowing again. When I don't instantly fall to the ground, my heart rate starts to settle back down to normal and my wobbliness begins to lessen. Then I'm brave enough to repeat the move with my right hand, and soon I'm able to start hauling myself up again.

I reach the escape window in one piece and take a few restorative breaths, resting my head against a rusty rung until I realise that it's going to add an additional dirty smear to my already grimy face. If I ever get back home in one piece, I'm going to wallow in the bath until I turn into a mermaid. But there's no time for daydreaming. I need to face my next challenge. I start pondering how I'm going to get the very heavy-looking sash open. From where I'm hanging, the barrier looks pretty impenetrable.

"There's a knack to it," calls up Fiona, as if breaking into a window on the second floor of a building is the easiest thing in the world. "Try putting some pressure against the bottom right corner of the window. No, not your right, my right."

I'd be a rubbish burglar. Fiona's confusing instructions are making things worse, so I tune them out and instead apply pressure to the whole frame. I'm now leaning precariously away from the ladder, relying on the fact that my left leg is wrapped around a rung to hold me in place. I am so relieved when finally I feel the frame shift and the window slides smoothly open. I hook my right leg over the sill. For a couple of seconds, I am suspended in splits formation in mid-air. Then at last I manage to heave myself inside, tumbling to the floor in a very undignified way. I lie there for a few moments to get my breath back. This paperwork had better be in here, after all the efforts I've gone to in order to rescue it. I close my eyes and savour the stillness. Maybe I could hide out here for the rest of the day and enjoy the peace and quiet I so desperately need?

A pebble flies through the window and lands millimetres away from my face. It's followed by a slightly larger rock, causing me to roll hastily to one side. Either Fiona is trying to attract my attention, or the heavies have launched an attack from the ground. Reluctantly, I heave myself up and lean out of the window.

"Everything OK? No trouble from below?"

"All good," hisses Fiona, trying to project a whisper loud enough for me to hear without attracting the attention of the guys at the front. "Maybe we should get the ladder looked at when the window is fixed. One or two of those rungs looked like they were about to give way when you were treading on them."

Now she tells me. I swallow and the film of my broken body slamming onto the ground starts re-running in my imagination.

Fiona doesn't appear to notice the blood draining from my face.

"By the way, Alexa," she says cheerily, "if you check the cupboard directly opposite the room you're in, you'll find my trainers. Apologies if they're a bit icky. I used to wear them for my lunchtime gym sessions, but given that I've not managed one of those in quite a while, you'll probably be alright."

Now that is an excellent piece of news. I lean a bit further out of the window so she can see me giving her a thumbs up. I don't know what I'm more delighted by – getting back onto solid ground after the precarious ladder, or being offered a decent pair of footwear to wear. My feet are begging for some kind treatment. The podiatrist is going to do well out of me when this crazy day is over.

Shoes first, and then paperwork. I cautiously poke my head out into the corridor in the manner of a police officer checking a room in a covert raid. There's no reason why anyone would be in the building after it's been padlocked shut, but my experiences today have taught me to be super cautious. I don't fancy bumping into one of the heavies' mates unexpectedly. It's not like there's any way of me making a quick escape in this place when it's in lockdown.

When I'm reasonably satisfied that I'm the only occupant, I dash across the corridor to check out the cupboard. I'm so overjoyed to find the promised trainers, I nearly do a happy dance, despite my bruised toes. I pull them on and delight in the cushioned comfort of wearing proper shoes. The poor soles of my feet are blistered and red raw. The trainers are about an inch too big, but I do the laces up extra tight and hope for the best. Better too big than too small, and they've got to be preferable to the teddy bear slippers with their completely inadequate soles. I swear, the next pair of slippers I buy will be sturdy enough to run a marathon in.

Remembering Fiona's hastily whispered instructions, I slip down a floor to the main office, pulling my hood up as I go because for some bizarre reason it makes me feel like I'm more in stealth-mode. My steps echo loudly from my new footwear as I hurry down the stairs, and I force myself to slow down so I don't make too much noise. The windows are single-glazed, and from my experience of similar glazing at home, I know they won't be much good at blocking unwanted sound from travelling. And from a purely practical point of view, I'm unused to my feet being this size, so I need to be extra careful not to trip over them.

I arrive on the first-floor administration area of the charity, and I'm a bit thrown by the number of doors to choose from. But after a couple of false starts, I finally light on a room furnished with some ramshackle desks and several oversized filing cabinets which look like they've seen better days. This appears promising, but unfortunately, it's a room positioned right at the front of the building with large bay windows looking out onto the ongoing confrontation between Sam and the heavies.

I know I should keep to the back of the room rather than risk going near the windows for a closer look, but I need to check that Sam is OK. I couldn't forgive myself if my plan has led to him, or anyone else, getting hurt.

I can hear raised voices so I drop to my hands and knees, and crawl forwards until I reach the window sill. Slowly, carefully I raise my head and peek out. The heavies are still flexing their muscles. Sam, meanwhile, is in full-on journo mode, firing aggressive questions at the guys to the point where I'd almost feel sorry for them, if they hadn't already demonstrated that they can more than handle themselves.

Suddenly, his voice falters and I raise my head still further, trying to work out the cause of his discomfort. He catches my eye and does a weird pantomime to tell me that my silver unicorn horn is sticking too far up. Then he suddenly turns the gesture into a bizarrely exaggerated head scratch, presumably because the heavies looked like they were about to rumble him. I push my hood back, slide down onto the floor and crawl until I'm further away from the windows. Sam raises his voice again with his question bombardment to let me know that he's alright.

Cursing myself for my carelessness, I gaze around the room and assess my surroundings as my heartrate slowly returns to normal. I need to hurry up and get on with this. Sam can only keep the boys distracted for so long. They're going to start getting suspicious, and that will not end well.

The easiest course of action would be to find the iPad with the complete paper trail on it, then I'd have the documents all in one place. Fiona told me it would be securely locked away somewhere, but she couldn't remember whether it was in the desk drawers or the filing cabinet. The desk drawers are in a better position for me to maintain my covert status, but they provide their own challenge.

Unfortunately, while Fiona has been able to provide me with a key for the filing cabinet, the desk key is apparently with her colleague who is currently in hospital with his partner who's giving birth to their first child. When it comes to legitimate reasons for not being disturbed on a day off, that has to rate pretty highly.

And so, I turn my attention to the filing cabinet first of all, trawling my way through the drawers from the bottom up. Inevitably, the thing is filled with tons of bits of paper, but none of them look like eviction notices, and there's certainly not an iPad tucked in among them all.

That leaves me with one option. I need to find a way to break into the desk drawers. In spy dramas, women in this situation always manage to magically produce a hairgrip from their locks and then bend it into a skeleton key. Alas, I'm still sporting the tangled bed-head style that I woke up with, and I haven't had a bobby pin near my hair since I failed my first ballet exam for talking back to the teacher.

I'll have to think laterally. I pull hopefully at the top drawer but it doesn't want to give. Then I remember an incident in secondary school when my locker stuck shut, and Charlie used a ruler to prise it open for me. A desk is a different kind of beast, but it's worth a try. Fortunately, the Phoenix Homeless Shelter seems to have a ready supply of stationery in here, and I quickly find what I'm looking for.

Holding the metal ruler firmly, I slip it into the narrow gap between the body of the desk and the sliding part of the drawer. When I find a point of resistance, I start levering it back and forth, all the while increasing the pressure on the lock by pushing the drawer down towards the floor. It holds firm for a few endless minutes, during which time the disappointed faces of Frank and Hercules haunt my thoughts, but eventually I detect it starting to give. And then, at last, there's a final snap and the lock breaks free from its wooden surround and the top drawer slides open.

Unfortunately, the contents are in no better order than those of the filing cabinet. I wonder if Sam uses this desk when he's here? I scrabble through the reams of detritus, and then finally feel the cool metallic surface of the iPad. Progress at last. I'm even happier than when I pulled on Fiona's trainers.

The next challenge is getting access to the documents saved on the darn thing. Fiona failed to mention that it was password protected and I'd really rather not have to climb back out of the window to ask her for the code. I try a couple of obvious options, like four zeros, and one-two-three-four, but neither of them works. If I'm not careful, I'll lock the thing permanently.

I gaze around the room, searching for inspiration. The iPads at work are all given to us with the same passcode – the year in which Richmond Woods was established as a law firm. We're told on pain of death to change the default setting, but half the members of staff end up forgetting. Maybe Phoenix has a similar problem, although it would be a definite advantage if it allows me to get into the iPad. There's a poster on the wall detailing the history of the charity to celebrate its anniversary. I key in "1990" and hope for the best.

The screen springs into life and I congratulate myself on my excellent hacker ability. I'm developing quite the criminal skillset. The backdrop of the home screen is another picture of the clients happily engaged in a cookery workshop. I detect the photography skills of Sam in their relaxed poses. It's yet another reminder of the importance of the task I am engaged in. I settle myself more comfortably at the back of the room so I can concentrate properly, and start to read.

When I first joined the legal profession, I found legalese absolutely baffling. It's a very precise form of language, designed to make sure that everything is completely clear to those in the know, without leaving any room for ambiguity. The emphasis there is on "those in the know" because it is pretty baffling to anyone without the benefits of legal experience. It's also deadly dull, and in my early student days, it used to send my attention wandering at best, and at worst set my eyelids drooping.

Now I'm a couple of years into my career, I like to think I've got a better handle on it all, and so what might seem like an incomprehensible document to your average punter is normally clear to me. There's a beauty in the efficiency of legal documents, everything meticulously expressed in black and white with all space for misinterpretation removed. But there's nothing precise or beautiful in this paperwork. I pride myself on my ability to translate confusing legalese into language which a small child could understand. But I'd really struggle to explain these documents to anyone, because I can barely understand them myself. Basically, they're a complete mess, clauses all over the place and random declarations which make no sense. The more I read, the more I'm convinced that whoever has prepared them for the landlord can't be from a legal background. I suppose that at least lets me off the hook in terms of the concern about him being a Richmond Woods client. If that were the case, these documents would be crystal clear and legally sound. The fact that they aren't can only help our cause.

I would hazard a guess that the landlord has prepared them himself, by copying and pasting random bits of legal-sounding jargon from Google. No wonder Fiona and the Phoenix team were so baffled by it all. But this definitely works to our advantage. As far as these documents detail, there is no justification for the eviction, and the proper processes have not been carried out to make the action of the heavies out the front in any way legal. And now that I know that, all I need to do is confront the heavies, take the key off them, and send them packing. Easier said than done, I fear.

Chapter Twenty-Eight

6.26 p.m.

My mind is buzzing with adrenalin. After once more engaging stealth-mode and crawling backwards out of the office, I zip upstairs so I can lean out of the window and fill Fiona in on all the latest developments and how I plan to confront the heavies. She looks slightly dubious when I announce my first idea, but she's so relieved that the eviction isn't legal that she's prepared to go along with it.

"I knew there was something dodgy about the whole thing," she bellows. Then she remembers that the thugs are only a few metres away, and lowers her voice. "I'm kicking myself for not consulting with a lawyer before now, but our cash reserves are so low at the moment that it never seemed like an option. Thank goodness Sam knows a top lawyer from one of the best firms in the city."

It gives me a bit of a buzz to be described like that.

However, I don't enjoy it for long, because Fiona's expression suddenly changes and the delight in her face switches back to concern.

"Goodness, sorry Alexa, but that's another thing I failed to think of." She hesitates. "What's your rate for this kind of work? I hate to say it, but I'm not sure we can afford to pay the usual Richmond Woods prices. I don't know if there's some kind of payment plan we can arrange? Otherwise we might really struggle. I'm so sorry, this is really embarrassing."

I nearly fall out of the window in indignation.

"What do you take me for, Fiona? Of course I'm not going to charge you for this, I promise. I wanted to help. I volunteered, although maybe I would have thought twice when I realised how much physical hazard there was involved in the job! But trust me when I say I'm absolutely delighted to do what I can. And from a purely selfish point of view, you guys have made me feel really good for being able to assist."

It's true, the endorphins are happily buzzing around my body, and I'm feeling inspired and uplifted. It's good to have made a tangible difference to something that's so important to a group of people who are normally overlooked by the rest of society. What I've helped with is only small in the great scheme of things, but I'm glad to have done my bit.

I say that, but I'm still locked inside with two thugs standing between me and the building being re-opened. There's no point in putting it off any further. I need to confront them. Fiona crosses her fingers and sends good luck vibes my way before heading to the front to await the next part of my plan.

I duck back into the centre and make my way downstairs once more, although this time I don't bother to keep my movements subtle and quiet. I stamp along doing my best to sound as loud and confident as possible. When I arrive at the front door, I pause for a brief moment to run through my next move, then I reach up and bash my fist against the wood panels.

"Open up in the name of the law!" I shout, hoping it comes across as authoritative rather than ridiculous. I'm banking on sounding impressive enough to cow the heavies into following my bidding.

The rumble of voices outside goes quiet for a moment and I knock on the door once again.

"Open this door without delay," I demand, amazed at my own audacity.

"What the effing hell is happening in there?" says someone with a brash East End accent. "I thought we cleared out the place when you set the fire alarm off?"

"We did. They even did a register while the siren was sounding, the morons. That's how I got the padlock on the door."

I hope Sam is taking shorthand during this exchange, as it's proving to be even more revealing and damaging to their cause.

"If you've finished comparing notes, could you please open the door?"

I wish I was wearing skyscraper heels like Zara normally does so I could impatiently tap my feet on the floor. It doesn't really have the same impact when one is wearing oversized trainers.

"Not until you've answered the question. Who the hell are you?"

"You guys are like a stuck record. I'm Alexa Humphries, legal representative for the Phoenix Homeless Shelter, and if you don't open this door in the next thirty seconds, there will be serious consequences."

Mr East End lets out a guffaw. "You appear to have been breaking and entering, darlin'. Why don't you stay exactly where you are while I get the police to come along here and sort you out?"

I put on my most cut-glass accent. "I would delighted, sir, if you did call the police. I'm in possession of a very interesting set of documents which I'm sure they would like to see. Namely ones which illustrate how your boss has falsified information and paid absolutely no heed to proper legal processes in order to carry out this supposed eviction. And by locking out the staff, volunteers and service-users from the building they are legally entitled to be in, you have in fact broken the law yourselves. So, I shall take great pleasure in watching the police arrest you, rather than me."

There's silence from the other side of the door, and I can almost picture them scratching their heads in confusion as they try to decide whether I'm bluffing or not. I press my ear against the wooden panel, straining to make out their now whispered conversation. I think I hear Sam asking them for a comment for the newspaper, and then comes the welcome sound of a key being turned in the padlock.

I leap back and fold my arms, trying to maintain an air

of studied calm as the door swings open towards me. As I've been standing in dim surroundings, at first, I can only see silhouettes of the people standing on the other side of the threshold. I have to crank my neck back to take in the full frames of the two heavies. I blink a couple of times to allow my eyes to adjust to the light from outside. Unfortunately, that rather undermines the confident manner I'd been hoping to project.

"That's right, little girl, you should be scared," says one of them in a manner which I would have found threatening if I hadn't been so amused by being referred to as a "little girl". He follows up his words by cracking his knuckles.

Honestly, these guys are almost parodies of the thugs they're trying to portray themselves as. The realisation gives me an extra surge of confidence and it makes me get a bit gobby with it.

"You should be careful doing that," I say, pointing at his knuckles. "It's really not good for your joints. My grandma always says it can cause you to get premature arthritis, but she's not actually a doctor, so feel free to ignore her words of wisdom."

"I don't give a stuff what your granny thinks," says the other heavy, although I notice his mate has now stuffed his hands in his pockets to stop himself doing it.

"She will be disappointed," I say.

I notice Sam shake his head at me slightly to warn me not to provoke them too much. He starts shuffling closer, trying to put himself between me and the heavies, like he's my own personal bodyguard.

While I'm grateful for his consideration, I can look after myself.

"Anyway, to get back to the issue in hand, can I check that you are the official representatives of Mr Darren Whittaker, the registered landlord of this building?"

I fix my gaze on them sternly.

"Yeah, we represent Daz," says the knuckle cracker with a horrible grin. I dread to think what other tasks come under their remit.

"Perhaps you'd like to get Daz on the phone or, even better, tell him to come down here? As the lawyer for Phoenix Homeless Shelter, I am duty bound to inform you that Mr Whittaker is in breach of several regulations, and has in fact carried out this eviction illegally."

"Bollocks he has," says Mr East End.

"Let's try and keep things professional, shall we? There's no need for that kind of language," I say in the snootiest voice I can muster. "Perhaps we can sit over at that bench there where it's a bit lighter, and I can talk you through these supposed legal documents in greater detail and explain exactly how they are invalid."

"Be my guest," says Knuckle Cracker. He even does a mock bow in my direction as I sashay out of the building. I lead them as far away from the main front door as possible.

What he and his mate don't notice is that as soon as I've got them tucked out of the way, the volunteers, staff and service-users are able to file happily back in to occupy the building once again. They do say possession is nine-tenths of the law, after all.

I sit down on the bench with a heavy on either side of

me, my wannabe-bodyguard Sam still hovering in the background taking careful notes of what's going on. And then I proceed to take them through exactly why the paper trail of this entire eviction fiasco is a complete load of nonsense.

By the end of my explanation, they're deflated and practically eating out of my hands. Suddenly they don't seem quite so big and threatening as they did before.

"So basically, Mr Whittaker has a long way to go before he can legally evict these law-abiding, decent tenants from his building." I pause so that my final threat can have good effect. "And if he does choose to go down the legal route, let me assure you that I will be representing Phoenix until the bitter end, and we won't go down without a fight. Plus, my friend Sam is always on the lookout for a story, so I'm sure he'd be delighted to cover every cough, spit and splutter of any legal battle. Are you happy to pass that message on to Mr Whittaker, or would you prefer for me to explain it to him myself?"

The boys look at each other and shake their heads.

"It's alright, Miss, we'll make sure he gets the message," says my friend the knuckle cracker, in a distinctly subdued voice. He knows the news is not going to be well received.

"Excellent. It was a pleasure to meet you both," I say, standing up and shaking their hands in a way which makes it clear that they're being dismissed. "And no offence, but hopefully we won't be meeting again."

They nod sheepishly and slink off. If they were wearing unicorn onesies, their tails would definitely be between their legs.

Chapter Twenty-Nine

6.47 p.m.

"Oh my God, that was epic!" says Sam, rushing towards me and sweeping me up in a hug so big that he actually lifts me off the pavement. The relief that the Phoenix Homeless Shelter will live to fight another day is written all over his face. I'm feeling pretty stunned myself. I can't believe my scheme actually worked. All at once I feel a surging sense of achievement and pride as the full realisation of what we've accomplished hits me. I've actually made a positive difference for a change. Instead of being obliged to help the fat cat, I've been able to support the underdog, and it feels wonderful. This moment will stay with me for the rest of my career, and I promise myself that it will spur me on to become the kind of lawyer I always imagined I would be – someone who gives a voice to those who need it most.

Sam twirls me around, whooping loudly. His face is lit up with sheer exuberance.

"You're an actual genius, Alexa. I could kiss you right now, I'm so happy."

His sentence starts out full of joy, but by the time he's finished speaking, there's something deeper in his voice, a huskiness that wasn't there before. His mention of kissing makes me hyperaware of how close we are to each other and something flutters in my stomach. Sam stops spinning, but his arms are still wrapped around me, holding me up in an embrace, surrounding me with his warmth. I look into his eyes, and the atmosphere changes from one of elation to something quieter, deeper. There's an intimacy between us now, the product of shared triumph over a common enemy, and perhaps something else as well. I can feel the warmth of his breath against my mouth and if I move just a millimetre closer, our lips will be touching. His heart is pounding against my chest as my fingers trace his broad shoulders, almost of their own volition.

"Alexa..." he breathes the word out, an unspoken question in his voice.

I answer it by making that millimetre move. I feel his intake of breath rather than hear it.

"Well done, Alexa, you saved our bacon."

Fiona's voice sounds as if she's speaking from very far away. Then she says, "Oh heck, sorry to interrupt, I'll leave you alone," and I hear her tiptoeing away.

But the moment has passed. Sam lets go, and my feet land on the ground with enough of a thud to bring me back to my senses, and we leap apart from each other. Sam clears his throat and looks away, while I brush some dirt from my onesie, concentrating closely on the furry surface as if I'm suddenly really concerned about my personal appearance.

"Yes, well done, Bambi," he says. There's still a slight husk in his voice. He clears his throat again and shuffles awkwardly on the spot.

I roll my eyes in mock irritation at being called Bambi again, but secretly I'm finding a bit of enjoyment in the nickname now. At least there's a softer note of affection in his tone, unlike his earlier stinging mockery.

"You didn't do too badly yourself, Hack Man," I reply, causing him to mirror my eye roll of a moment ago, although his lips twitch with the ghost of a smile. Using the nickname makes me think of something else. "I reckon you should write about Phoenix rising from the ashes. They deserve the publicity and it might bring in some extra much-needed donations. Don't forget to remind Sir Clive of his promise, too. We've scared off Mr Whittaker for now, but I wouldn't be surprised if he comes back for round two at some point in the not too distant future. We should think about what we can do to safeguard the service for the long term."

Sam nods and shows me his notebook. It's gained several extra pages of scrawled shorthand. "Already ahead of you with that idea. But I thought you didn't want to be in the paper," he says. "I can't really tell the story of today's developments without including you. Although as you know, I do have some excellent photos of you for illustrative purposes, were you to change your mind."

"There's no chance of me changing my mind," I say

quickly. "Definitely not for the climate change thing. And you'll have to keep me out of this, too, as I'm officially ill in bed. But maybe you can gloss over my involvement and talk about a lawyer intervening without being too specific in the details."

Sam purses his lips. He doesn't look too sure about the idea. For a moment, I imagine what will happen if he goes ahead and publishes without my permission. I thought I was starting to see a different, more understanding side to him, but maybe I was mistaken.

Eventually, he nods his head. "No, that's fine, I understand why you want to remain incognito. You've got to watch your position." He scans through his shorthand notes again and sighs. "Although it seems a shame not to include your involvement when you were key to the whole thing happening. It would be a much better story, and you deserve the credit for what you've achieved today. Maybe I could imply you worked in an advisory capacity from afar? And I could be sketchy about when all this happened? Those thugs aren't likely to contradict the exact chain of events, and the guys at the centre are so happy that the situation has been resolved that they'll keep quiet too. Getting the story out there is what matters most."

"You, a serious journalist, being sketchy about when something happened?" I laugh and make light of his suggestion, but I can't help feeling a little burst of hope at this sign that he might be backing down from his earlier stance of refusing to compromise about anything. "Can you really get away with that? In fact, do your highfalutin morals allow for that?"

Sam holds his arms up as if in surrender. "OK, OK, I give in. You've been badgering me enough. If you really insist, I guess I could be persuaded to delete the pictures of you battering the policeman at the protest."

I gape. Did he really say what I think he did? He nods again, answering the unspoken question in my eyes. I can't believe I'm off the hook. The fear of being arrested and/or subjected to a serious disciplinary which has been hanging over me all day now diminishes slightly. There is still hope for me and my future. The relief I'm feeling right now is indescribable. In fact, I could snog the man. And properly this time.

Sam doesn't seem to object to the hug I settle on giving him.

"As I said, I guess I could be persuaded to delete the photos," he says, a cheeky glint in his eye as we break apart. There's a pause, then we both start speaking at the same time.

"Would—"

"I—"

We laugh.

"You go first," he says.

"No, you," I insist. I'm not quite sure exactly what it is I'd been planning to say. I just know that I don't yet have the courage to articulate the strange thoughts that have been swirling around in the back of my mind for the last few minutes.

He leans back and puts his head on one side. "OK, if that's what you want." He takes a deep breath, as if he's steeling himself for something difficult. When he finally speaks, his words come out in a great rush, so that it takes me a moment to work out what he's saying to me. "What are you doing on Friday night once you've miraculously recovered from your current ailments?"

"Probably catching up on lost sleep after all the stress of today. Why?" I ask. I'm half-hoping I know the reason, but I tell myself that I'm letting my imagination run away with me.

He shuffles on the spot, looking even more unsure of himself. He takes his glasses off, polishes them on his shirt and replaces them before he answers me. "Just wondering if you fancied going out for a drink with me?" he says, sounding uncharacteristically nervous. He's speaking quietly, giving me the get-out of pretending I hadn't heard what he asked.

At first, I'm delighted, and about to rush in with an enthusiastic "Yes" that would have surprised the me of a few hours ago, but then an unpleasant thought occurs.

"What, as in a date? You're telling me you'll delete the pictures if I'll agree to go on a date with you?" I ask suspiciously. It does seem to be a big turnaround from threatening to go public with the pictures to asking me on a date. Did he ask because he genuinely wanted to spend more time with me, or is this a tabloid trick and he's pursuing an agenda of his own? I'm feeling pretty confused. I've spent most of the day worrying about those pictures, and I can't quite believe, after him being so stubborn, that he's suddenly going to turn around and delete them, even though I have just helped save the shelter. But then again, he's been blunt all day, to the point of rudeness sometimes, so if the drinks invitation did come with strings attached, he probably would have come out and said it, wouldn't he? I think I might be overthinking things again.

Sam turns pink and puts his hands on his hips. His face is full of outrage.

"What do you take me for? I don't know who you've been mixing with in the legal world, but I certainly wouldn't blackmail a girl into going on a date with me. For a start, I have no need to."

He puffs himself up, acting like the great I Am.

"Alright, Mr Full of Yourself," I retort, defensive because I'm regretting having accused him in the first place.

Our stand-off lasts a few minutes, neither wanting to be the first to back down. Eventually, Sam runs his hand through his hair.

"Forget about it. Ignore the drinks thing. It was a stupid idea anyway."

He turns away and heads back into the centre.

I want to call after him, but in the distance, I can hear a church clock striking. I count out seven clangs of the bell with growing horror. I curse loudly, the panic rising in my throat. I had no idea it was that late. I'm still miles away from home, and regardless of the situation with the pictures, if I don't get back before Zara does, she'll make sure I'm given my P45 faster than you can say "P45."

Even if I start running – which is a stretch given my oversized trainers, lack of bra and general absence of fitness – I stand little chance of making it back to Bethnal Green in under an hour, and then there's still the problem of the locked front door to contend with. If it came to it, I suppose

I could land on the doorstep and claim I've only just locked myself out, but it would definitely arouse Zara's suspicions about why I'd been out there in the first place. No, I need a key and I need some way of getting me home which doesn't involve any more physical exertion on my part, and fast.

I look through the open door of the shelter. Someone has turned the radio on, and service-users and staff are dancing together in celebration at their stay of execution. I'm loath to break up their party. I'm going to have to ask Sam to help me get home. But have I already burnt my bridges there, and should I really be trusting him?

Chapter Thirty

7.01 p.m.

I take a deep breath, and head inside, my eyes darting around to spot Sam in the crowd. I'm met with cheers and whoops as soon as I step foot over Phoenix's threshold. The group, who had looked so depressed and deflated only half an hour ago, are now buzzing with exuberance, faces creased in smiles rather than frowns. Even Hercules seems to have caught the party spirit; his tail wagging so enthusiastically his entire body is vibrating with joyful energy. He runs up and gives me a big slobbery lick on the leg, delighted that everyone else is so happy, even if he doesn't quite understand the source of their pleasure.

The celebrations are in full flow, and I find myself being passed from person to person, receiving so many affectionate slaps on the back that I strongly suspect I'm going to have a bruise in the morning. It's worth it. For a few brief moments, I get swept up in the joyful atmosphere and enjoy feeling part of the community. But then a glimpse of the clock on the wall brings me crashing back to reality, and the panic claws at my stomach once again.

"Frank, I'm so sorry, I've got to go," I say, doing my best to extricate myself from his arms as he leads me in a surprisingly confident waltz around the room, Hercules bouncing at our heels and barking with every turn.

Frank twirls me one final time, and then lets go.

"You young ones should learn to relax and go with the flow," he says. "When you get to my age, you realise most of the things you regret are from times where you were running around trying to please other people, rather than yourself."

"Wise words, Frank, but I'm not going to be able to relax and go with the flow if I haven't got a job. And more importantly, I'm more likely to be able to help the Phoenix further from within the institution of Richmond Woods than outside of it."

"You seemed to do pretty well by yourself just now," is his response. "Fine, off you go, but I'm only letting you leave the party because I'm a romantic at heart, and I can see young Sam hovering in the doorway, waiting for you with a soppy expression on his face."

I spin round. Sam's expression looks more like that of a man with indigestion than anything else, but I'm glad to see he hasn't disappeared completely.

"I'm sorry for earlier. I didn't say I wouldn't go out for a drink with you," I say. As an opening gambit, it's not my best, but my head is still all over the place.

"Perhaps we should just gloss over that," says Sam

eventually. "I've filed the story about the protest, by the way."

I can tell he's dying for me to ask which pictures he included with the copy, and for that very reason, I perversely decide to do the exact opposite of what he expects, even though I'm desperate to know the answer.

"Good for you," I say, in as breezy a fashion as I can muster, although my stomach is flipping as I imagine the pictures of me, mid-snarl at a police officer, winging their way around the world.

The silence hangs between us. I'm about to cave in and ask the question anyway when Fiona breezes up.

"There you both are. Can I interest you in a celebratory mocktail? We're a dry drop-in centre, of course, but Joe over there used to work at a health club in the West End before he lost his house, and he makes a mean virgin mojito."

Joe smiles a toothless grin and enthusiastically shakes the thermos flask which he's commandeered for his mocktails.

"It sounds great, but I've got to fly. I'm on a deadline to get back home, I'm afraid," I say.

Fiona's face falls.

"Oh, but we'd love for you to stick around for the rest of the evening. I have an ulterior motive, naturally. I was hoping to rope you into volunteering for us. Sam will testify that once we've got our clutches into you, we are very reluctant to let go."

"I'd love to." I don't even have to think about my answer. Whatever the future may hold for me, I know I'd like to spend more time at the Phoenix. "I'm not a brilliant cook, but I can help with the washing-up, and I'm more than happy to apply my legal brain to any complicated forms that require deciphering. And, as I said earlier, I guarantee that I'll be here at the very first inkling of any further trouble you have from Mr Whittaker."

Fiona hands over a form, which I tuck into my onesie pocket for later.

"You're going to regret making that offer." She smiles. "I have a list of tasks as big as this room, but thankfully our volunteers have an amazing tendency to get hooked on coming to this place. I'm sorry, I'm babbling on, you mustn't let me keep you. Are you going to be able to get back home OK?"

"Well, I was hoping that you could help me with that, Sam."

It's underhand of me to say it in front of Fiona, but I really need his assistance, and I'm not convinced he would agree in any other way.

"Naturally," he says, in a flat voice, recognising my tactics of old.

Fiona looks between the pair of us, not quite able to follow the undercurrent.

"I'll leave you to it. Don't be a stranger, Alexa." She waves cheerily, and then goes to join Frank on the makeshift dance floor.

Sam leans against the doorframe.

"Once again, I'm to be your knight in shining armour. How may I be honoured to assist you now?"

He pretends to doff an invisible cap, enjoying playing the humble rogue far too much.

I hesitate. I'm about to take a calculated gamble, but the more I think about, the more I'm certain I don't have any other option. I'll have to trust that he'll do the decent thing.

"I need the house keys. Please can you help me get them?"

"We're miles away from my base, and consequently my set of keys. Believe me when I tell you, this is the first and last day I head out on assignment without taking my keys with me. My day would have been so much easier." Sam spreads his fingers wide to emphasise his empty palms.

"But we're only about ten minutes away from the Richmond Woods headquarters on Gray's Inn Road."

"Your point being?"

"That you could go to my office, pretend you've lost your keys and ask Zara if she'll let you borrow her set."

Sam whistles through his teeth. "That's a big ask. Zara's super scary. Did you know that when I moved in, she muted the television in the living room so I couldn't hear the sound, just because I hadn't got round to paying my share of the licence yet?"

I laugh. "She did that to you too? Glad I wasn't being singled out for such treatment. But seriously, she has no reason not to accept you at face value."

"But surely she'll be on her way home any minute? Won't she just offer to accompany me back? And failing that, don't you think she'll be rather suspicious that I'm suddenly turning up on the doorstep asking her for a favour? We're not exactly on matey-matey terms, and she'll wonder why I haven't called out a locksmith, or rung the doorbell and asked you to let me in."

I throw my hands up in the air in frustration. "Fine, if you don't want to help me, at least be honest and come out and say it, rather than making all these excuses. Couldn't you pretend you can't afford a locksmith? And you were in the area anyway for a job and thought you might as well call in?"

The corner of Sam's lips twitches. Is he laughing at me?

"I suppose it is realistic that an impoverished journalist such as myself would rather brave the lion's den than fork out for a locksmith," he muses. "I'll do it. But you're probably best off coming with me, and lurking around the corner while I go in. After all, you don't want to waste valuable time waiting for me to come back here with the keys, rather than being able to set straight off home."

The thought of going any nearer to my office makes me very jumpy. The whole area is bound to be crawling with my colleagues, and if any one of them spots me in the wild, then I'm in big trouble. But my options are limited, and I'm wasting time by hesitating. I'm going to have to rely on Sam coming up trumps. I hope it's not a mistake to place my trust in him.

Chapter Thirty-One

7.13 p.m.

S am checks his watch. "What time is it you need to get back home? I have to warn you that as a journalist, I'm very deadline-oriented."

"Any time from now," I reply. "You know what Zara's like with working late, but I have a feeling she might make an exception and leave the office on time today. She'll want to assess how likely it is she'll have another Alexa-free day at work tomorrow." And after accidentally calling me earlier, I have a strong suspicion she'll also want to get home early to double-check how much I overheard.

"Should we hire bicycles to get there a bit quicker? I suppose it will have to be my treat, of course." He makes a great show of patting his pockets in a parody of my gesture at the National Theatre.

I'm not sure I trust these trainers on the pedals of a

bicycle. It feels like a recipe for disaster. Besides, I'm still traumatised from the abuse I got earlier in the day when I last attempted using that form of transport.

"Thanks, but let's do it at a jog instead. By the time we've managed to get the bike locks free, we'll be halfway there anyway," I say optimistically, hoping that wearing trainers will somehow miraculously imbue me with the ability to run fast.

I'm wrong of course. Sam sets off at a punishing pace, and I follow in his wake at a distinctly less vigorous tempo. Our different speeds make it look like I am pursuing him while he's desperately trying to get away, and I get a few suspicious looks from passers-by, although thankfully most of them are too wrapped up in phone conversations to actually intervene.

Although the soles of my feet are no longer pounding directly against the pavement, I still haven't quite adjusted to having what feel like the equivalent of clown shoes on. It's a most disconcerting experience, and after experimenting with several different running styles, I end up lolloping in an ungainly fashion, picking my feet up in an overexaggerated way in order to make sure I know exactly where I'm putting them down again so I don't trip.

"Are you actually running back there?" calls Sam over his shoulder, while somehow managing to effortlessly increase his pace. He doesn't even sound out of breath. While he is gracefully weaving his way in and out of the other passers-by with apparent ease, I'm having less luck at getting people to move out of my blundering way. I narrowly avoid two near misses with besuited business types, and then end up getting clobbered on the side by a delivery rider speeding off to hand over someone's takeaway dinner. It completely knocks the wind out of me, leaving me unable even to shake my fist at her retreating form. I let out a strangled sound of protest, but the woman doesn't even turn back to apologise. Still stunned by the shock of the collision, I stagger over to a handy wall and prop myself up against it.

"What's the matter now?" asks Sam as I double up, clutching my side and wincing at the impact. I'm only thankful that I have a bit of protective cushioning there, otherwise I dread to think what would have happened to my ribs.

"Give me five seconds to catch my breath, and I'll be fine," I wheeze, still feeling startled by the cycle-by assault. This is the last thing I need when I'm up against such a tight deadline.

Sam jogs back to my side. He hasn't even broken a sweat.

"I swear I've never met someone so accident-prone as you. Never a dull moment when you're around, is there Bambi? Come on, you got this."

And to my surprise, he loops his arm around my waist and helps me to carry on hobbling. I try not to lean too heavily, but the tenderness in my side is still making me wince when I make any sudden movement. I take a deep breath and try to walk normally, but end up sucking my breath in as my side protests. Sam takes more of my weight in his arms and we stagger on a few paces until the pain starts to fade.

"I bet you didn't think your day would end up like this when you got up this morning, escorting a wounded unicorn to a place of safety." I attempt a joke to hide my embarrassment at yet another cringey situation.

"It's certainly been more interesting than my usual diet of photographing politicians and snapping celebrities as they do their morning coffee run," he says. "Although, you'd be amazed at some of the bizarre scrapes they can get themselves into, so I guess you could say that this isn't my first time at the rodeo."

I wonder who he's referring to.

We stagger around a corner onto the main road. After the relative peace of the side street, the noise of the traffic here is a shock to the system. The rush hour is still in full swing and there are a lot of grumpy drivers around relieving their feelings by hooting impatiently at each other. I don't know what they think they're going to achieve by it, but it certainly creates a tense atmosphere.

I feel very exposed with all the cars crawling past. No one is moving anywhere fast, and I'm convinced that they'll be fighting the boredom by staring at people on the pavements. I'm under no illusion that I will be able to blend into the background. Every time I see a Mercedes or Jaguar, the favourite mode of transportation for partners at Richmond Woods, I have to fight the urge to shrink back against the wall. If only I had chameleon powers which would allow me to fade seamlessly into my surroundings.

Sam seems to sense the tension I'm feeling.

"Tell you what, why don't you find somewhere to hide around here, and then I can call you when I've got the keys from Zara?" he suggests.

I take my smashed-up phone out of my pocket.

"Call me on what exactly? I think this thing is long past having the last rites read to it."

Sam examines it carefully. "I smashed my screen worse than that, but it still managed to work. They're sturdier than you think."

"Trust me, I've tried pressing all the buttons it possesses, which alas, isn't many, and there isn't a spark of life in it. The only thing I haven't tried is charging it, but my capacious onesie pockets sadly do not conceal a charger or power pack."

"Now that is something I can help with." Sam heaves his rucksack off his shoulder, and we move to the side of the pavement so we're not in the way of all the commuters hurrying on their way home. "I carry a lot of junk around in this thing, but the last time I checked, there was a power pack in here. Let me take a look."

He rummages around for a while, grimacing when his fingers come into contact with the orange peelings.

"You could have a cure for cancer growing in that thing," I say.

He pulls a face. "Quite possibly. Blame the life of a journalist on the road. It's got half my worldly possessions in there, or at least, it feels like it sometimes. I'll clear it out one day. But in the meantime, I think this might be what we're looking for."

He heaves out a power pack with the aplomb of a

magician pulling a rabbit out of a hat. He dusts off the connections and then plugs it into my phone. We stare at the screen, hoping for signs of life. It remains stubbornly black.

After a few moments, the churning in my stomach starts up again. I'm really not good at waiting for things to happen.

"It's not working. We should get going, Sam," I urge him, glancing nervously about. "We're right out in the open and there's a high chance some of my colleagues could be collecting takeaway coffees in that café right opposite us."

"Just give it thirty seconds more," he says. "I have a good feeling about this."

I have no idea what he's basing that on.

"Buried within that cynical journalist exterior, there's a bit of a secret optimist lurking, isn't there?" I can't resist teasing him.

Sam looks about and puts his finger in front of his mouth. "Shh, don't tell anyone you've discovered my secret."

His exhortation to be quiet coincides with a lull in the traffic just long enough for me to hear the tell-tale beep as my phone splutters back to life.

"It lives, it lives!" I say jubilantly. I'm so elated I briefly forget my cares and punch the air in delight. It's amazing how cut off from the rest of the world I've felt without it. I've only been without my phone for a couple of hours, but it's made me realise how completely reliant I am on the thing. It can't be healthy. Maybe indulging in a digital detox would be another way of improving my lifestyle going forward? But in the meantime, the reincarnation of my phone gives me a burst of hope that maybe, just maybe, I might be able to get home before my deadline.

"Perfect," says Sam in satisfaction. "You keep hold of the power bank and let it continue charging up, and then I'll go to track down Zara and sweet-talk her into lending me her keys. I'll call or text you to let you know when I've got them and the coast is clear."

But while the thought of going anywhere near the office makes me feel incredibly nervous, I'm no more relaxed at the prospect of skulking around here by myself until Sam returns. There's a whole range of people marching around on this street, but I've yet to see anyone in an outfit as distinctive as mine. I've clocked at least two drivers slowing down to get a better look at me, and I'm sure I've been snapped in a couple of selfies. At least if I stick with Sam for a bit longer, then I have my own personal six-foot-something of man to hide behind. He does have his uses.

I double-check our surroundings and finally get my bearings.

"We're nearly at the office now anyway. I'll stay with you until we get around the corner, then I'll duck out. There's a wall near a block of flats there that I can go and sit on."

I am far too well acquainted with that wall. When I first joined Richmond Woods and hadn't cottoned on to the status quo, I used to go and take my lunch breaks sitting on the wall. Yes, I know, actual lunch breaks, what halcyon days. It became my favoured spot, not because it was particularly comfortable or in beautiful surroundings, but because it was sufficiently far away from the office to give me an hour free from my colleagues. And it wasn't because any of them were being particularly obnoxious or unpleasant to me at that time. It was purely because I needed an hour to get away from it all and feel like I wasn't being observed, which I would certainly have felt if I'd gone and sat in the canteen. In retrospect, maybe if I had gone to sit in the canteen, I might have made more friends among my co-workers, but I didn't, and that's probably part of the reason why I feel so isolated nowadays. Correction, why I felt so isolated. I realise that in the last few hours, things have in some ways changed for the better for me. One of my housemates is definitely growing on me, despite his irritating ways, and I have a whole bunch of pals to hang out with at the Phoenix Homeless Shelter. My future in London is looking much brighter. I make a silent vow to make more of an effort to hang out in the work canteen as well, if Sam and I manage to pull off this next feat.

That thought gives me the strength to pick up my pace again, and we continue our jog along the street, Sam holding back so he's by my side rather than striding ahead. It feels strangely companionable, and trust me, I'm not a girl who's into working out with a companion. Or working out full stop.

The area around the wall is busier than when I last spent time here, and a new office seems to have opened with an unhealthily large contingent of smokers hanging around outside, but I settle myself down with the phone and charger and try to ignore the strong feeling that I'm being stared at by people in the neighbouring flats.

Sam looks around warily.

"Are you sure you're happy to stay here by yourself?" he says pointedly, as he narrowly avoids crushing what looks like a used syringe under his foot.

I'm not sure there's anywhere within a two-mile radius of the Richmond Woods offices where I'd feel completely safe right now, so I figure it's as good a place as any to lurk.

"I'll be fine. Anyone who is up to no good will probably be more scared of me than I am of them. Besides, didn't you realise that the onesie has magical protective qualities?"

He doesn't look convinced by my light-hearted attitude.

"Trust me, I can look after myself. Did you see what I did to the policeman who tried to assault me? That's a joke by the way, and not an admission of guilt."

I so nearly ask about the contents of the article he's filed. But now I've got a functioning phone, I can check for myself, and I don't want to delay him any further. I experience another pang of nerves.

"I certainly wouldn't want to come up against you in a fight," he says, eyes twinkling.

Nevertheless, he still seems reluctant to leave me there.

"Well, Mr Hack Man, do you think you'll be able to prove your hunter-gatherer credentials and rescue those keys for me?"

I reach out and tweak his hair, catching myself and him by surprise.

"What's that in aid of?"

"Just trying to make you look slightly less disreputable," I improvise quickly. "Don't want Zara to call security on you when you turn up. You claim your newsroom has standards too high to let me in, but I can assure you that Richmond Woods sets the threshold ten times higher."

"Touché. But trust me, I'll have them eating out of the palm of my hand. My ability to charm my way past the front door is legendary, I'll have you know."

"I hadn't noticed," I retort.

"I save the charming act for work and for people I'm completely indifferent to," he says obscurely. For the briefest of seconds his gaze softens in a way which sends a tingle through my body.

"Which way do I need to go?"

It takes me a moment to collect my thoughts.

"End of the road, turn right and walk for about fifty yards, and then you'll be at Richmond Woods."

He salutes and does a neat about-turn.

"Please be careful," I call after him, as if he's a soldier about to head to the front line.

He spins around, a carefully blank expression on his face.

"Still don't trust me?" he says in an overly light tone.

"All I'm saying is, Zara's not stupid. If she has the slightest suspicion, she'll go on at you until she finds out the truth. So, please, watch every word you say."

He salutes again.

"Contrary to popular belief, journalists are the soul of discretion, when they need to be. You wouldn't believe the number of other people's secrets I would go to prison before breathing a word of."

He blows a cheeky kiss in my direction and disappears towards Richmond Woods. I'm glad he's not close enough to see me blush.

Chapter Thirty-Two

7.22 p.m.

Now that I have a means of connecting with the outside world again, my first priority is to check the contents of the article that Sam has filed to his newspaper. Although my phone is charging without any problems, the smashed screen makes it a challenge to navigate my way onto the internet and then to read the pages once they load. My heart is pounding so hard, I can feel blood pulsing in my forehead. I scroll through the newspaper site, scouring the headlines, torn between dread and hope at what I might see. The homepage is full of adverts and pop-ups, and my poor phone is struggling with information overload. Every time I think I'm making some progress, the screen freezes, and I have to reload the page. It's like there's a conspiracy to prolong my agony.

Eventually, the site stays working long enough for me to scroll down and spot the headline, "Protesters turn wild at climate change demo". I swallow nervously. This is it. My finger hovers over the screen. I'm not sure I dare to look. The contents of this article could dictate my entire future. Sam won't have dropped me in it, will he? I gaze into the middle distance, trying to psychologically prepare myself for either outcome.

Ever since his kindness to me after my panic attack at the school, I've been nursing a growing hope that Sam's attitude towards me has softened, as mine has towards him, despite his unerring ability to wind me up. The more I analyse that moment where he asked me out, and I defensively thought he was doing it on a quid pro quo basis, the more I'm convinced I overreacted. After all, there have been several points today when he could have caused trouble for me without putting himself out, yet he chose not to. He had no need to get more information out of me for his article, so maybe his drinks invitation was motivated purely by a desire to spend more time with me. I know I'd like to get to know him better. Despite everything I've gone through today, I have laughed more than I have done in months, and Sam has played no small part in that.

But then a vision of Genevieve flits into my mind, Genevieve asking me what on earth's going on as she reads the newspaper and sees a glorious technicolour action shot of me grappling with a police officer at the heart of the climate change scrap. I know that what I did was nowhere near as dramatic as that, and I was acting in self-defence, but having spent so much of the day worrying about the incident, it has blown up out of all proportion in my mind. I can see her standing there with a face of thunder, livid at my actions. I can see her standing there...

And then I realise with a terrifying jolt that I really can see Genevieve standing just metres away from me. I'm so startled that I let out an involuntary yelp, and tumble over the wall like a soldier diving for cover as a bombardment is launched. I lie on the ground, my heart pounding and my brain going at a million miles an hour. I squeeze my fingers into fists and take a few deep breaths as I try to talk myself down from this heightened sense of terror.

I tell myself I'm overreacting, yet again. I have a big imagination, but it's not powerful enough to actually summon a person's presence. It's not possible that could have been Genevieve. She's in Japan clinching a deal with Richmond Woods' next big client. There is no way on earth that she's skulking in a back street around the corner from the office. It was just another woman in a sharp business suit, like the tens of thousands of other businesswomen who work in the capital. Yes, her brown hair may have had a similar style to the one sported by Genevieve, and there was definitely something familiar in the determined set of her shoulders, but how many other women adopt that demeanour in order to be taken seriously in a world which is still suspicious of an ambitious female?

Yet, however many times I tell myself that I've hallucinated the whole thing, I still can't bring myself to stand up and check. In fact, I hug closer to the wall, curled up nearly in a foetal position as if it will somehow make me invisible. I'm bracing myself for the cold tones of Genevieve's voice asking me what on earth I'm doing. The ground is sandy and covered in shards of broken glass, but in my freaked-out mind, it feels safer to be nose deep in smashed-up bottles than sitting on the wall and running the gauntlet of being confronted by a random woman who is definitely not my boss. I mean, Genevieve is probably sipping Champagne with the client. Or is it the middle of the night there? I'm so discombobulated that I can't work out the time difference between here and Tokyo. Maybe instead of downing the cocktails, she's tucked up in her five-star hotel room, luxuriating on a memory-foam mattress while I become intimately acquainted with a slab of concrete and the gnarled roots of a sickly-looking tree. Wherever she is, she's certainly not here in central London.

Slowly, my heart returns to its normal beat, and my hands stop wobbling like I'm about to take a piano exam. I stretch out slightly to relieve the cramp in my lower back. Now my senses are no longer overwhelmed by flight or fight response, my nostrils start twitching at the overwhelming smell of urine in the air. Trust me to take refuge in the local pissoir for drunks caught short on their way home from a night out.

But just when I think it's safe enough to emerge from my makeshift hideaway, there's a peal of laughter from over the road. There's something about the high-pitched nature of it that once again sets alarm bells ringing at the back of my mind. I've never been face-to-face with Genevieve when she's been laughing, but I have heard it echoing down the corridors in the office. That makes it sound like she's regularly in a genial mood, ready to share a joke with her colleagues. Alas, in my experience, the laughter is normally a prelude to someone running down the corridor with a fearful expression on their face. In other words, the laughter is the warm-up act before she lays into someone and rips them apart for some misdemeanour or other. I think she genuinely enjoys lulling people into a false sense of security and then catching them when their guard is down. Maybe this is what she's doing right now?

I once again remind myself that Genevieve is living it up in Japan, but I'm seriously starting to doubt the veracity of that. I didn't check my emails properly this morning, and I've only got Zara's word for it that Genevieve's flight had landed. What if there was a last-minute change of plan and Genevieve is really in this country still? What if she's standing on the other side of that wall waiting to ask me why I'm lying on the ground in a unicorn onesie instead of sat behind my desk in Richmond Woods checking the wording of a contract for her?

Chapter Thirty-Three

7.26 p.m.

I need to do something. I can't stay curled up on the dirty ground for the rest of my life, and if I wasn't in enough of a pickle, I'm starting to get cramps in my legs. They're not used to doing as much exercise as has been forced upon them today, and the chilly concrete I'm currently concealing myself on is not helping the situation. I try flexing my toes to ease the pain, still too terrified to make any bigger movements. Unfortunately, that only worsens the situation. My feet constrict into a claw-like position, sending arrows of agony shooting up my legs. It feels like someone is stabbing me in the shins. I stuff my fist in my mouth and try to swallow the moans of anguish which I can't help uttering. Normally, my pain threshold is pretty high, but this cramp is something else. My right leg is going into a proper spasm now and I can't even straighten it out. I let out a yowl like a cat giving birth.

There's a rustling on the other side of the wall, and then the unmistakable sound of someone walking over to check what's going on. The footsteps are getting louder, but I'm frozen to the spot. If it is Genevieve, then she's about to catch me right in the act of my illicit duvet day. It's now or never. I've got to get moving. I roll over like a clumsy ninja and heave myself up onto all fours, my brain telling me I need to sprint off like an Olympic athlete. But my feet are still cramping like mad and with the additional hazard of my clown-like trainers, I don't trust myself to be able to stand up without causing some serious damage. In this battle of mind over matter, matter is definitely going to be victorious. I take the next best option and start bear-crawling along the length of the wall, trying to look as inconspicuous as possible while I complete the ungainly manoeuvre, bum sticking up in the air in a manner which would have army sergeants yelling at any recruit for failing to keep close enough to the ground. Every couple of metres, I pause and stretch out my legs, hoping that the cramp will eventually fade away.

"What's going on over here?"

The voice is unmistakably Genevieve's, those crisp vowels, that cut-glass accent which wouldn't be out of place in the Queen's drawing room at Buckingham Palace. She's always had the ability to make her voice carry through the biggest of crowds without having to raise it, and she's demonstrating that skill right now. Every single syllable makes me flinch and my limbs feel like they're dissolving into jelly. I feel like a naughty schoolgirl about to be hauled in front of the headteacher. I reach up and pull my hood down low over my head, trying to conceal as much of my face as possible. Somewhere at the back of my mind, there's still a vague hope that I might be able to get through this without being recognised. After all, business-Alexa is very differently turned out to my current hot mess. Genevieve barely even acknowledges my presence in the office, I tell myself, so why would she associate the mousey junior in the anonymous suits who is normally up to her eyes in legal tomes with the crazy-haired, wild-eyed unicorn currently crawling around on a patch of wasteland?

"Excuse me, you there."

Genevieve's voice is full of an authority that there's no arguing with. There's an expectation of obedience in her tone, a confidence in her ability to get anyone to stop and follow her bidding. I'm sure it's my imagination, but it feels like all the rest of the ambient noise in the street has quietened down to a dull roar, that the cars are no longer driving past, and the commuters are hurrying away from the confrontation which is inevitably about to happen. I wouldn't be surprised if the temperature hasn't dropped several degrees as well.

My right foot goes into one last spasm, as if in reaction to Genevieve's voice, and then I feel the circulation mercifully starting to return, going through the horrid pins and needles phase first and then finally reaching something resembling normal. Maybe the rapid tempo of my heartbeat has helped revive it. I'm still full of panic, but now at least I feel like I can make a run for it. But is that the right thing to do? Can I get away quickly enough without her seeing my face?

I risk a brief glance upwards. I've well and truly backed myself into a corner here. The wall is to my right, admittedly it's not a very high wall, but it does have an angry Genevieve pacing along its perimeter and I'm not convinced that I can successfully vault it without risking some kind of injury. Knowing my luck today, the odds of that happening are pretty high. And to my left is a very solid, very high iron gate with spikes on top of it and a code-pad buzzer entry system. Whoever installed that meant business. Unless someone happens to emerge from the block of flats with very good timing, there's no way I'm getting through there.

"Excuse me, you there. Yes, you in the rainbow outfit. Are you injured?"

There's no point pretending to myself now that she hasn't spotted me. But there's something which might be a note of concern in Genevieve's voice which gives me the tiniest burst of hope. I remind myself that presumably she didn't get to the lofty position of being head of pro bono work at Richmond Woods without having some kind of social conscience. After all, there are far more prestigious departments to work in, ones which are much more lucrative. I briefly toy with the idea of feigning injury and throwing myself on her mercy, but then quickly dismiss it as much too far-fetched to work. Even if I used my best acting skills, I still don't have a good enough explanation for why I'm here, hiding in the undergrowth a few hundred metres from the office, rather than in my sick bed at home cuddled up to a hot-water bottle. And that's not even touching on the issue of Sam's article. Why didn't I read it when I had the chance rather than wasting time sitting there and dithering?

I take a deep breath and give myself a pep talk. If I move back the way I've come I will get to the dip in the wall, where I reckon it's much safer for me to leap over. And if I make that move fast enough, then all Genevieve will see will be a flash of rainbow whizzing past her eyes. The bagginess of the onesie conceals my body shape and if I make sure my hair is tucked into the hoody, then there's every chance she won't be able to tell even the gender of the person running past her. And here my large trainers might also play to my advantage, giving the illusion of me being bigger than I actually am. Besides, they make me move in such a different way that her subconscious won't even be able to recognise my gait, right?

I make my decision, and as if on cue, the general hubbub of the street comes flooding back to life. I'm suddenly aware that I'm going to be leaping out into quite a crowded environment. More people equals more witnesses, but on the plus side, there will also be more obstacles between me and my hunter. Hopefully that will work to my advantage. As long as I can get in and among the commuters as quickly as possible, then maybe Genevieve won't be able to catch up with me. I may be wearing giant trainers, but surely they'll be easier to run in than Genevieve's trademark stilettos.

I tap my pocket, checking that my phone and the power pack are still in there as if they are my lucky charms. They certainly feel like a lifeline. I'm going to have to find somewhere even more obscure to hide if I get out of this situation in one piece, and I need to have the means to contact Sam and get the keys off him. There's no point in him wandering around wasting time trying to find me. It's even more important than before that I get home and tucked up in bed before Zara returns. If there's even the slightest niggling thought at the back of Genevieve's mind that she's seen me lurking in the bushes, then Zara returning to the house and finding me absent would set in motion the means for that suspicion to be confirmed. I am determined that my career in law will not end with me being ignominiously fired on my front doorstep while I'm still dressed in a stained and bedraggled onesie. I am worth more than that, and if nothing else, my brothers will never let me live it down.

OK, this is it, the moment of action, the moment where I am going to take control of my own destiny and take the fight to the enemy, rather than waiting for them to come to me. Or something like that. My adrenalin is pumping and I've psyched myself up to go. Nothing is going to stop me now. I take a deep breath, and channel the unswaying confidence and determination of an elite marathon runner about to cross the finish line in a record-breaking time. And then I leap up and go for it, moving from completely horizontal, to standing tall and running in the space of milliseconds. I'm going so fast, it feels like I've left part of me behind still curled up on the ground, and the strange sensation of an out-of-body experience adds to the surreal nature of the situation. It's like I've stepped out of myself and am a spectator watching, from a distance, the effect my sudden appearance from behind the wall is having on the innocent passers-by.

I'll be honest with you. In their position, I would have been terrified and assumed the worst too. A few shoppers clutch their bags to them in fear. An elderly woman with a Zimmer frame screams and shakes her fist. One bloke actually flinches and crosses himself, as if unsure whether this apparition is real or imagined. A businessman on his phone has to move out of the way so quickly that he's startled into spilling his orange juice down the front of his pristine white shirt. But there's no time for an apology. I swerve out of his way to avoid causing further trouble. And that's when I collide with the person on the moped, knocking them flying to the ground.

Chapter Thirty-Four

7.31 p.m.

Everything goes still and the only thing I can hear is my own ragged breathing. Now, I'm no longer a casual spectator watching the chaos I'm causing from a detached distance. I am fully back in my own body, the hot horror of what I have accidentally done flooding every vein. I am frozen to the spot, unable to fully process the sight in front of me. It's like my brain is trying to protect me from the consequences of my actions by flatlining my thoughts into a big empty nothingness.

I take another shuddering breath and press my fingernails into the palms of my hands, focusing on their sharpness against my skin. Today has been a day full of disruption and chaos, but I never set out to hurt anybody badly. Through all my clumsiness and scrapes, I've been focused on my goal of getting back home by causing the minimum amount of trouble possible. Yes, things have not been going my way, but at no stage have I done anything as terrible as this. Now I've ended up colliding with an innocent passer-by and knocking him off his bike. I could have killed him.

As my brain slowly starts functioning again, I begin to process the scene in front of me and confirm that my victim is male. He looks young, barely out of his teens. I imagine his parents waiting for him at home, the table set for his tea, wondering where he's got to. Instead, he's lying spread-eagled on the ground, his face a concerning shade of paleness. Everyone's attention is on him. This would be the opportunity for me to flee into the distance, but I'm not going to leave the scene of an accident, whatever the personal cost it entails.

"I'm so sorry," I find myself saying on repeat, unable to form any other words as I scan the ground in terror for what I'm sure will be a growing pool of blood. He wasn't wearing a helmet, just a bandana wrapped around the lower part of his face, and I'm convinced he must have bashed his head as he tumbled to the ground. Between the hard edge of the pavement and the broken-up tarmac of the road, there wasn't much to break his fall gently.

Thankfully, there's no blood that I can see, but that doesn't mean that he's alright. Haven't there been countless stories about people who got knocked on the head and were conscious and talking, but died hours later because it turned out they'd been bleeding internally ever since?

I scour the rest of his body for signs of damage. His jeans are scruffy – I know, I'm one to talk – but on the plus side, they look thick and sturdy enough to have protected his skin from grazes. None of his limbs are at odd angles, and the moped has fallen in the opposite direction to him, so thank goodness he hasn't been crushed by it. Is his stillness because he's been stunned by the crash, or is something more sinister at play?

I can sense a crowd gathering around us, but no one else is rushing forward to check that he's OK. It's definitely the kind of occasion where I wish I'd chosen medicine over law, as the knowledge from my Girl Guide First Aid badge is really rather rusty now. But as nobody else is volunteering to step forward, I've got to do what I can, and hope my offbeat appearance doesn't freak him out further.

I bend over my victim, hands shaking as I reach down to pull the bandana from his face to check that he is breathing. He blinks at me as my fingers near his face and then he scowls. The bandana slips lower as he bares his teeth, gnashing them together like a guard dog warning someone about to encroach on its territory. I snatch my hand back, startled by his unexpectedly aggressive behaviour.

And then I am unceremoniously shoved out of the way by the elderly lady with the Zimmer frame. She leans forward, wobbling precariously, and snatches a handbag lying half hidden between the moped rider's arm and the pavement. Then she prods him with one leg of her Zimmer frame.

"Take that, you brute," she says. With a burst of strength which belies her fragile appearance, she plants a well-aimed kick at the man's backside. There's a smattering of applause.

I gaze around me in confusion. Surely the accusations of

being a brute should be coming in my direction? And that's when I realise that I am the centre of attention of the small crowd gathered around, rather than the man lying on the ground. Once again, the camera phones are pointed at me, lights glowing as they film my every move. But whereas I would have expected their faces to be filled with condemnation, they're smiling at me. Someone even gives me a thumbs up. They're actively cheering as this elderly lady clutches her bag in one hand and shakes her other fist at the moped man.

Then she turns and heads for me. I instinctively take a couple of steps backwards. I'm completely confused about what's going on, but this woman, however benign her exterior, has just tried to beat up a man lying potentially injured on the ground. I'm not sure that I want to hang around and find out what punishment she has in store for me.

"You there," she says in a shrill, no-nonsense voice. I can sense the crowd growing around us, the lights from the filming mobile phones are starting to dazzle. But I daren't move my gaze from this woman. I swallow nervously.

"You there, I'd like to say thank you," she says, raising her voice still louder. "That thug had snatched my handbag. It's got all my pension money in it, and my late husband's watch which is irreplaceable. You saw him do it and at great personal risk, you tackled him." She turns to address the crowd. "This person saw that hooligan assault me, and without thought for personal safety, intervened. My unicorn hero didn't hesitate, just advanced into the affray and defended me."

"But I—" I try to interrupt, to explain that it was a complete fluke, that I hadn't even been looking when I collided with him.

She seizes my hand and raises it to the sky like she is declaring me the victor of a boxing match.

"My unicorn hero," she repeats. And then a couple of people in the crowd start taking up the chant. I look around in growing horror. I can hear the shutters snapping, the beep-beep-beeps as people start texting and tweeting. Someone is already muttering about starting a unicorn hero hashtag.

A couple of burly guys move forward and haul the moped man to his feet. The way he's struggling suggests there's nothing physically wrong with him from the collision with me. I'm slightly worried that he may end up feeling less great once these two have finished conducting their citizens' arrest on him. Given the commotion, I reckon the police will be turning up at any moment. The protest at the Bank of England earlier already feels like a lifetime ago, but I can't risk hanging around to find out if there's an all-points warning to look out for the strange girl in a unicorn onesie.

But if that wasn't enough to worry about, at the back of the crowd, I can see Genevieve staring straight at me, her expression unreadable. Our eyes meet and with the worst possible timing, there's a gust of wind and my hood falls back, throwing my face out of shadow and revealing my hair.

I daren't wait to see the recognition pass over Genevieve's features. I extract myself from the elderly woman's steely grip and desperately look for a gap in the crowd. But there's a sea of people before me, and I have no idea how I'm going to get through them all. I pull my hood back up, lower my head and just go for it, charging away from Genevieve for all I'm worth. Hands clutch at me, trying to slow me down. I'm entreated to stop and take a selfie with at least two people, but there's no time to politely decline. I've got to get a move on. The applause is still going, and the crowd is whooping for the "Unicorn Hero", enjoying this unexpected interlude of drama at the end of their busy working days.

I can almost feel Genevieve's gaze boring into my back and the thought of her wrath spurs me on to put on an extra burst of speed. I've lost count of the number of times today that I've ended up running apace away from some scene of chaos. My phone starts buzzing in my ridiculous onesie pocket, and for a horrible moment, I imagine that Genevieve is already calling to give me my marching orders. I put on a sprint past the Royal Mail depot and run down the middle of the paved street, dash across a road and then dive into what looks like a former graveyard. And then, I find a secluded spot between a gnarled tree stump and a headstone which is teetering at a crazy angle, and sit down to get my breath back.

I'm not the only disreputable-looking figure in this little patch of parkland, so I reckon I can blend into the background for a bit. I wheeze away and replay the last few minutes in my mind, wishing, not for the first time, that I could rewind the clock and change the outcome of what happened.

I tap out a quick text letting Sam know I'm not at the wall any more. It's too complicated to explain why I've had to move on, so I keep things brief. I don't want to start his journalistic senses twitching again. Besides, describing how I assaulted a thief and then got hailed a hero would confirm his view that I'm a crazy lady. I wouldn't blame him if he hands in his notice at the house and moves out as soon as possible after all this.

A tramp wanders past with his dog and gives me a friendly nod. I wave in return. I'm beginning to think that I've found my tribe in London. It may come in useful when all the trouble finally catches up with me.

My phone buzzes, and I check the battered screen. The text is rather distorted by the cracks in the glass, but I manoeuvre it around until I find the optimum angle to read it at. There's a definite flutter somewhere internally when I realise it's a message from Sam. My emotions soon change to something else altogether when I read it. There's no update on how the key collection mission is going, but the contents still send me into a spin.

"Is this you?" the message says, and then there's a link to a tweet. I get a sinking feeling from the URL alone. I don't want to look, but like a rubbernecker at the scene of a motorway crash, there's this terrible compulsion to do so. With a horrible feeling of inevitability, I click on the link. It seems to take forever to load, and while the little grey circle of doom spins around, my imagination runs riot.

Finally, it starts playing, and I see some shaky video of the elderly woman having her handbag snatched. It's grainy, and the smashed-up screen doesn't help the image, but it's still clear enough to see the dramatic moment the moped speeds past her and nearly knocks her flying as the thief seizes her bag. Seconds later, the camera swings around at sickening speed, just in time to catch me apparently throwing myself in the moped's path and shoving the perpetrator to the ground. Even I can appreciate the drama of the footage. The sequence of events and the angle it's been filmed from do make it look like I was playing the role of a have-a-go hero. Plus, it has that added soupçon of excitement in that the have-a-go hero is dressed in such a ridiculous outfit. It's only a matter of time before it becomes a meme.

Now I've seen what happened before I knocked the moped man over, I feel a little less guilty about colliding with him. We're regularly getting emails at work warning us about gangs of thieves on mopeds in the area, but I'd always been lucky never to encounter them personally. And I suppose a naïve part of me liked to think that there was some kind of honour amongst thieves whereby they wouldn't target elderly, vulnerable people. More fool me. Now I've seen one of the little sods in action, I feel decidedly *Daily Mail* in my response to how they should be treated by the law. Well, he's certainly not going to get away with his crime this time, although his notoriety is going to be tied hand-in-hand with my own.

I glance down and see the tweet is already going viral, with thousands of retweets and likes. The number jumps up another score while I'm looking. How do these things happen so quickly? It seems astonishing that an incident that occurred around the corner barely minutes ago is already being viewed and discussed by people around the world. When I click onto the general Twitter feed, I immediately spot that the unicorn hero hashtag is starting to trend, alongside dozens of tweets asking, "Who is the Unicorn Hero?"

If they knew the truth, they wouldn't be hailing me a hero, that's for sure.

Chapter Thirty-Five

7.39 p.m.

I watch the footage again, this time trying to view it dispassionately, paying forensic attention to every frame, reminding myself that most people will be watching it on screens in a considerably better condition than mine. Thankfully, the person behind the camera didn't have the steadiest of hands, but there are at least two shots in which most of my face is visible. I scroll through other tweets, and see that some bright spark has already done a screen grab of these particular bits of footage and zoomed in on them. Another internet geek has offered to use special software to tighten up the details of the pixels. Yes, it's only a matter of time before someone I know spots it and answers the question as to the identity of the Unicorn Hero.

I've been so wrapped up scrolling through the wormhole of Twitter that I haven't replied to Sam. In typical journo fashion, expecting an instant answer, he sends another message repeating his question, this time in shouty capital letters. Concern starts to swirl in my stomach once more. Why is he so keen to know? I still don't know what he published in his original article, but even I, a lawyer with only a smattering of knowledge about how journalism works, can recognise that what's just happened is a gift of a story, especially if it was a follow-up to the climate change coverage. People love a have-a-go hero, and a have-a-go hero in fancy dress who earlier assaulted a police officer at a climate change protest is the icing on the cake. It's exactly the kind of thing I'd be chatting about on the phone to Charlie if I wasn't the one at the centre of the whole ridiculous mess. A reporter getting their by-line on a story unmasking the Unicorn Hero would probably get to bask in the praise of the news editor for a few hours at least. The question is, which way does Sam's loyalty lie? I'm not sure I like the answer which presents itself to me. You don't get a job at one of the most famous, or rather, infamous, tabloids in the country without having to develop a fairly ruthless streak.

I check Twitter again, and spot that his newspaper has already cottoned on to the story. They've put out a sensationalist tweet calling on members of the public to identify the Unicorn Hero. How did they find the footage so quickly? They're obviously wanting to make a big deal of it, sending out three tweets in quick succession. They'll be offering a reward next. But why? Is Sam behind this? I tell myself that I'm being paranoid, but his involvement does seem to be an obvious explanation. After all, he's the only one who would be able to make the connection so quickly.

Well, him and Genevieve; but as far as I know, she doesn't have anything but contempt for the tabloids, so she'd hardly be likely to go running straight to them.

I try to reload the main newspaper website to read the article about the protest, as I should have done in the first place, but once again, the pop-up ads crash my browser and scupper my plan.

The more I think about the newspaper's tweet about the Unicorn Hero, the more I worry that Sam could be behind it, drumming up extra interest among their hundreds of thousands of online followers, so he can then publish his own article revealing my identity and the story of my exploits today. It would be perfect clickbait, and being behind a viral article could only help his standing in the newsroom. It would definitely distract them from the whole fake pregnancy gossip.

But surely he wouldn't drop me in it like this? After everything we've been through today, I'd hoped we'd come to an understanding, that we were friends, friends with that tinge of excitement that there could be something more. I feel disloyal for questioning his behaviour in this way, but if I'm being completely honest with myself, what do I really know about him? We've spent a few hours together, during most of which we have been at each other's throats, engaged in a game of dangerous one-upmanship which neither of us have wanted to show weakness in backing down from. Is that game still on? I thought we'd called a truce when we came together to save the Phoenix, but it wouldn't be the first time someone had been taken in by a good-looking guy with an easy manner.

I don't like the way I'm thinking. I realise that I'm finding the thought of Sam's betrayal as upsetting as the idea of exposure, perhaps even more so. I need to get a grip on myself and focus. The important thing is to decide what to do now. I check the time on my phone, but sadly, the clock hasn't miraculously stood still. It's still ticking inexorably towards my deadline. To be honest, it's probably past my deadline, and the game is up anyway, but I'm not prepared to crush my last little bit of hope just yet. The next few minutes are going to be make or break. I'm at least three miles from home. If I get moving in the next five minutes, then there's still a tiny chance that I can make it back in time, provided I can summon up some form of transport. But if I don't set off in that direction very soon, then I might as well just walk into reception at work with my hands up in surrender and confess all. I need those keys from Sam, and I need them now. And at the back of mind, I can't help thinking that if I see his face again, then I'll be able to read the truth there, however painful it might be.

I type out a quick message letting him know the exact location of the wasteland, completely ignoring his question about the Unicorn Hero. Neither confirm nor deny, that's the mantra of Richmond Woods, and it's one I'm going to stick to now. Hopefully his curiosity will bring him here in a hurry, and then I'll just have to seize the keys and make a run for it before he has the chance to pry any further.

A little voice at the back of my head tells me that I'm being ridiculous for immediately assuming he's betrayed me, that Sam is a decent guy, and that he wouldn't do this to me. I think about the look on his face when we managed to save the Phoenix Homeless Shelter. A man capable of expressing that unbridled joy and relief couldn't possibly be capable of cold-bloodedly betraying someone he'd shared that wonderful experience with only half an hour later, could he?

The sudden ringing of my phone startles me out of my reverie. I look down at the screen, expecting to see Housemate Sam popping up. But it's a landline number, and one that is all too familiar – the switchboard for Richmond Woods, the number which shows up regardless of which extension you're dialling from. Someone at work is calling me on my personal mobile. This is it. I'm about to be dragged over the coals. It must be Genevieve, returned to the office in a rage, ready to give me my marching orders. Or could it even be Zara, fresh from a conversation with Sam, about to confront me about my adventures today? The timings would work. After all, Sam must have been in the Richmond Woods building when he saw the footage. What if he turned his phone around so Zara could watch it too? Were they laughing together, two people united in ridiculing their third, hapless housemate?

My fingers hover over the screen as I wonder whether I should answer it. Maybe it's time to acknowledge that the game is up and accept my fate.

And then I clock Sam as he hesitates in the gateway to the park. The sun is starting to dip, and the light is that lovely golden colour, bouncing off his head, making him look like he's grown a halo. Chance would be a fine thing. I firmly remind myself to keep things business-like and not allow myself to be taken in by his good looks. He may know how to turn on the charm when it suits him, but I need to be on my guard. I check his hands carefully. No sign of Zara's massive bunch of keys with their distinctive, and rather uncharacteristic, pink fluffy keyring. But on the plus side, he's not clutching his camera either. A guy with his brains would know I'd want to run as soon as I could, so he would take the first opportunity to get a new picture of me for his article.

The longer I sit here dithering, the less my chances are of getting back home, tucking myself up in bed and giving myself plausible deniability. OK, maybe not so plausible, but a girl has to have something to live for. Taking a deep breath, I stand up and reveal myself from behind the gravestone, brushing bits of moss from my backside, as if that will make all the difference at this crucial moment. I try to read his body language as he hurries towards me.

"Alexa, are you OK? It was you wasn't it? I knew the second I saw Unicorn Hero start trending online that it would be something to do with you."

There seems to be genuine concern in his voice. His eyes are raking over me, as if he's checking to see whether I'm injured. My hand moves to my hip, and massages the bruise which is forming there, subconsciously answering his query about my physical state.

He glances around the park, and hustles me back behind the gravestone, making sure we can't be seen from the gateway. Who is he expecting to have followed him here? The feeling of unease in the pit of my stomach starts making its way further up my body. His hand is still resting on my arm, and he's standing very close to me in the shade of the ornate gravestone. The sun is dipping in the sky now and the lengthening shadows make it hard for me to read his expression properly. His thumb is against my forearm. Is it my imagination, or has he slightly increased its pressure, a massage so subtle and gentle that I'm questioning its existence, even as my skin reacts?

I'm finding his proximity a dangerous distraction.

"The keys?" I ask, my voice coming out hoarser than intended. I clear my throat, and repeat myself in a firmer tone.

"I couldn't believe it when I saw the footage," he says, completely ignoring my question. "They made me sit and wait in reception for Zara. Apparently, I looked too disreputable to be allowed into the building without an escort, although let me tell you, some of the people they ushered in were extremely questionable. Trust me, we've got dossiers on half of that lot back in the newsroom."

His mention of the newsroom reminds me to get my act together. I twitch my arm out of his hold, and take a step backwards. My backside is now flush with the grave and I can feel the dampness from the moss starting to seep through my onesie to my bum, while a carved angel is digging into the small of my back.

"Richmond Woods only accepts clients whose businesses are absolutely squeaky clean," I say. "Typical journalist, assuming there's something dodgy going on around every corner."

"There's a difference between legally right and morally right," retorts Sam, unknowingly parroting back an argument I have used on many occasions in the office.

"That's how the little organisations like the Phoenix Homeless Shelter get shafted from on high."

"Stop getting away from the point. Did you get the keys from Zara or not?"

I'm beginning to think he's using deliberate delaying tactics. He keeps glancing around him, as if he's expecting someone to join him. Is this all part of some elaborate set-up?

"Zara was in a meeting when I arrived. She was pretty reluctant to leave it, hence me whiling the time away scrolling through Twitter. They really didn't get your best angle, you know, whoever shot the video."

"Thank goodness. I could do without high definition, close-up footage of that particular debacle," I say, unthinkingly.

"Ha, I knew it was you," says Sam, clearly delighted to have tricked me into confirming his suspicions. "Have you anything you'd like to say to the legions of people who are now heralding you as a hero online?"

I shrink even further back against the gravestone. The stone cherub is going to leave an imprint on me if I'm not careful. But there's no time to waste thinking about such trivial considerations. I need to get away from this park, and soon. Everything Sam is saying is making me feel more and more uncomfortable. It really does sound like he's confirming my worst suspicions, that he is going to write an article naming me as the Unicorn Hero. There's still a small part of me that hopes that Genevieve hasn't put two and two together and realised my identity. Yes, there was that one moment when we locked eyes, but everything was chaos, and that could be enough to make her give me the benefit of the doubt. But there's no room for benefit of the doubt when your employee's name is plastered across the tabloids and trending on Twitter.

"No comment," I say, like I'm a defendant in court.

"Aw, Bambi, the way you took out that thug on his moped... I mean, it was extraordinary. I actually whooped out loud in reception. I don't think that did my chances of getting into Zara's office any good, unfortunately."

Sam is still bubbly with excitement, as if this whole situation is a hilarious escapade that he's relishing every second of. Is it the thrill of the chase that he's revelling in? I've seen him like this before, when he first encountered me at the climate change protest and threatened to publish pictures of my confrontation with the dodgy police officer.

I shake my head as if it will shake the anxious thoughts out of my skull.

"You whooped out loud? Could you have done anything more to draw attention to yourself?" He tries to look contrite, but I can see the corners of his mouth are still twitching. "It was meant to be a stealth mission, Sam. In, get the keys, get out; not draw as much attention to yourself as possible. And speaking of keys, where are the bloody things?"

I'm getting irate now. The man has no concept of the situation I'm facing right here.

Sam taps his pockets as if he's forgotten where they are. Infuriating guy.

"Keys, keys, now where did I put them?" he says, then he starts searching through his bag. When he whips his camera out, it's like I've been punched in the stomach. My last vestige of hope melts away.

"Don't you dare," I say. I feign to the left and then duck away to the right as soon as he moves in the wrong direction. The bastard. He's set this whole thing up so he can get another picture of me.

"Alexa, wait a minute..." he starts, but I'm not waiting for anyone.

I do the only thing which seems to be an option in that moment of panic. I grab his bag and set off at a run.

He calls my name again, and his bellowed, "Sorry, I can explain," causes a few people wandering through the park to stare in my direction, but I'm not falling for that trick. I know without turning back that he's still got his camera in his hands, and there's no way I'm going to give him the opportunity to take a picture of me, let alone another one of my face in full flight mode.

I dash out of the park and then pound down the road until good sense, breathlessness and out-of-control boobs bring me to a halt. Gasping for air, I squat down on the pavement and search through his bag, hoping to find the keys hiding somewhere in it. I have no plan, no clue what to do next, and if the keys aren't there, then I have no hope whatsoever. And on top of that, I'm already feeling guilty. By running off with Sam's bag, I've behaved in no better way than the moped thief. How have I descended to that level of lowlife?

Sam's bag is no tidier than it was earlier, but despite my best searching efforts, there's no sign of the keys anywhere. I could cry with sheer frustration.

And then a pair of pointed shoes stop in front of me and start tapping the ground impatiently. I'd recognise those lethal Rosa Klebb-worthy heels anywhere.

In slow motion, I look upwards, a cold sweat breaking out over my body.

"Looking for something?" asks Zara.

Chapter Thirty-Six

7.47 p.m.

There are no words. I mean, there are literally no words I could use to express what is going through my mind right now, because my brain has just experienced so much sensory overload of panic and horror and guilt that it's shut down altogether, and I have no idea what I'm feeling any more. The cavity between my ears might as well be playing lift music, such is the lack of anything resembling coherent thought which is going on in there.

My mouth opens and closes a few times, as gormless as a goldfish in a bowl in the waiting room of a dentist's surgery. I blink, as if closing my eyes and opening them again will miraculously change the scene in front of me. Maybe this is a hallucination, generated by my guilt at stealing Sam's bag.

"Fancy seeing you here, Alexa," says Zara.

So, it's definitely not a hallucination. Her voice is sugary sweet, and although I'm hypersensitive, bracing myself for it, my ears can't detect even the slightest edge in her tone. It's like she's bumped into me in the shared kitchen on the second floor and is striking up conversation to be polite while we wait for the kettle to boil. Somehow, that makes it all the more scary.

The silence stretches between us. How am I meant to respond to her? I am at a serious disadvantage, literally on my knees on the pavement looking like a tramp, as she towers above me, cool, calm and collected after a day spent cloistered in the temperature-controlled offices of Richmond Woods.

I rest back on my ankles, not quite trusting my legs to support me if I attempt to stand. There's also a small part of me which is still deceiving myself that if I continue lurking down here on the ground, then she'll get bored and move away. Who am I fooling? This is probably the most exciting thing to have happened to Zara all day, and I can only imagine how gleeful she must be at the prospect of seizing victory in our ongoing office juniors' rivalry. And what a victory she will gain. With me out of the way, there'll be nobody standing in her way for whichever promotion she chooses to go after, and with all the brownie points she'll gain for exposing me, I expect she'll be able to negotiate a handsome pay rise as well.

The tongues of my oversized trainers are starting to dig into the top of my feet, and I'm beginning to get pins and needles in my toes again. I rock forward a tad to try to get the circulation flowing, then accept that I'm going to have to stand up and face the music.

As I haul myself up, my legs are pretty wobbly, whether from nerves at the situation, or the aforementioned pins and needles, I wouldn't like to say.

"Oh, hi, Zara," I say in as casual a manner as I can muster, reflecting back her relaxed tone, but bracing myself for the inevitable confrontation.

I fold my arms, but quickly realise that standing like that makes me look defensive, and so put one hand on a hip and end up looking like I'm about to sing "I'm a little teapot". Sam's bag is still on the ground at my feet. It falls to one side, and for one glorious moment, I think I catch a glimpse of Zara's pink keyring in its deepest depths. If I'm right, then Sam was at least true to his word about getting the keys for me, not that it makes a jot of difference to the situation I'm in right now.

Zara smiles thinly, and I automatically take a step back, immediately kicking myself for showing any sign of weakness in front of her. My mind is now racing with possibilities. Should I try to continue the illness thing, and attempt to make her believe that I've travelled across London in a feverish state and have no idea where I am or what I'm doing? I've dismissed the plan almost as soon as it's occurred to me. There is optimism, and then there's just ridiculous. That definitely falls into the latter category.

Or maybe I could pretend I've dragged myself from my sick bed after being summoned into the office by Genevieve? But again, I quickly dismiss that option too. It's too easy to disprove, and while it might work in the short term, there's no way I can get away with it longer term.

No, I am all out of options. And so, by default, I settle

for doing nothing at all. I am at her mercy, and it is up to her to decide what she is going to do with me. In some ways, it is a liberating thought. The sword of Damocles has hung threateningly over my head all day. Now it has finally fallen, at least I don't have to dread the sickening blow any more. The worst has happened. I've been caught. It's time for me to wait to see what fate has in store for me now.

"Sam had quite the story to tell me," says Zara, finally admitting defeat in our little battle by being the first one to break the silence.

I'm irritated by the visceral reaction the mention of his name provokes in my treacherous body. Why is my heart starting to beat faster when I have a horrible feeling the object of its foolish affections might have betrayed me? I shift on the spot.

"Oh really?" I say in as disinterested a tone of voice as I can muster. I'm still hoping against hope that she is fishing for information, that she's put two and two together about us both being in the area and worked things out for herself, rather than being told about my exploits by a traitorous tabloid hack on the lookout for a good story.

My phone buzzes and we both automatically glance towards it, programmed to respond instantly like any good Richmond Woods lawyer. But I decide not to read the contents of the message. Getting distracted by whatever it says is not going to help me in my current situation.

Zara sucks her breath in, demonstrating her disapproval of my actions.

"Yes, Sam had quite the story to tell," she repeats, in case the implied threat hadn't got through to me clearly enough.

"The thing we need to establish here, Alexa, is: what is it worth?"

I really don't like the way she says my name, overemphasising each syllable so it ends up sounding like "Al-hex-ha", cursing and laughing at me simultaneously.

I try to keep my expression neutral. It sounds awfully like she's trying to blackmail me. For a few seconds, I actually consider going along with it. But good sense quickly kicks back in. I know Zara. This is another way of her exerting her authority over me. She knows I'm in a difficult position, and she is making the most of that. Even if she promises to keep quiet, she won't stick to that promise for long. She'll spy an opportunity which will be better for her, and she'll sell me down the river without even a second thought. I decide to buy a bit of time by playing dumb.

"Sorry, you're going to have to enlighten me. What do you mean?" I ask.

If she's going to threaten me, I'm going to make absolutely sure of her position before I decide my next move. I've recognised the classic lawyer power-play she's made, implying she knows a lot, when in reality she could be fairly clueless. Besides, given that Genevieve has seen me in action as the "Unicorn Hero", worrying about what Zara's going to do is child's play in comparison.

We stand there in silence, a mismatched pair if you ever did see one. Zara unruffled and collected in her smart suit, as immaculately turned out as when she left the house this morning; me, well, quite the opposite. But as we stare at each other, I start to notice the little details which are, in their own way, quite revealing: the faint smudge of darkness under her eyes which is showing through her concealer, the pallor of her complexion that the carefully applied bronzer doesn't quite counteract, the slight stiffness of her shoulders which speaks of a day hunched up in front of a screen. And I think about how different our days have been. Zara has spent her hours being a slave to the stresses of the office, navigating the treacherous waters of the internal politics, reading between the lines of every exchange, and battling to satisfy the whims of some of the most demanding individuals in the country.

As for me, well, I've been experiencing quite a bit of stress too, but of a very different kind. Despite my misadventures today, I have had moments of sheer joy. I've seen more of the city in the last ten or so hours than I have since I first moved here. And I've made connections with actual, real people (not that I'm saying that lawyers aren't real people, of course), people who I very much hope I will continue to be friends with. Having walked and run miles on these streets, blagged my way into some of the city's most prestigious institutions, and helped some of its most vulnerable inhabitants, I finally feel like I am happy to call London my home.

With this realisation, there comes a growing sense of self-assurance. Despite everything that has been thrown at me today, I've been more resourceful and confident in dealing with these tests than I would have ever thought possible. I am a survivor, a hard grafter, and I will rise to the challenge of whatever is thrown at me. Zara may look the part right now, but I'm just as highly qualified as she is, and I know I'm just as good at my job. I've worked hard to get my role at one of the most prestigious law firms in the city. I may be about to lose that job, but I'm not going to go down without a fight. One duvet day and its associated dramas should not be enough to counteract all the hard, good work I've put in since I signed on the dotted line and became a lawyer at Richmond Woods. And if Zara thinks it is, then she is mistaken. I will not throw away my dreams of making a difference. I will fight for my position and I will stand up for myself.

Zara rolls her eyes and checks her watch. "Really, Alexa? Do you really think you're in a strong enough negotiating position to start playing games with me?"

My hackles raise. Zara is looking at me as if I'm some dog mess she's walked in and even as she tries to blackmail me, she's talking down to me as if I'm barely worth her time or consideration. It's the final straw. I've had enough.

"What exactly is it that you've got against me?" I say. I don't raise my voice, but the frustrations of two years of being downtrodden give it a distinct don't-mess-with-me vibe.

I think I see the briefest expression of uncertainty flit across Zara's features, but they soon settle back into her normal snooty sneer. This time she's the one to attempt a lack of understanding.

"I don't follow," she says. I can tell she's annoyed with herself for rising to the bait, for following the rules of my game rather than her own.

"You know exactly what I mean," I respond. "Ever since I arrived at Richmond Woods, you've been out to get me, setting me up for trouble, and basking in my failures. Why? I don't understand."

"It's nothing personal, that's just business, honey," Zara says, a sting in her voice despite her apparently affectionate way of addressing me.

I could stamp my foot, I'm so frustrated.

"But it's not 'just business', is it? We're meant to be colleagues, working together for a common goal, rather than competing against each other. As women, we should raise each other up, rather than try to tear each other down."

I realise I sound like I'm quoting one of those Instagram accounts full of #inspo, but the sentiment is genuinely meant. Blame my idealistic tendencies.

Zara curls her lip.

"You're pretty naïve if you think that," she snaps back. "I've got no time for that kind of stupid pseudo-feminism. Raise each other up? Yeah right, in cloud cuckoo land. That's not how it works. You know what people see that kind of behaviour as? A weakness. And I refuse to be seen as weak. Do you think Genevieve got her way to the top by being happy-clappy and nice to everyone? No, she knew what she wanted, and then she went after that goal, and hang the consequences for anyone who got in her way."

Somebody clears their throat.

"That's an interesting interpretation of my route to promotion, Zara."

I swear those cool, crisp tones make the temperature drop ten degrees. I shiver despite my furry outfit. Zara and I automatically take a step back as we realise that the woman herself has arrived without us noticing, exuding authority from every pore. While being bullied by Zara was hardly fun, it's going to seem like a walk in the park in comparison to being hauled over the coals by Genevieve. The moment I have been fearing all day has finally come.

I try to stand a little taller, straightening my back and attempting to smooth down my hair as if a sleek style is going to make the slightest bit of difference to the outcome of this confrontation.

Zara doesn't look like she's feeling much better than me. I can almost see the thoughts whirling through her mind as she wonders at which exact point in our conversation Genevieve arrived. The one thing she doesn't look, though, is surprised, which tells me that when she informed me that Genevieve had landed in Japan first thing this morning, she was lying to me. I guess that's another example of her putting her theories about how to get ahead into practice. It makes me feel all the more anxious about what is going to happen next.

Genevieve's face is inscrutable.

"Ms Baxter, Ms Humphries."

She gives the slightest of nods at each of us in turn.

I try to respond naturally, but fear I end up baring my teeth at her and jerking my head as if I've developed a tic. Zara, meanwhile, gives such a deep nod in return that she practically bows.

The silence stretches out. Genevieve walks around us, like an army officer inspecting the troops on parade. Zara's fingers pluck nervously against her suit trousers. My heart is beating in time to Genevieve's footsteps.

"I see you're starting to recover from your earlier ailment, Ms Humphries," says Genevieve. "How are you feeling now?"

Is that a trick question? Her tone is so neutral, I can't decide what to make of it. I realise I'm bracing myself, clenching my muscles as if I expect her to suddenly turn around and punch me in the stomach.

"A lot better, thank you," I say quietly, realising that it is true. Despite this current level of peak stress, my head feels so much clearer than it did first thing this morning.

Genevieve acknowledges my response with an efficient nod.

"You've had quite the day of it," she says softly.

Somehow, this seems worse than if she was shouting at me. I swallow. The back of my throat has started to hurt. My feelings of guilt are making me develop psychosomatic symptoms of the illness I faked this morning.

"I... I..." I start to speak, then abruptly close my mouth again as I realise that I have no idea what I'm intending to say. Besides, in these circumstances, I might be better off remaining silent for as long as possible so I don't incriminate myself still further.

Her phone chirrups, the cheeriness of the message alert tone in contrast with the seriousness of the situation we are currently in.

Genevieve glances down and checks the text. The faintest shadow of something like amusement crosses her features before her face once again becomes inscrutable.

She turns the phone towards me. My mouth falls open when I see a picture of me, waving a placard and clearly mid-protest song. Although it's only a few hours since I took part in the climate change demo, it feels like a lifetime ago already. I'm in bigger trouble than I feared. And as for that slimy toad Sam – for where else could Genevieve have got this photo? – he's going to be on the receiving end of some rather choice words from me the next time I see him. I dash away an angry tear. Actually, I'd much prefer not to see him ever again. My feeling of betrayal is almost physically painful.

"Quite the day of it," she repeats.

"I can explain," I say, although I realise as soon as the words are out of my mouth, I can't. How am I meant to tell my boss that I was so burnt out I had to take a duvet day? That my behaviour today is not representative of my genuine desire to progress at Richmond Woods and help people through the medium of the law?

"Maybe I can't." I abruptly shut my mouth, and stand there, shoulders sinking, while Zara smirks in the background.

"Try me." Genevieve fixes me with a stare which brooks no refusal.

"I'm going to enjoy this," says Zara, unable to resist the opportunity to stir things up further.

And that's when I figure I've got nothing to lose. If I'm going to get fired standing on a street corner in central London dressed in a grimy unicorn onesie, then I might as well go out with a bang. So, I launch into a no-holds-barred description of my actions today, and the stress and anxiety which triggered my decision to take a duvet day. I don't exaggerate, but neither do I shy away from articulating the full extent of the unbearable pressure I had been feeling.

Genevieve's features remain impassive throughout, and I can't tell if this is the precursor to her exploding with rage, but I take her silence as encouragement to continue, and so I do. Zara's grin meanwhile grows so broad, I'm worried it might split her face in two. Watching my downfall like this must be like all of her Christmases have come at once.

"And so that's how I ended up here, accidentally tackling a thief on a moped, rather than sitting behind my desk at work. I'm sorry. There's nothing more I can say."

I finish and await my fate. There's nothing more I can do now. The nervousness has gone and I feel strangely relieved. Saying everything out loud has been oddly cathartic.

The silence stretches out. And then, as Genevieve opens her mouth, about to declare her verdict, Sam barrels into view.

Chapter Thirty-Seven

8.13 p.m.

"Wait," he shouts, "things aren't as they seem." He skids to a halt in front of me. "I didn't betray you, I swear on my life."

"Nice try, Hack Man, but how can you explain my boss being in possession of one of those photos of me at the protest which you promised you'd delete?" I gesture for him to leave me alone, brushing him away like he's a fly that's buzzing around my head. "Anyway, it's a moot point. I am completely indifferent to what you did or didn't do. Your entire existence is utterly meaningless to me."

I'm being deliberately cruel, but after what he's done to me, he deserves it. It doesn't stop me feeling a pang of guilt as he staggers back, looking as hurt as if I'd physically lashed out at him.

"Just go away," I say, although I'm worried my voice lacks conviction.

Sam turns to Genevieve. "You must be the boss. I'm Sam Harris, and I write for a newspaper with one of the biggest circulations in the country. If you upset Alexa, I will dig until I find whatever dirt you've got hidden, and I'll make sure it's published."

I'm both touched and really quite pissed off at his attempts to intervene on my behalf.

"Don't be ridiculous, Sam," I hiss. "You're really not helping, and if you think some stupid grand gesture is going to make me believe your lies, you've got another think coming. And I can fight my own battles, thank you very much."

Genevieve clears her throat. "If you don't mind, perhaps I could speak?"

The three of us fall into line like children standing before the headteacher's desk. She scans each of our faces, then seems to come to a decision.

"First of all, you, Sam, whatever your name is. I'm a personal friend of Sir Clive, and I don't think he would be very happy that one of his journalists was going around threatening members of the public."

Sam folds his arms defiantly, but I can see the worry in his expression. Genevieve stares him out for a while, assessing him with her piercing, all-seeing eyes. Then she nods briefly, seemingly satisfied at the effect she's having on him.

"However, I do have a potential story which I wouldn't mind speaking to a journalist about," she says. "As you're here, you might as well do it. I'd like to contribute a piece about Richmond Woods' commitment to its corporate social responsibility policy, and how its values are particularly exemplified by the actions of one of our most talented young lawyers."

I can sense Zara starting to swell with pride beside me.

"This young woman is passionate about the causes she believes in, and more to the point, she takes action, rather than merely talking about them."

I'm starting to get a funny feeling.

"Yes, she'll even go to the extent of wearing a ridiculous unicorn outfit in order to get her point across."

My mouth falls open.

Genevieve turns to me, a wicked spark in her eyes. "While I certainly do not condone skipping work, I must admit that you've been extremely productive during your impromptu day off. I believe you encountered my husband Graham earlier. He's the one who sent me the pictures of the 'charming girl dressed as a unicorn' that he met at the climate protest he attended. According to him, the police behaved like complete brutes, and you did very well not to lower yourself to their level."

I shuffle nervously on the spot, trying to look worthy of Graham's glowing description of my character.

"Graham is very passionate about the cause, and he was most impressed by your commitment. He's gradually working on me," adds Genevieve, with what I can only describe as an indulgent chuckle. "I've him to thank for cancelling my trip to Tokyo so I don't increase what he calls my 'grossly large' carbon footprint. I suppose a video conference call does allow one to avoid the horrors of jet lag, although I am missing out on my *sake*. But that's by the by."

She gestures at Sam. "I don't know this young man from Adam, but I can vouch that he is not the source of my knowledge of your affairs today."

Sam nods his head vigorously. "And I swear I didn't tell Zara either."

"He so did," says Zara, apparently determined to carry on being difficult until the bitter end. But I've already decided who is more believable. Whether he's prepared to accept my apology for misjudging him is another thing altogether.

"Give up, Zara," I say quietly.

"Yes, if I were you, I would remain quiet," says Genevieve. "I'm seeing a side to you that I don't like very much, Ms Baxter. Integrity is the most prized quality at Richmond Woods, not ruthlessness. I'm disappointed that you haven't worked that one out for yourself yet."

She turns back to me. "There will, of course, be consequences for your adventures today. Would you accept having this day marked down as unpaid leave?"

I nod meekly, too shocked at the turn of events for words. I know I am getting off very lightly indeed.

"Very good. And on your return to work, let's have a chat about a position I've got coming up on the fifth floor. The pro bono department is always on the lookout for new talent, if that's something you're interested in."

I nod my head so vigorously, my unicorn horn bounces up and down. This is everything I've ever dreamt of, and I can't quite believe it's actually finally happening, even after all that I've been through today. And then I decide I'm not content to wait for that chat with Genevieve. It's time to seize the initiative. If there's one thing I've learnt from my duvet day, it's that it's better to take control of my own destiny. There's no point in sitting back and allowing things to happen to me. I am more than capable of making things happen for myself.

"Speaking of that, Genevieve, I'd like to approach Cordelia Cheng about her charity fund. I know she's moved on to Harrington's, but their pro bono department doesn't have the expertise that ours does. When she was first setting up the project, she spoke to me about it. I'd love to approach her again and see if she's interested in working together on it. I've got some ideas about how her fund could assist smaller charities, perhaps those reaching crisis point, or facing challenges like being evicted from their premises."

Genevieve looks impressed. "A good suggestion, Alexa. The Cheng Foundation has a lot of potential. The right person with legal know-how and a strong sense of compassion could help them really make a difference." She nods her head, decision made. "Please do make that contact. I'll look forward to your report on how it goes."

The "Yes!" of delight is out of my mouth before I can stop myself. But then again, given my current state of attire, it's pointless pretending to be a super-cool professional.

Genevieve's mouth twitches with barely suppressed amusement as she hands her business card to Sam. "Perhaps you could contact me tomorrow to write the story of Richmond Woods' very own 'Unicorn Hero', the approachable face of the business. It will be excellent PR for the company. We will catch up properly tomorrow, Alexa. I have no doubt you'll be refreshed and raring to go." She fixes me with a stern look. "Stress is a bugger, my dear. Never feel like you can't speak out about it. I think perhaps some of us have been turning a blind eye to what has been going on in the office, and it's time for us to reassess our work culture. I hope you'll help us with this."

With that I am dismissed, and then it's Zara's turn to come under the spotlight. "As for you, Ms Baxter, could you accompany me back to the office? I think we need a conversation about integrity."

She strides off, Zara trailing miserably in her wake.

I flump down on a nearby bench and try to process what has just happened. After all the drama, and the stress and strain of today, it turns out knocking a thief off a moped and going viral on social media as the "Unicorn Hero" is just what Richmond Woods wants out of its lawyers. "The approachable face of the business." I snort out loud as I recall Zara's face when Genevieve uttered those words.

Sam collapses beside me, casually resting his arm along the back of the bench.

"Well, Miss Unicorn Hero, that was quite something," he says. He really does have the warmest voice. But I'm not going to let that distract me.

"I thought I made it quite clear that I don't need you to save me."

Sam's face creases into a grin.

"I know," he says simply. "You're more than capable of

saving yourself, as you've demonstrated on more than one occasion today."

I nod my head, the wind rather taken out of my sails by his compliment.

"Too right," I mutter.

"And it's not just yourself you've saved. You've been helping people out all day. Campaigning to save the planet, then rescuing Briony from the vile Katherine at the school. And let's not forget the guys at the Phoenix, plus the spectacular way in which you stepped forward when that old lady had her handbag nicked."

I'm bracing myself for the catch here.

"You know that was a mistake," I protest.

"But I'm fairly confident that if you'd seen what had gone down, you would have taken that action anyway," he says.

I shuffle awkwardly. "You don't know that."

Sam smiles, and thumps his hand on his chest for emphasis. "I do know that. Despite the angst you've put me through today, I do know that. You've shown me over and over again that you're a kind person, that you put others first, and that I'm lucky to know you. In fact, I'm kicking myself for not having got to know you sooner."

"Ten hours, give or take, does not full knowledge make," I say. "I think you'll find I'm a complex, multi-faceted individual who has a lot more going for her than prancing around London in a unicorn suit will ever have shown you."

"Well, give me the chance to get to know you better," says Sam, inching ever closer. I'm finding it hard to concentrate when he's sitting so close to me, doing his attractive man thing.

"And why should I want to do that?" I can't help saying, although various parts of my body are telling me strongly that they can think of at least a dozen reasons why it would be nice to spend some time letting Sam get better acquainted with me, and I with him.

I don't give him the chance to answer, but instead I close the distance between us and for a few minutes, the delicious softness of his lips against mine proves thoroughly distracting.

As his mouth takes an exploratory detour to investigate the nape of my neck, I remember something.

"Out of interest, what did you do with those of photos of me at the protest?"

His soft laughter tickles my skin. "I deleted them, as I told you I would. Turns out I had a much stronger picture to illustrate the article, showing that police officer holding a penguin in a headlock. I think he's going to have to do a course on how to police a peaceful protest before they let him out on the front line again."

"In which case, I believe I owe you a drink," I say.

I feel Sam's lips curve into a smile against mine.

Chapter Thirty-Eight

9.02 p.m.

"I've imagined this moment for so long. I thought it would feel good, but not this good."

I reach out and tenderly stroke my hand along the firm, tough exterior of our open front door.

"Do you want me to leave you two alone for a moment?" asks Sam.

"No fear, Hack Man. I'm not letting you out of my sight, especially not as you've got the food in your clutches."

"And there was me thinking the lure of my incredible good looks and dazzling personality was enough."

I look him up and down, and purse my lips in mock criticism.

"I've seen worse, I suppose," I concede, then soften my words by giving him a quick peck on the cheek, which rapidly turns into a rather more lingering affair. It's only when we hear a wolf whistle from the street that we reluctantly move apart.

"I think I've had enough of making a public spectacle of myself for one day," I say as we shut the door on the outside world. I'm about to spring the latch closed when I hesitate. "What should we do about Zara? She doesn't have her keys since we used hers to let ourselves in."

"I'm not sure I'd dare come back here, if I were her," says Sam.

"Me neither, but perhaps we're better off leaving it unlocked, just in case." I'm not sure she'd do the same for me, but I'm not going to lower myself to her level.

"Desperate to get some undisturbed time with me?" Sam waggles his eyebrows, playing up to the suggestiveness of his question for all of his worth.

"You, and the beer and that rather delicious selection of barbeque goodies you're holding. Plus, I really don't feel like facing her at the moment."

Sam tweaks my unicorn horn. "She should be the one dreading seeing you again, after all she's done. If she's got any sense, she'll find somewhere else to stay until she can move on. You've got nothing to be afraid of. Besides, you're the Unicorn Hero. You can take on anyone."

I laugh. "True. After today, I do feel like I can take on the world. But to be honest, I think it's about time I shed this unicorn skin and put some normal clothes on. It's so grimy, it could probably walk its own way to the washing machine. Or perhaps I should chuck the bloody thing on the barbeque."

Sam pulls a face of genuine disappointment. "But I was getting to love the unicorn look."

"I'll ask Charlie to order one for you. In fact, I'll get him to send it to your work. I'm not getting myself locked out again to rescue another of your parcels. I hope the contents were worth all the angst they've caused me."

It's hard to tell in the gloom of the hallway, but I think he's blushing. Now I have to ask.

"Go on, 'fess up, what was in the parcel?"

He mutters something and I have to lean in closer, convinced I've not heard him right.

"Sorry, you're going to have to say that again."

He clears his throat. "A light sabre," he says sheepishly. "It's not for me, honest."

I take a step back in faux horror. "You're telling me that I went through all that trauma, all that stress, so you could run around pretending to be a Trekkie?"

"Light sabres are *Star Wars*, actually." He can't help correcting me, although he looks embarrassed to be doing so.

"Ha, got you! And you claim it's not yours. I bet you're a superfan. Perhaps we could get you a Chewbacca onesie, seeing as you've revealed yourself to be such an admirer," I say, unable to resist continuing to tease him.

"Would it make it any better if I said it was for one of the lads at Phoenix?"

"I'll ask them to confirm that for me next time I'm there, which won't be long," I say, taking the volunteer application form out of my pocket, along with Nige's business card, and placing them carefully on the hall shelf.

I'll fill out the form and pay my taxi fare to Nige first thing in the morning. While I want to settle my debts and make my fresh start, tonight I just want to enjoy being in the moment and spend some time with Sam when we're not both running around like mad things. "Are you OK to light the barbeque, while I go and have a quick shower?"

Sam nods his agreement, and hurries off towards the garden. I resist the urge to tease him about checking that his light sabre is in one piece.

I haul myself upstairs, and hesitate on the threshold of my room, suddenly nervous that if I go back in there, everything will return to how it was before my duvet day. Although it feels like a lifetime since I was last here, it looks like I left only seconds ago. The abandoned jar of Nutella is still on my bedside table, the spoon balancing precariously on the lid. The laundry pile has not miraculously cleared itself, and the stacks of law books are still taking up nearly every spare surface. I wait, half-dreading the familiar crushing sense of disappointment and personal failure catching up with me. But it doesn't. My room hasn't physically changed, but I feel like a very different individual from the person who reluctantly rolled out of bed this morning to answer the door. Somewhere in my wanderings around London, I found a sense of purpose and self-belief. I've acknowledged my stress and shortcomings, but I realise now that they don't make me less of a person, and I'm determined not to allow them to overwhelm me again.

As I peel off my unicorn onesie, I try my best to hold my breath. Twelve plus hours of dashing around London at full throttle have taken their toll on the fabric. The fluff is matted and grubby, and great big chunks have fallen off altogether, leaving thinning clumps of dirty fleece behind. The silver horn is grey and mushy, and the tail is hanging on by a thread. And don't even get me started on the smell. The thing needs to be sealed up in a "hazardous waste" bag and destroyed. But instead, I fold it carefully and place it back on the cheery paper Charlie originally wrapped it in. I'm not naïve enough to think that everything from here on out is going to be all blue skies and shiny rainbows. I have a lot to look forward to, but I know there will be challenges along the way. I decide that I'll keep hold of my unicorn onesie, just as a little reminder to myself that I do have the strength to face whatever life throws at me. I leave it by the rickety windows. Hopefully the draught will help dissipate the pong.

When I emerge into the garden ten minutes later, hair still dripping from the shower, but otherwise respectably attired in jeans and a jumper, Sam does a pretend double-take.

"I knew I should have locked the front door. I can't have strange women wandering in off the street when I'm waiting for a date with the Unicorn Hero."

"The Unicorn Hero is taking a well-earned rest upstairs. But if you're happy with plain old Alexa, here I am."

Sam's eyes twinkle. "More than happy."

He passes me a bottle of beer and we settle down on a pair of camping chairs, watching the burgers start to sizzle on the glowing embers of the barbeque. Somewhere in the distance, a police siren is wailing. The dogs in the back alley are growling and scrapping, and a suspiciously grassy smell is drifting through the air from the squat over the road. As the darkness closes in around us, the city is gearing itself up for the night. It's a crazy, loud, dirty place, but there's nowhere I'd rather be right now. I reach across and clink my bottle against Sam's.

"Cheers."

It's not been too bad a duvet day, all things considered.

THE END

Acknowledgments

One of my favourite things about writing is that it lets me escape into a whole other world, something which has felt particularly valuable during this time of the pandemic. I've had so much fun telling Alexa's story, and no small part of that joy is down to the lovely people who have cheered me on along the way.

Thank you to editor extraordinaire Charlotte Ledger and the rest of the One More Chapter team for all your wonderful insight and support. And thank you also to Federica Leonardis and Amanda Preston for your enthusiasm and encouragement.

A big shout out to my Book Camp girls. You are such a talented, supportive group of friends, and I can't wait until we can all be reunited at our next writing retreat.

Liz, thank you for letting me bombard you with questions about corporate life. It goes without saying that Alexa's experiences at work are not yours, and any errors are my own.

To my beloved family, you inspire me in everything I do. Thank you for always being there for me. And thanks to my four-legged best friend for lending a very important name to the story – extra biscuits heading your way!

And finally, thank you to you, lovely reader, for picking up *Duvet Day*. I really hope you enjoyed Alexa's adventures.